BRIGHT LIGHTS

A JOHN MILTON THRILLER

MARK DAWSON

This one's for Team Milton.

PART I

1

John Milton settled himself into the black bucket seat. The vinyl had cooked in the California sunlight and was warm through the already damp cloth of his shirt. He put the key into the ignition and turned it. The engine rumbled to life.

The owner of the lot opened the passenger door and leaned in. "Well?"

Milton ignored him, listening to the growl, the burble and pop from the exhaust.

"Well?" the man repeated. "What you think?"

Milton allowed himself a smile. He could feel the rumble of the engine through the chassis and the bucket seat. "She sounds good."

"'Good?' You been smoking, man? Please—just *listen* to it. That's the original in there. Ram Air III cam, roller rockers, Edelbrock intake with Holley carb..."

The man went on, listing the improvements that he had made. Electric choke. Dual snorkel air cleaner with chrome lid. Milton tuned him out, dabbed his foot on the gas and felt and heard the engine respond. It felt alive—*primal*—and

Milton couldn't help but think how much fun it would be to take the car out onto a quiet desert road and bury the pedal. Fun? The prospect was intoxicating.

"So," the man was saying, "when you say she sounds good, what you meant to say was...?"

"All right," Milton conceded. "Better than good."

Milton assumed that the man's name was Sam. A vinyl banner with SAM'S CUSTOM MUSCLE CARS had been draped over the lot's entrance, and the man's denim overall bore a patch with HI – I'M SAM across his left breast. Milton couldn't decide whether that was ironic or authentic. The man was short, with a head of unruly black curls and a stocky build. His overalls were stained and, somewhat incongruously, he wore rubber flip-flops on his feet and had a half-smoked cigarette tucked behind his right ear.

The lot, in Oakland, was as scruffy as its owner. Milton would not usually have chosen a place like this to make a significant purchase, but he had something special in mind, and the Craigslist ad had suggested—a little dishonestly, as it had turned out—that this would be a private sale. Never mind. He was here now, and the car was exactly what he had in mind. At least *that* part of the ad was correct: it had described the car as a prime 1969 GTO, and it was.

Sam smiled as Milton ran his fingers against the rough stitching of the leather-trimmed steering wheel. "Want to take her for a quick spin?"

Milton said that he did. He waited for Sam to get in next to him before releasing the emergency brake and nudging down on the gas, rolling the car out of the lot and onto the street.

"She's not perfect," Sam said, "but she's solid. Won't let you down."

Milton smiled, thinking that sounded like a description that he might put on himself.

The lot was on Twenty-Sixth Street. Sam directed him until he was on the John B. Williams Freeway, heading north towards the interchange with the 580. He turned to the east and followed the MacArthur Freeway.

"Go on," Sam said. "Give her a little juice."

Milton pressed down on the gas and pushed the speed up to forty and then fifty. The steering wheel was tight, the Cooper radials stuck to the road, and the rumble beneath the hood did indeed sound new.

"You said you did the rebuild yourself?" Milton asked.

"Yeah. Took me six months." Sam shrugged. "Took the engine apart, replaced what needed to be replaced, then put it back together again. You got—"

Milton sensed he was about to start listing components again, and cut in. "It'll get me to Las Vegas? Across the desert?"

"It'll get you to New York if you want, man. Guaranteed. Something goes wrong, bring it back. I'll be here."

Sam pointed to an exit ramp and Milton took it, following Broadway to the south and then hooking back onto Twenty-Sixth. Milton drove back to the lot and reversed the car back into its space. He got out and walked around it again. The paint was Cortez Silver that had been sanded and wheeled until it was as slick as glass. The vinyl top was in good condition; there was a Judge rear spoiler, new weatherstripping and window felts; and the tinted windshield was free of chips or any other imperfections.

"New," Sam noted, rapping his knuckles against the glass. "I was gonna restore the interior, maybe put in a new radio, trick it out a little more. But here you are."

Milton didn't care about the interior or the radio. "I like it."

"You can drive her away today," Sam said, rubbing his chin.

"How much?"

"Thirty."

"Fifteen."

"Don't be crazy." Milton stared at him. "Twenty-five."

Milton stared at him some more. "Fifteen."

"Twenty-three, and that's as low as I'm going."

"Sixteen."

"I can't do sixteen, man."

Milton said nothing.

"Can you think of a better way to get to Vegas?"

Milton shrugged. "I was going to get a Greyhound."

"The fucking Greyhound," Sam repeated with mock incredulity. "You're killing me. Twenty."

"Seventeen." Milton stared at Sam for a long moment until the man had to look away.

The air went out of him. "Fine," Sam said. "You got it. Seventeen."

"Excellent. Cash all right with you?"

"Cash would be perfect."

Milton opened his satchel and took out the money. He decided not to mention that it was dirty. He had liberated it from a dealer in LA who had been foolish enough to try to sell his goods to the son of a woman Milton had met at the early morning AA meeting in Pasadena. The woman had shared about how her inability to save her boy from his addictions was leading her back to the bottle. Milton had listened quietly, not saying a word, but had taken her aside when they went to the café on Fremont for breakfast afterwards. He'd asked her for the bare minimum—the dealer's name and where he did his business—and then had gone to fix the problem.

The dealer was an emaciated crackhead, foul-smelling but with a vermin cunning that glinted in his eyes. Milton delivered a stern rebuke and, when the dealer had called his bluff—had actually *threatened* him—Milton had underlined his warning by breaking three of the man's fingers and putting enough torque on his wrist to very nearly break that, too. They had reached an accommodation after that, but Milton had still taken his stash.

He counted out the seventeen grand and handed it over. Sam took it into his office and returned with a receipt.

"You decide to do the interior, bring it back to me," Sam told him. "Give you a discount and I promise no one will make it look better."

Milton nodded. "I will. Keys?"

"Seventeen. Jesus, man. You're killing me." He made a show of his reluctance to hand them over, but, as Milton readied another icy glare, he tossed them across.

Milton caught them. "Thanks," he said. "One more thing."

"Yeah?"

"There's a cassette deck in the car, right?"

"A Kraco. Would've been an eight-track out of the factory, but whoever owned it before must've got it fitted."

"Don't suppose you got any tapes?"

"Wait there."

Sam went back into the office and came out again with a small cardboard shoebox.

"Haven't played these in years," he said.

Milton took the box and removed the lid. He saw a selection of cassettes. There were albums by the Beach Boys, the Righteous Brothers, Dionne Warwick, The Foundations, The Animals and others.

"How much for the box?"

"You think I want to negotiate with you again?" he said. "You can have 'em."

2

Milton headed under the freeway on Fourteenth and turned onto Market, the engine of the GTO rumbling as if in remonstration that it was not being given the proper workout that it deserved. Milton thought of the long drive ahead of him and smiled; it had suddenly become a lot more interesting than might otherwise have been the case. He would have taken a Greyhound, but driving himself in a car like this would be a pleasure.

This trip was a little last minute, but perhaps more exciting because of that. He had been in London for a month when he had seen a news story on the BBC website. The talented young boxer Mustafa Muhammad had attracted the attention of promoters in the United States, and, when a fighter on the undercard of the upcoming world championship fight at Mandalay Bay had pulled out due to injury, Muhammad had been installed as his replacement. Milton knew Muhammad as Elijah Warriner, a youngster whom he had tried to help in the immediate aftermath of his renunciation of his government work.

Milton was a fan of boxing and had realised that he could combine a trip to see the bout with his long-cherished dream of taking a classic American muscle car on a cross-country road trip. He had persuaded himself that this was the perfect occasion to do that. He would start in San Francisco and buy a car, and then he would drive to the east coast, stopping in Vegas along the way.

He had arrived a few days earlier and had taken a room at El Capitan in San Francisco. He had stayed there before, months ago, when he had foolishly thought that he might be able to make a life for himself in the Bay area. He had been holding down two jobs—delivering ice and driving a cab—and had even found himself a woman before he had been embroiled in a series of murders after a girl whom he had driven to a party had disappeared. He had been on the run from the Group then, but the events of the succeeding months—most notably the death of Control—had removed the threat to his future prosperity that his discovery would have entailed.

He had enjoyed his time in the city. He had visited the tourist sights, walking for miles up and down the hills until his legs burned. He had attended a meeting every day, subconsciously hoping that he might bump into Eva, the woman with whom he had spent time before. He'd asked around, eventually discovering that she had taken a job with Netflix in New York. That was probably for the best; the last time they had met, she had been kidnapped in an attempt to put pressure on him. He told himself that there was no reason why she would want to see him again, and had put the notion out of his head.

His wandering had been interrupted while he had taken care of the errant son and the drug dealer, but now he had nothing else to do. The fight was in two days. He would go to the hotel and check out and then start the long drive and see where it took him.

~

MILTON HAD JUST CROSSED the Bay Bridge and was driving southwest towards the Mission District when he saw an elevated billboard at the side of the highway. It was bright red with a picture of an old man in a Stetson standing next to a steer, his hand resting between the beast's horns. The headline proclaimed THIS IS NO BULL.

Milton couldn't stop looking at it and, as the sign rushed at him, he noticed a glare of red out of the corner of his eye. He turned back to the road and saw that the cars in front had slowed down to a crawl. He stamped on the brakes and brought the car to a stop with just a few feet to spare.

The billboard was immediately to his right. The rest of the text announced that Baxter's Bail Bonds had just opened a new office on Bryant Street, in SoMa. Milton remembered the geography of the city from his previous visit and knew that Bryant Street was close, near the Hall of Justice.

The driver behind him sounded his horn. Milton turned back to the road and saw that the traffic was moving again. He held up his hand in apology and pushed down on the gas, sending the GTO ahead. He saw an exit sign up ahead for Ninth Street/Civic Center and, without really thinking about what he was doing, he flicked the indicator and turned off.

3

The newly opened branch of Baxter's Bail Bonds enjoyed a spectacularly good location. Bryant Street was nothing special, with auto shops and industrial units on one side of the road and cheap cars parked nose-to-tail as their owners conducted their business. The other side of the road, however, was taken up by the vast Thomas J. Cahill Hall of Justice. Police vehicles were slotted amongst the civilian cars that were parked on that side of the road, and clutches of people—many of whom were clearly unhappy that they were here—filtered in and out of the double doors that were set back from the street and accessed by way of flights of concrete stairs.

There were a number of bail businesses opposite the municipal building, and with good reason. The men and women who had just been processed were often unable to find the money that the court had set in order for them to be bailed. The bondsmen up and down this stretch of road would offer that money, often at ten per cent interest. Business was clearly brisk.

Milton parked the GTO a little way down the road from

his destination and then walked back toward it. The building was not much more than a storefront that had been erected on the corner of Bryant and Boardman. It was single storey, with white-painted walls and a steeply pitched shingled roof. The signs on the walls announced that it was open twenty-four hours and that Spanish was spoken. The name of the business—Baxter's Bail Bonds—was arranged so that the three words were stacked on top of one another. The three Bs were drawn so that they were all interlocked.

The office was accessed from the pavement by way of a flight of four steps. Milton climbed them and paused at the door. He hadn't seen Beau Baxter since he had last been in San Francisco. The old man had introduced him to a mafia family that had helped him to solve part of the problem that Milton had been facing. Their first meeting had been some time before that, when Baxter had been sent over the border to Juárez in an attempt to track down a man named Santa Muerta, the psychotic cartel *sicario* who had massacred members of that same Italian family. Milton had been impressed with Baxter's dry sense of humour, his toughness, and his very obvious capability.

Milton was still persuading himself that he should go inside when the decision was made for him.

The door opened and Beau stepped out. The old man saw him and froze. His weathered face, lined and wrinkled through age and a life spent chasing miscreants across inhospitable territory, broke into a wide smile.

"Well, fuck me," he said. "If it ain't English."

4

Beau led the way back into the office. The building appeared to have been split into two. There was a public space for entertaining potential new clients, with a reception desk, a leather sofa with wooden chairs on either side of it, a water cooler and a rack of magazines. There was a closed door behind the desk that looked as if it offered access to a back room where, Milton guessed, the administration of the business was carried out.

"Take the weight off," Beau said, pointing to the sofa. "Got some coffee brewing in back—want one?"

"Thanks."

"Coming right up."

Beau went into the back. Milton heard the sound of low conversation. He looked around. The office looked newly decorated. The paint on the walls was fresh, the magazines were all up to date, and the sofa hadn't yet been marked with the indentations of the clients who would, no doubt, come to rest on it while they waited for Beau to pronounce whether or not he could help them with the matter of their liberty.

Beau came back out with two cups in his hands. He hooked the toe of his cowboy boot around the door and pulled it closed. He handed Milton one of the cups.

"I'll be honest, English," he said. "I didn't ever think I'd see you again."

"I have a habit of popping up," Milton said. "Like a bad penny."

"You been in San Francisco all this time?"

Milton told Beau what had happened since they had last met. He skipped over the denouement of the events in the city and his involvement in the disgrace of the presidential candidate whose unfortunate extramarital proclivities had been kept out of the public eye by way of a murderous chief of staff, and moved on to provide the briefest sketch of where he had been: Russia, the Australian outback, New Orleans, London, Manila, Rio de Janeiro.

Beau was wise enough not to ask Milton to explain what he had been doing in those places. "So what are you doing back here again?" he asked instead.

"Just passing through."

"And how'd you find me?"

Milton grinned. "I saw the sign on the freeway."

"Oh, that." Beau shook his head and chuckled. "That nonsense ain't got a thing to do with me."

"Really?"

"You think making a fuss like that's the sort of thing I'd do? It was my fool son's idea."

"I didn't know you had children."

"I never told you. His name's Chase." He lowered his voice and nodded at the closed door; Milton guessed that the subject of the conversation was inside the office beyond it. "He's a good man, honest and hard-working. He was in the military until he got shot in the leg and discharged. He was drifting around aimlessly with not much purpose in life, so I suggested he set up shop as a bondsman."

"Like you?"

"Not *exactly* like me." Beau grinned.

Milton remembered: Beau had decided that he was never going to make his fortune paying the sureties for felons who were just as likely to abscond as make their trial dates, and had taken the commercial decision to search out other forms of employment, including what might once have romantically been described as bounty hunter.

"You're not sharing the old clientele with him?"

Beau tutted. "This is my boy. It's got to be as straight as an arrow. Last thing I want is him getting caught up with some of the people I've worked for over the years. Anyway—I'm keeping my office in San Diego, least for a while. 'Frisco? This is all on him."

The door opened and a tall, younger man stepped through it. He was wearing a chambray shirt with a white undershirt beneath it. He had on a single-breasted jacket with slim peak lapels that worked down to a single button, and a pair of blue jeans with a leather belt. He had a white cowboy hat on his head and was wearing cowboy boots that were the equal of the snakeskin pair that Beau sported. The mix of a sharp suit jacket and cowboy accessories was something of a clash, and Milton was left with the impression that the man was struggling to ape the natural style that Beau had unconsciously adopted over decades.

"Ah," Beau said. "Speak of the devil. This here's my boy, Chase. Chase, this is John Smith. John's an old friend of mine."

Milton was about to stand, but Chase held up a hand for him to stay where he was. "Good to meet you," he said, reaching his hand down.

Milton shook it. "Likewise."

Chase had a strong grip, and he looked Milton in the eye when he spoke.

"We were just talking about that foolish sign you've got next to the highway," Beau said, his tone belying the admonishment.

Chase smiled. "You see it?"

"I did," Milton said. "Hard to miss."

"Ain't that the truth," Chase said, pleased.

"He didn't mean that in a good way," Beau said. He leaned back, stretched out his legs and glanced over at Milton. "You see, Chase read a book about branding, and now he's an expert. He thinks that a picture of me with my hat on my head is the kind of thing that'll draw attention to the business—like the tweakers and dopers he'll end up bailing out will choose us over any of the others on the street because it looks like they'll be doing business with a good ole boy. I told him most of those dudes are gonna be black, and that's probably not the image he wants, but he didn't listen. I was madder than a wet hen when I saw it."

"But it worked, Pops, didn't it?" He looked to Milton. "You saw it, didn't you?"

"I certainly did," Milton said. "It's very striking."

"There you go," Chase said triumphantly. "Striking."

"He didn't mean that in a good way, either."

Beau gave Milton a theatrical wink and got up. "I was just on my way out," he said. "Chase had his first skipper last week, didn't you? Got a kid name of Anwar who was caught with eighty-two wraps of meth, coke and fentanyl down in the Tenderloin. He gets charged and his mom comes in and says that she don't have the fifteen grand the judge has set for bail. Chase fronts that, Anwar gets out, and the next thing you know"—he clicked his fingers—"*poof*, he's gone."

"There was no way I could've known," Chase protested.

"So Chase gets on the phone to me and asks for my help in finding Anwar so we can deliver him to justice and get the fifteen back again. I make some calls and find out that Anwar has friends in Vegas and that he's gone there in the optimistic hope that if he lies low for a while, this'll all blow over. I've just booked a ticket to fly over there so I can pick him up. I've got a friend on the Metro Police who knows where he's at."

Beau leaned back and gave Milton a theatrical wink.

"Come on, Pops," Chase protested. "Give me a break. I said I'd go get him."

"I *would* send Chase to clean up his own mess, but, on the balance of it, his time is better spent here finding more business. So it's on me."

The two of them had a nice interplay, Milton noted. He could tell that Chase's protestations were exaggerated and Beau's criticism was manufactured. There was a warmth between father and son that was attractive and, not for the first time, Milton regretted the fact that he would never have a relationship like that with anyone, much less a child of his own.

Beau turned back to Milton. "Plus, I love Vegas," he said, with a grin. "I got a couple of hours before my flight. You wanna grab a bite to eat?"

5

Beau led the way underneath the highway and onto Folsom Street. He pointed to a restaurant on the other side of the road.

"Fondue Cowboy?" Milton said.

"What about it?"

"Fondue?"

"Why are you pulling that face?"

"What is this? The seventies? And what does fondue have to do with cowboys?"

"You coming in, or are you gonna stand outside bitching all day?"

Milton followed Beau across the road and into the restaurant. He was expecting something that would appeal to the San Franciscan hipster, and he wasn't disappointed. The decor was done out in tones of brown and black, with cowboy paraphernalia positioned around the room. There was a saddle near the kitchen, a lasso strung out across the ceiling, and a set of steer's horns hung from the wall. Beau led the way to a booth that was furnished with padded leather banquette seats beneath a large portrait of a smouldering Clint Eastwood. A waitress welcomed them and delivered a pair of menus before taking their drink orders—a beer for Beau and a glass of iced water for Milton—and then leaving them to choose their food.

"So you're going to Vegas?" Milton said.

"That's right. Why?"

"I'm headed there too."

"Seriously?" Beau said.

Milton nodded.

"You're not saying that because you want to help me out again, are you?"

"Not this time."

"You remember that guy from before?"

Milton did remember. He couldn't recall the man's name, but he remembered going into the house and flushing out the skipper. The man had retreated and walked straight into Beau's stiff right hand.

"Doubt I'll need you this time. Anwar's not like Ordell. He's a hundred pounds dripping wet."

The waitress came back to take their orders. Beau—without even the barest hint of irony—selected the Rawhide, a fondue that featured Dolce Gorgonzola, Emmental and bacon. Milton, still trying to work out whether Beau was pulling his leg, chose the Traditional with Gruyere, Emmental and nutmeg. The waitress complimented them on their choices, took the menus and said she would be back with their food.

"So, what are you going to be doing in Vegas?" Beau said. "You don't strike me as the gambling type."

"I'm not," Milton said. "A friend of mine is a boxer. He's on the undercard of the fight at Mandalay Bay."

"He any good?"

"*Very* good," Milton said.

The waitress returned with their food. She set up fondue lamps on the table and then placed small bowls atop them so that the flames could melt the cheese inside. She set out the sides—bread, roasted potatoes, cured meat, sausage, broccoli, pickles, olives, grapes and apples—and left them to their meals.

"You fix the problems that you had in Juárez?" Beau asked.

"I did," Milton said.

Beau had been there when Michael Pope and his detachment of Group Fifteen operatives had descended upon the cartel mansion in an attempt to bring him back. Milton had escaped with the help of a friendly Mexican police officer; Beau had fought his way out, disappearing in the chaos.

"You ain't ever gonna tell me what that was all about, are you?"

"I'm afraid not," Milton said. "If I told you..."

"Yeah, I get it. You'd have to kill me."

They shared updates as to what they had been doing as they started on the food. Milton had always enjoyed Beau's company, and today was no different. And to his considerable surprise, and still unsure as to whether this was a joke that his companion was playing on him, he found that the meal was delicious.

When they'd finished, Beau wiped his mouth with a napkin and looked at his watch. "I'd better jet," he said. "I need to get to the airport, and traffic at this time of day can be a pain in the ass."

He reached into his jacket pocket, took out a card and laid it flat on the table in front of Milton. Milton looked down at it: it was the same garish red as the billboard sign, and there was the same picture of Beau next to a steer.

"I know," Beau said, wincing. "Branding, right? Chase is taking this all *very* seriously."

"It's a memorable picture," Milton said.

"Don't," Beau said with a grin. "Look—when are you heading to Vegas?"

"I've got to go and get my stuff from the hotel," Milton said. "I was going to leave after that."

"All I was gonna say was if you want to meet when you get in, then that there's my number." He jabbed a finger at the card. "I'll be in the city for a couple of extra days. I like to play a hand of poker now and again, and they've got a decent weekly tournament at the El Cortez. You get a lot of tourists coming to play—these hotshot lawyers and accountants who think they know how to win at hold 'em—then you get the pros turning up and skinning them. It's fun."

"You're one of the pros?"

"I sure as shit ain't one of the fish."

"Gambling's not really my thing," Milton said. "But thanks."

Milton took out the roll of notes from his pocket and peeled off three twenties to cover the bill.

"No, no," Beau said, reaching for his wallet. "I got this."

"No," Milton insisted, laying the money on the table and pocketing Beau's card. "Good luck with bringing your man in. If I get a moment in Vegas, I'll give you a call."

They both stood. Beau extended his hand and Milton took it, shaking it firmly.

"Good to see you again, English. Stay out of trouble."

"Always."

PART II

6

Milton went back to the hotel to check out. He packed his meagre possessions into his bag, settled his bill and went down to the GTO. He slung his bag into the back seat, climbed into the driver's seat and set off, going back over the Oakland Bridge and heading east. He filled the tank at a Shell gas station just outside San Leandro, then went back to the car and plotted his route: the best way to reach Vegas appeared to be to follow I-5 south to Bakersfield and then continue east. He would pass through Barstow, skirt the northern boundary of the Mojave National Preserve and then turn north to cross the border into Nevada. It was five hundred and sixty miles. He guessed it would take him ten hours, with three stops to refuel. He looked at the long stretches of highway that he was going to have to traverse, and squeezed the leather-trimmed steering wheel, pleased that it would be a decent drive.

He wouldn't worry too much about the police when he was out in the desert.

This was going to be fun.

~

THE CAR DROVE like new across the high desert, gobbling up the highway that cut through the California sand. Milton found *The Beach Boys Today!* in the box of music, took the cassette out of the case and pushed it into the slot. The introduction to 'Help Me, Rhonda' started to play as he pulled out to overtake a truck.

Milton flattened the pedal and watched the speedometer as the needle moved around the dial. The engine purred, easily bringing the car up to a hundred and then a hundred and ten. Milton was almost constitutionally averse to official attention, but there was nothing out here but sand stretching away in both directions; he relished the thought of letting the car stretch its legs a little.

He took out the Beach Boys tape and replaced it with a compilation from The Animals. 'Please Don't Let Me Be Misunderstood' started, replaced in short order by 'The House of the Rising Sun.'

Milton tapped out the beat on the wheel and let his thoughts drift. He felt good, better than he could remember feeling for a while. He had always been happy with his own company, latterly choosing solitude over the seemingly inevitable strife that sat on his shoulder and attached itself to anyone who came across his path. He was content with what he had: the car, the open road and a selection of choice music. Eric Burdon's voice rang out of the ancient speakers, a warning to mothers so their sons might avoid the things that he had done, and Milton rolled down the window to let the afternoon zephyrs blow the stuffy air out of the cabin.

He arrived in Bakersfield at five and stopped for fuel and a sandwich. He didn't dawdle, hungry to get back to the drive. He got back into the car and set off again, now heading east. He passed out of the city limits and picked up speed again, the scenery rushing by on either side of the car.

7

H e was ninety miles from Vegas when he decided to stop for something more substantial to eat and to top up the tank. He pulled the car off the interstate just as he passed through the town of Baker, found a gas station and filled up. There was a restaurant attached to the gas station, the sign hoisted high above it announcing it as the Mad Greek Café. Milton had checked the route before he had set out in order to learn a little about the landmarks that he would pass along the way. This particular establishment was a well-known highlight; it was familiar both to hopeful visitors looking forward to reaching Vegas, and also to bitter refugees running from the casinos, their luck spent.

Milton drove over to the parking lot, slid the GTO into a space next to a shiny new Tesla Model S, and went inside.

His guidebook had revealed that the Mad Greek had been a fixture in the desert since the late nineties. It was a reasonably small building, and, as Milton looked around, he counted twenty tables, most of them empty.

A waitress in a branded shirt came over to greet him. "Afternoon," she said. "How you doing?"

"I'm good," Milton said.

"Take a seat," she said, gesturing to the empty tables. "I'll be right over."

She gave him a menu and went over to deliver a pot of coffee to a table where two grizzled truckers were working on plates of chili. Milton found a table at the window where he could look outside, and sat down. The menu was a large laminated card and he scanned up and down it. The café was known for its gyros, but the menu offered a much wider selection in addition. There were burgers, pastrami and cheesesteaks mixed in with falafel, dolmadakia and spanakopita. The baba ghanoush that two chastened gamblers had ordered looked particularly good, and Milton decided that he would order that and a strong coffee.

He sat back and checked out the other diners. Apart from the truckers and the gamblers, there was a table of four raucous young men, early twenties, hyped up about the prospect of a night in Sin City; there was an older man, his eyes hidden behind a purple visor; and, in the corner, there was a younger woman sitting by herself. She was facing him and, as he glanced over at her, he saw that she was crying.

The waitress came over. "What you having, darlin'?"

"The baba ghanoush looks good."

"*Is* good," she said. "You want something to drink?"

"Coffee, please."

"Be right back."

She made her way to the open kitchen counter. Milton kept his eye on the girl on the other side of the room. She took out her phone and swiped her finger down the screen. She took a moment to compose herself, tapped the screen and then put the phone to her ear. Milton watched her as she spoke. The diner was too noisy for him to hear her side of the conversation, but he could tell that whatever it was that she was being told did nothing to alleviate her unhappiness. She frowned and then scowled, and then, her voice raised, she snapped that whatever had been said was "completely unacceptable," before ending the call and laying the phone back down again.

The waitress returned with a mug and a pot of coffee. She put a napkin down on the table and rested the mug atop it.

"Going to Vegas?"

"That's right," he said.

"That your GTO out there?"

"It is."

"Seventy-two?"

"Sixty-nine."

She sucked her teeth appreciatively. "Had a boyfriend once; he had one just the same. Nice wheels. How did it handle the desert?"

"Like a dream."

"Like I said—nice car," she said. She poured out a mug of coffee. "You see the Tesla next to it?"

Milton said that he did.

"It's hers," she said, pointing to the girl in the corner. "She can't start it. Been here an hour already. I don't know... You wouldn't see me taking an electric car into the desert. I don't care how expensive it is. Something goes wrong, what you gonna do?"

She went back to the kitchen. Milton sipped his coffee, watching as the young woman laid a banknote on the table and stood. She wiped her eyes with her napkin before balling it up and dropping it onto her empty plate. She made her way to the exit, passing right by Milton's table. He looked away as she approached. Empathy was not one of his strong points, and he wouldn't have known what to say if she had stopped to talk to him. He heard the door open and close and watched her as she made her way across the lot to the Tesla. She aimed her phone at it, stabbing at the screen, before aiming a petulant kick at the rear wheel. She put her back to the car and slid down it, leaning back against the chassis with her legs bent.

The waitress arrived with Milton's food. "Here you go," she said, depositing the plate, a knife and fork wrapped in a napkin, and a glass of water on the table. "Get you anything else?"

"I'm good," Milton said. "Thanks."

"No problem. Enjoy your meal."

Milton picked up the knife and fork and took a bite. The eggplant was perfectly cooked, succulent with juices, and delicious. Milton swallowed and took a second bite, glancing over at the young woman once more. She had the phone to her ear again and was in the midst of a second conversation. She was crying, her head dipped down. She finished the call, wiped the back of her hand across her eyes and got up. She tried the door, couldn't open it, and kicked the car again.

Milton tried to turn his attention back to his food, but couldn't; he was distracted, thinking about the girl and wondering whether there was anything he might be able to do to help.

8

T he girl was still there when Milton had finished his meal. He laid a twenty on the table to cover his meal, added a five for a tip and made his way outside and back to the GTO. It was eight o'clock and still warm, although there was a chill in the air that suggested that night in the desert was going to be cold.

She looked up as Milton approached.

"Hello," he said.

She looked up at him. Her mascara was streaked with tears. She didn't speak.

"What's the matter?"

She shook her head.

"You've broken down?"

"Piece of shit's fucked," she said at last.

"How?"

"I can't even open the doors."

"If I'm overstepping, please say," he said. "But is there something I could do to help?"

"You an engineer?" she asked him.

"Afraid not."

"Then I doubt it."

She was brusque, but not rude. There was something in her face—something open—that endeared her to him.

"Is it yours?"

She nodded. "Six months old."

"You know what's wrong with it?"

"The battery's dead."

He looked at the car and scratched his head. "If it had a normal engine, I might have been able to help, but I wouldn't know where to start with this. These are expensive, right?"

"Ninety grand."

"Don't you get roadside service for that?"

"You do, but apparently not for another five hours. Which would be fine if I had five hours to waste, but I don't."

"Why?"

She rubbed her eyes again. "I'm supposed to be at home to pick up my father. We've got a flight to catch. I'm not going to make it."

Milton looked at her and bit his lip. He had been enjoying his own company, but she had been dealt a bad hand and obviously needed a favour. He had covered most of the distance to Vegas and would have as long as he wanted in his own company if he took the car coast to coast like he had planned. He was on the home stretch now; there was only another ninety minutes to go before he hit the Strip.

"You want a ride?"

"You're going to Vegas?"

"I am. Where do you need to go?"

"Summerlin."

"I can take you there."

"You sure?"

"It wouldn't be a problem. Happy to help."

She looked at him, her despair from moments ago now replaced by a hopefulness that was quickly suffused with suspicion. "This is just you offering me a ride because you're a nice guy, right? No other reason?"

Milton knew what she was suggesting: what did he expect in return? "I'm not that kind of guy," he said. "I'm going to Vegas; you want to go to Vegas. You'll have to put up with my taste in music, but that's it."

She glanced at her inert car. "I guess I could leave it here and get the garage to pick it up."

"Well, the offer's there."

"My stuff's in the back."

"And you can't open it?"

She shook her head. "The doors, the trunk—they're locked. But I don't suppose it's a big deal. I can get what I need in Vegas."

Milton waited for her to make up her mind.

"What's your name?" she asked him.

"John Smith."

She narrowed her eyes at him.

"Scout's honour," he said. "You'll be safe."

She sighed, got to her feet and put out her hand. "Thanks, John. Appreciate it."

"And you are?"

"Jessica Russo," she said. "Nice to meet you."

9

M ilton stepped aside so that she could get into the car. He went around to the other side, dropped into the seat and started the engine. It rumbled happily, ready to devour the miles once again. Milton almost made a comment about the enduring benefits of the internal combustion engine, but held his tongue. He put the car into reverse and edged out of the parking space. Jessica gazed out at the Tesla as Milton put the GTO into drive and rolled out onto the freeway.

"I was going to get a Porsche," she said. "I wish I had."

She took out her phone and cancelled the roadside assistance. She finished with that and made another call. Milton could only hear her side of the conversation, but could tell that she was speaking to her father. She told him what had happened with her car, that she had hitched a lift back to Vegas, and that she would be a little later than planned. She engaged in a little extra small talk and then ended the call.

"All okay?"

"Fine," she said.

They were on the fringe of the Mojave National Preserve. The road was two lanes going northeast and two lanes going southwest. The traffic was scarce, and all Milton could see to the left and the right were the wide-open plains, tickled with scrub, running all the way to the mountains that loomed in the gloomy distance.

Jessica grew quiet and brooding.

"Is everything all right?" he asked her.

"I'm sorry," she said. "I don't mean to be antisocial. It's just…"

"Whatever it is, we don't have to talk about it."

"It's fine," she said. "I can't pretend like it's not happening. My dad has cancer. The same type my mom had."

"I'm sorry," Milton said, abashed.

"The doctors say he's got a year. He's told them to stop the treatment so he can enjoy the time he has left. He's leaving the country."

"Where to?"

"Italy."

"Russo," Milton said. "You've got Italian blood?"

She nodded. "My family came from Siena, back in the 1900s. Dad wants to go before… well, you know, while he still can. That's why Mason and me are going back."

"Mason?"

"My brother."

"You're both going with him?"

"Yes," she said. "It's why I was upset back at the truck stop. I don't usually burst into tears in front of strangers. I was just worried that I wouldn't be able to get back in time."

"What time's the flight?"

"Eleven. I'm picking Dad up and meeting Mason at the airport."

Milton looked at his watch. "You'll be there in plenty of

time."

Milton decided to put on some music to help lighten the mood. He reached down for the tape that he had dropped into the storage bin in the side of the door. It was Donovan's 'The Hurdy Gurdy Man,' and as he pushed the tape into the player, the title track played out.

"You weren't kidding," she said.

"About what?"

She gestured at the stereo. "Your taste in music."

"What do you mean?" Milton protested. "This is a classic."

"I don't even know who it is."

"You've never heard of Donovan?"

She shrugged. "Should I have?"

Milton handed her the cassette box. She took it and held it out in front of her with an expression of exaggerated curiosity.

"Don't tell me you've never seen a tape before," Milton said.

"What can I say? I'm twenty-two. This is practically an antique."

"Come *on*," Milton said.

She shone him a bright, white smile. "Relax," she said. "I'm kidding."

Jessica brightened now, visibly relaxing. She was attractive, in that wholesome and hearty way that he had observed in so many American women. Her skin was clear and her teeth were perfect. She wore her hair long, down past her shoulders, tying it into a ponytail to keep it out of her face. Her eyes were lively, too, especially now that the redness from her tears had started to fade.

"Put something else on if you like," Milton said. "There are more tapes in the glove box."

She opened the compartment and sifted through the tapes. "I've never heard of any of these," she complained. "The Kinks. The Small Faces. Manfred Mann."

"What do you like?" Milton said.

"Beyoncé," she said.

"Don't have any Beyoncé."

"This'll do."

She ejected Donovan and pressed in a Creedence Clearwater Revival compilation. 'Bad Moon Rising' started.

They listened together, Jessica tapping her finger to the beat. The GTO leapt forward hungrily, and Milton had to make an effort not to let it race ahead.

"Tell me about your brother," Milton said.

"What do you want to know?"

"Younger or older?"

"Five minutes older," she said. "We're twins."

"What does he do?"

"He was army."

"He got out?"

She paused for a moment. "Got a discharge."

There was something there that she wasn't saying. Milton guessed that her brother had not left the army on the best of terms, but saw no point in prying into something that might be uncomfortable.

She changed the subject. "Where's your accent from?"

"England."

"What are you doing here?"

"Holiday. I've always wanted to drive cross country."

"And you're stopping in Vegas?"

"It's been a while since I was here. I thought I'd spend a day or two."

They reached Halloran Springs; they were approaching the state line. Milton allowed himself to succumb to temptation, pushed down a little on the gas and watched as the speedometer slid around to ninety. Jessica was comfortable; she sat with her legs drawn up and her arms around her knees.

She looked over at him. "What do you do when you're not on vacation?"

"For work? Nothing much."

"You don't have a job?"

"I'm a cook," he said. "I have a job in London."

"Seriously?"

"Seriously."

"You weren't always a cook, though?"

"Why do you say that?"

"You were in the military."

He looked over at her, surprised by her perspicacity. "How'd you work that out?"

"Like I said—my brother was military. All the soldiers I've ever met have the same look. I saw you in the diner and thought you were military."

"That was a long time ago. I've been out for years."

"Working as a cook," she said, apparently still finding that difficult to credit.

"For part of the year," Milton explained. "I save up; then I spend that travelling around. Sometimes I work while I'm on the move; other times I don't."

There was an eighteen-wheeler ahead of them. Milton flicked the turn signal and pulled out, stamping down on the gas and pushing ninety as they blasted by it. He pulled back into the right-hand lane and let the speed bleed down to seventy again.

Jessica grew quieter as they drew closer to the city. She seemed to be thinking about something. Milton listened to the music and concentrated on the road ahead.

10

Milton pushed the speed limit until he judged the risk of being pulled over had grown to an unacceptable level. As a result, they made excellent time. It was a quarter past nine when the neon lights of the Strip glowed in the distance, a hue of golds and pinks smudged against the dark, beckoning people with the promise of luck and fortune. Milton had interest in neither. In truth, it was with some trepidation that he looked on those monuments to gambling and excess. He felt secure in his sobriety, but he knew that there were few places on the planet that were designed to encourage a lapse better than Vegas.

Jessica directed him onto the Bruce Woodbury Parkway and then to the west of the city and Summerlin. She took them into a neighbourhood where the houses grew in size the deeper inside they went. The properties on the outskirts were modern, two-storey stucco homes with small yards, but, as they drove along the enclave's quiet roads, those residences mutated into sprawling mini-mansions set in generous grounds. The properties had circular drives and privacy walls and water features and all of the other foolish things people surrounded themselves with when they found that they had more money than they knew what to do with and tried to show it off.

"It's nice here," Milton said. "What does your dad do?"

"Did," she said. "He worked in IT. Network security. For the casinos."

The streets were quiet, but as Milton followed Jessica's directions, he saw the lights of two cars approaching them. He observed the lead vehicle and then the one in the rear; they were identical Chevrolet Suburbans. The driver of the first SUV stared at Milton as they rolled by one another. Milton got a good look at him: hair cut short, appeared to be reasonably large, wearing a dark top.

He felt a quiver of disquiet.

"What is it?" Jessica asked him.

"You recognise either of those cars?"

"No," she said. "But I don't live here."

Milton watched them until they passed out of sight around a corner. The two vehicles didn't belong here. They felt out of place.

"Why?" she asked him.

"It's nothing."

He drove on. The Russo home was at the back end of a cul-de-sac formed by two other homes. It had been built on a small rise, the expansive lawn spilling down toward the street with a paved path offering access. The property had been built in a Mediterranean style, two storeys tall and with the main body of the building bracketed by identical wings that looked as if they were used as garages. A half-moon-shaped drive curled in front of the white stucco struc-ture. The majority of the house was dark, save two windows to the right. The double front doors were nearly ten feet tall and looked like they belonged on the front of a small castle rather than a house, even a house as expensive as this one. They were wooden and ornate, with metal studs and cross bands.

Milton parked and looked up at the house, searching for anything that might be a reason for the unease he was feeling. The door was closed; the windows were closed; there was no sign of activity in any of the rooms that he could see into.

He thought of the two SUVs. Something still didn't feel right.

"Does anything look out of place?" Milton asked.

She looked at the house and frowned. "Maybe a little quiet."

"What would it normally be like?"

"The blinds downstairs would usually be down. And my father would usually have the sprinklers on. Why are you asking?"

Milton got out of the car, shut the door quietly and listened again. There was silence, and, given the proximity to Vegas, that was surprising. Milton knew they were on the fringe of the desert here, but it was still uncanny how the noise of the Strip had been smothered by the simple expedient of travelling a few miles to the west. He heard the whoosh and chug of a sprinkler in the garden of one of the other houses and, in the distance, the howl of a coyote.

She got out, too, and came to stand beside him. "What is it?"

Milton shook his head and put a smile on his face. "Forget it. You've got a flight to catch. I hope Italy is great."

"Thanks," she said. "I appreciate it. You've been amazing."

"Please pass my best wishes to your father," he said.

She leaned in to him and placed a kiss on his cheek. "Goodbye, John."

"Goodbye."

Milton stood beside the car, watching as Jessica climbed the rise and reached the front doors. There was a small keypad on the left of the doors, and an overhead light flashed on as she reached it. She tapped out the code on the keypad and pushed the doors open. She turned back to give him a final wave and then she went inside.

He waited.

11

Oscar Delgado stared out of the windshield at the GTO as it rolled slowly in the other direction, heading toward the cul-de-sac that they had just left. The car was distinctive, but that wasn't what had given him pause. It wasn't the driver, either, although there had been something in the man's expression that had made Delgado's hackles rise as he had driven by.

No.

It wasn't the car or the driver that had arrested Delgado's attention.

It was the woman in the passenger seat.

The GTO passed them, the engine rumbling, and continued toward the Russo house. Delgado let it go, waiting until it had turned the corner and was out of sight.

He turned to Higuaín. "Stop."

"What? Now?"

"Yes, *now*."

Higuaín pulled over to the side of the road. Pérez was driving the Suburban behind them and he pulled over, too.

Delgado took the radio from the dash and held down the button to transmit.

"Pérez," he said.

"Yes, boss."

"Go back."

"What?"

"Go back to the house."

"I don't get it. What's wrong?"

"You see that GTO that just went by?"

"Sí."

"Jessica Russo was in it."

"Shit," he said. *"I didn't—"*

"Go back and get her." He thought about the driver. "There's a guy with her," he added.

"What you want me to do with him?"

"Bring him, too."

Pérez acknowledged the instruction. Delgado looked in the rear-view as the second Suburban performed a three-point turn and started to roll back toward the house. Delgado watched for a moment and then allowed his focus to draw in and drift down to the other men in the back of the vehicle. The SUV had the two seats up front, then a row of three, and then, at the rear, another two. He had four of his men with him: Higuaín was in front and Castellanos was in the back, with Grande and Araujo in the row of three. Grande was in the leftmost seat and Araujo was in the rightmost, with a fifth man wedged between them. He wore a hood over his head, and his hands were secured behind his back with two cable ties. He was wearing shorts and a T-shirt, and there was blood on his right leg from where he had fallen into the glass table during the struggle to subdue him.

He had fought, and that was not surprising. Richard

Russo had worked for the cartel for two years and, in that time, he must have realised what would come to those who were crazy enough to cross them. Delgado was the cartel's representative in Las Vegas. Russo's betrayal did not look good for Delgado, and fixing the mess that had been caused —and finding the money that had been taken—was his highest priority. He needed to get it done before La Bruja found out just how serious the situation was.

Delgado was confident that he could persuade Russo to cooperate now that he had him in his custody.

But having his daughter, too?

That wouldn't hurt at all.

Higuaín put his hands back on the wheel. "What you want me to do, boss?"

"Follow them," he said.

Higuaín nodded and turned the Suburban around.

12

Milton waited outside the car. He rolled his shoulders forward and back, working out the tension, loosening the knots from the nine-hour drive, forcing himself to relax. He watched as the light for the hall switched on, and then another, and then a final one in what he assumed must have been the living room. He leaned back against the car, enjoying the cool edge to the night, wondering whether he might be able to take a swim when he arrived at the hotel. It had been a long day, and he knew that a little exercise before bed would guarantee a deep and restful night's sleep.

He was contemplating what he would like for his evening meal when the front door was flung open and Jessica walked quickly back outside. She came down the path and made her way straight for him. Her face was white.

"What is it?"

"Something's wrong."

"What?"

"Really fucking wrong."

He pushed himself upright. "What is it, Jessica?"

"He's not there. My father—he's not inside."

"He couldn't have gone to the airport?"

"I'm meeting him *here*," she said, her voice quivering. "And the house has been wrecked."

"What do you mean?"

"I mean the table in the living room is smashed. The drawers have been pulled out. The books in the bookshelves are all over the floor. Someone must have broken in." She paused, her face twisting with a mixture of realisation and fear. "Those SUVs that passed us—you said they bothered you."

"I thought they looked strange," he said.

"Jesus," she said. "What the fuck is going on?"

"I don't know," he said carefully. He wanted to tell her that there was nothing to worry about, that there must have been an explanation for what she had seen, but if the house had been turned over like she said... She was no fool. "Show me."

Milton scanned the cul-de-sac as they approached the bottom end of the drive. There were no cars on the street, and the other two homes were dark. He could hear the sprinkler nearby, but that was it. He spotted a Jaguar parked in the drive of the house on the left, but it was the only sign that he could see that indicated that the neighbouring homes were lived in.

They reached the top of the drive. Milton listened for sounds inside the home.

Nothing.

"Show me around," he said.

Milton went inside first and Jessica followed. They were standing in a large foyer. The floors were made of marble and there were large portraits on the wall: Milton saw a younger Jessica, a teenage boy who looked like her—he remembered that she and her brother were twins, and guessed that it must have been him—and an older couple who he guessed were her mother and father. There was a circular staircase to the left and a ceiling light above.

Milton listened.

Nothing.

Jessica led him through the foyer, across an open passageway and through a set of decorative pillars into a vast living space. A huge marble fireplace was off to the left, and a long wet bar made of matching marble was to the right. Two leather sofas faced each other in the middle of the room. A set of three shallow steps led up to a breakfast nook and, beyond it, a huge kitchen and family area.

"Look," she said, pointing.

The remains of a glass table lay between the two sofas. The glass top had been shattered, with large shards scattered beneath and around the wrought-iron frame. A smashed vase contributed its emerald-coloured glass to the debris, with books and papers similarly strewn over the floor. Milton approached the table and knelt down; there was a patch of red across the corner of the frame. He dabbed his fingers against it; it was tacky, and his fingers brought back a faint red stain.

There had evidently been a struggle. Someone had fallen back and cut themselves against the corner of the table. Not long ago, either, if the blood was still wet.

They were near a window. Milton went to it and looked out into the cul-de-sac beyond. There was his GTO and nothing else.

"Dad!" Jessica yelled. "Dad! You here?"

Milton put a hand on her shoulder. "We need to check the rest of the house."

"Dad!"

"Jessica." He needed her to be quiet.

"That's *blood*," she said, pointing down at the table.

She was on the edge of panic and Milton needed her to keep it together. "Let's just be sure he's not here," he said. "Do you understand?"

"He's *not*."

"Let's check."

Jessica stiffened and fell silent. Finally, she nodded. "Okay. Where?"

"Every room. We'll start at the top and work down."

13

They went back to the spiral staircase in the foyer and climbed it to the floor above. Milton followed Jessica up to an impressive landing that was carpeted in deep shag. They followed the hallway to a bedroom. It looked like a master suite, with a huge king-size bed in the centre of the room with a vaulted ceiling overhead. Jessica stayed where she was, while Milton carried on into the his-and-hers en suites, both done out in ostentatious marble with gold fixtures and fittings. Even the medicine cabinets had been turned out, with bottles scattered on the floor and in the sink.

He returned to the bedroom. Jessica was standing by the headboard of the bed, withdrawing her hand from behind it.

"Okay?" Milton said.

She nodded.

"What are you looking for?"

"My father kept a gun here."

"Behind the headboard?"

"Yes. But it's not there."

She led him to a second living room, then a third and fourth bedroom. Both these bedrooms were furnished with en suite bathrooms featuring marble floors and brass fixtures, and there was an enormous family bathroom. The rooms had clearly all been searched, with drawers pulled out and overturned, their contents scattered across the floors. Clothes had been yanked out of the wardrobes. The place had been ransacked. It was a mess.

"You think it's burglars?"

"It could be," Milton said.

"So where's my dad?"

"I don't know that yet."

They returned to the landing.

Milton gestured to the only door that they hadn't checked. "Through here?"

"Guest suite," Jessica said, opening the door.

Milton went inside. It was another vast bedroom, ransacked like all the others. The room was at the front of the house, and the view from the floor-to-ceiling picture windows was impressive. They were up high and the elevation afforded a magnificent vista; he could see the Strip in the far distance, the neon pulsing and throbbing, throwing coloured light up into the dark. Milton saw his Pontiac below and, behind that, the lights of an approaching vehicle. It was moving slowly and cautiously and looked big and boxy, the black paintwork glittering in the light from the streetlamps.

A second vehicle turned into the cul-de-sac and followed the first.

Milton frowned: it was the pair of Chevrolet Suburbans that they had passed earlier.

"John?"

Milton ignored her, his attention still fixed on the Suburbans. The second one stopped alongside the GTO. A man stepped out of the cabin, went to the door of the car and tried it. Milton had not locked it and, as he watched, the man slid inside the car. The first Suburban moved ahead, turning onto the drive that led up to the house. The doors opened and three men disembarked.

Jessica joined him at the window. "Are those the same cars?"

The men walked up the drive. The fourth man—the one who had checked out the GTO—followed them. The second Suburban stayed on the road. Both vehicles had killed their lights, but Milton could see the exhaust still swirling around their pipes. He knew what they were doing: the occupants of the second vehicle were standing sentry for the others and providing cover should anyone arrive at—or try to leave— the house.

"Come away from the window," Milton said, taking Jessica by the elbow and moving her back.

"I don't understand—who are they?"

"Doesn't matter for now. We need to get out. I don't think we want to be in here when they arrive."

"What about my dad?"

Milton had a very bad feeling about that. "We'll sort that out once we're safe, but now we need to go. *Right* now. Does your father have a car in the garage?"

"Yes," she said. "I think so."

"Which way?"

"There are two garages. He keeps the lawnmower in that one." She pointed over to the right, then to the left. "His cars are in there."

Milton led the way back to the landing. He paused at the top of the stairs, straining his ears for any suggestion that there was anyone else in the house with them, and, satisfied that there was not—yet—he started quickly down. The staircase wound around itself, and it was only as he reached the final few treads that he was able to look down into the foyer. There was a panel of glass on either side of the double-height front doors, and Milton froze as he saw the silhouette of a man in the window to the right of the door.

He reached back with his hand, stopping Jessica behind him, and held his breath.

14

The man in the window moved to the right, his silhouette no longer visible. Milton grabbed Jessica by the wrist and hurried her down the remaining steps. He moved as quickly as he dared, hurrying through the foyer and then into the central corridor that ran across the middle of the property from east to west. There were skylights overhead, and the moon cast its glow down onto them, silvering the antique side table and occasional chairs.

Milton reached a billiard lounge with no obvious way out.

"This way," Jessica said.

There was a door to the right, on the other side of the table. Jessica pushed it open and led the way through into a room that had been left undecorated, with a plain tiled floor and walls painted in neutral grey. The room was in the shape of an L: Milton walked ahead three paces. There was a laundry room to the right and, straight ahead, another door.

"Garage?" he asked.

Jessica pointed forward. "Through there."

Milton heard the faint sound of a voice from behind them, from somewhere near the front of the house.

The men were inside.

Milton walked up to the garage door. He listened.

Silence.

"Stay here," Milton said. "I'm going to check it out. Don't move."

She blinked several times, then nodded.

Milton put his ear to the door to the garage, listening hard, but still heard nothing. He pushed down on the chrome lever and pulled the door open.

A gleaming grey Cadillac Escalade and a navy Porsche Macan were parked next to one another underneath fluorescent lights. The epoxied floor looked as if it had been lifted straight from the showroom with not a single mark on it. Four mountain bikes were hung on the far wall. Sets of golf clubs rested in front of the Macan.

Milton took the two stairs down into the garage and then realised what was wrong.

There was no reason for the lights in the garage to have been left on.

He was on unfamiliar ground, in a situation he hadn't foreseen, and he had been unforgivably careless.

"Don't move."

The barrel of a gun pressed against the back of his skull.

Milton stood still.

The pressure of the gun increased against the back of his head.

"What's happening?" Milton said, feigning fright. "Who are you?"

"Hands against the wall."

Milton did as he was told.

The gun withdrew.

"Turn around."

Milton turned and saw his assailant. The man was the same height as him, in his late twenties, with hair buzzed so short it would have been possible to set a drink on top of it. He was Hispanic, with a big nose and a small mouth, and was clean shaven. His shoulders and chest had evidently received attention in the gym. He had a small earpiece in his ear, and a mic was clipped to the lapel of his black shirt. He held his Ruger like it was not his first time, the muzzle centred on Milton's chest.

"I have one male secured," the man said into the mic, "in the garage."

Milton glanced around for anything that might offer him a means of fighting back. There was nothing to hand, but he kept his thoughts focused and calm. The man had no idea who Milton was, nor what he was capable of. That was an advantage.

"Where's the woman?" the man asked.

"Who?"

"Jessica."

"I don't know," he said.

"So why are you here?"

"I'm just a friend of the family," Milton said, his hands up, faking the fear that the man would expect.

"You let yourself in?"

"I have a key."

"But why are you here?"

"I'm staying here tonight. I came in and saw the place had been wrecked."

The corner of the man's mouth flickered into a small smile. "Where's the girl?" he repeated.

"She's not here."

"She was in the car with you. We saw."

"No, she wasn't," he protested. "I'm on my own."

"You're gonna protect her?" The man shook his head. "That'd be a really bad idea."

"Please," Milton said. "There's no need to point that thing at me."

"Where is she?"

"I already told you—she's not here."

The man raised the Ruger so that now it was level with Milton's mouth. "This isn't doing you any favours, *cabrón*. You want to walk out of here? You need to tell me where I can find her."

"I told you—I can't help."

The guy shook his head, making a show of his disappointment in Milton's stubbornness. He stepped closer and pressed the small black earpiece with his free hand.

"*Es Pérez,*" he said. "*Estoy en el garaje. La niña está en la casa, pero no conmigo.*"

Milton took a breath, balancing himself, readying his body for sudden and violent action. His movements were small and subtle, and would have been imperceptible to anyone who didn't know what to look for. He bent his knees a little and leaned forward until his weight was directly over his feet; he straightened the four fingers of his right hand, bracing his forefinger with his thumb.

The man smiled at Milton, both corners of his mouth turning upward this time. "You need to tell me now."

"Okay," Milton said. "She's upstairs."

The man relaxed his arm just a fraction. He reached his left hand up to the broadcast button on his earpiece. His attention flickered away, just for a moment.

Long enough.

Milton moved.

15

Milton brought his left hand up hard into the man's elbow. The muzzle of the gun went straight up, and the weapon discharged into the ceiling. Milton followed with his right hand, striking a hard, straight-fingered jab into the man's throat. The gun fell to the ground and the man stumbled backward, clutching at his larynx, unable to breathe. Milton raised his knee and kicked out, planting his boot in the middle of the man's chest and sending him back into the Porsche. Milton bent down, collected the Ruger, and put one bullet into the man's forehead. He slumped to the ground.

Milton stepped over to the man and knelt down next to him. He was wearing a Motorola TETRA radio, with earpiece and in-line lapel mic. Milton plucked the earpiece out of the man's ear and pushed it into his own.

He overheard the conversation. *"Morazán, Lòpez. Pérez está en el garaje."*

A second speaker responded: *"Es Morazán. ¿Qué quieres que hagamos?"*

"Revisa el primer piso y luego encuéntrate con él."

"Afirmativo."

Milton's Spanish was basic, but he understood the gist of what he had heard. The man he had killed was Pérez. He must have breached the property through the side door to the garage. Morazán and Lòpez were the other men whom Milton had seen coming inside, through the front door. He had no idea where they were now, but if they were clearing the first floor, then they would discover Jessica in the laundry room before they got to him.

He had to move. He frisked Pérez and found a wallet and a cellphone. He put both into his pocket and then checked the Ruger. It was a nice weapon, compact and well made, with a precision-machined nitride stainless steel chassis and slide. He ejected the magazine and counted the load: there were eleven rounds in the mag and another one in the chamber. He pressed the magazine back into the well, climbed the steps, opened the door and made his way back to the laundry room.

～

JESSICA WAS HIDING behind the upright tumble dryer. She was pale.

"I heard shooting," she said.

"There are men in the house," Milton said. "They're looking for you. We need to leave."

"But the gunshots?"

"One of them jumped me in the garage."

"He fired at you?"

"No," Milton said. "But he would have."

"So?"

"So I shot him first."

"*Jesus!*"

They didn't have time for a conversation like this. There were at least two men in the house—probably more—and they were likely heading in their direction.

"We need to leave, Jessica. It's not safe for you here. For either of us."

He heard the sound of footsteps coming down the central corridor toward the billiard lounge. He grabbed Jessica by the wrist and pulled her through the door and into the garage. They went down the steps, and Jessica stopped in her tracks as she saw the body of the dead man. The bullet had passed through his head from front to back, and blood and fluids were leaking from both gory wounds. Milton dragged her on, taking her to the southeast corner of the garage, next to a set of shelves that held plastic boxes of junk and pots of paint. It was hidden from the door by the two vehicles.

"Stay down low," he said.

Jessica crouched down. Milton switched off the overhead lights and took up a position behind the Porsche, at an angle that allowed him a clear line of fire to the door. He dropped to one knee, raised the Ruger, took a deep breath to steady himself, then exhaled.

He blinked slowly, waiting for his eyes to adjust to the gloom.

There was enough light from the street shining through the window on the south wall for him to see across the space. The door opened and the first man appeared, followed closely by a second man. Milton waited for them to come fully into the garage. He had a visual on them both: they were dressed similarly to Pérez, all in black. They were both armed, too, each toting a large handgun.

"*Estamos dentro,*" the second man said. Milton heard it

from across the room and in the earpiece he had taken from the dead man.

The first man glanced to his left, in Milton's direction, and caught sight of the body on the floor.

"*Mierda.*"

The earpiece buzzed. "*¿Qué es?*"

Milton changed his aim, drawing a bead on the second man. The target was too far away for Milton to risk a headshot, so he aimed into the middle of the inverted triangle between the man's head and waist. He pulled the trigger, just once, and hit him squarely in the gut. The man's body fell back, blocking the door. His colleague must have noticed the muzzle flash; he turned toward Milton and brought up his weapon, but Milton had already taken fresh aim. He squeezed off a second shot, and the man was drilled in the side of his torso. He stumbled forward and Milton fired again, dropping him to the ground.

He kept a running tally: four shots, four hits. Nine rounds left.

His earpiece crackled. "*¿Qué es?*"

Milton went over to the two men, the Ruger trained down on both of them. They were both still alive, but they were bleeding out from their wounds. Milton shot them both at close range. Seven rounds left.

He stood, took another deep breath in, and then exhaled. He felt no regret for what he had just done. Three men were dead. Another three to add to a very long list. But these men were not as helpless as some of those who had paid the price for crossing his path. These men were armed, and they had forced their way into the house with bad intentions. Milton didn't know where Jessica's father was, but the blood in the living room suggested that he had been hurt and removed from the premises. Milton did not enjoy violence. He never had. But here, tonight, he had been left with no choice. He would have been a dead man if he had hesitated. Kill or be killed.

He also knew that his ruthlessness would mean nothing if they did not move quickly. He frisked the two men, taking their weapons and ejecting the magazines. He pocketed both.

The radio crackled again. *"¿Qué es? Pérez?"*

Milton went back to where Jessica was hiding.

"Lòpez, qué esta pasando?"

The window of opportunity to get out of the house was closing. Milton had no idea how many more men were inside and outside the property. He had seen two SUVs. How many men were inside them? It was impossible to do anything other than guess, but Milton always worked on the worst-case scenario. He would assume there were at least another four, meaning that, together with the man in charge, he was looking at a minimum of five hostiles. If they came in heavy, knowing that three colleagues had gone quiet...

Milton didn't like those odds very much at all.

"Higuaín, hemos sido atacados. Acérquese al garaje inmediatamente con precaución."

Milton gestured for Jessica to stand. She did. She was white, and he saw that her hands were trembling.

"I need you to focus," Milton said. "Can you do that for me?"

She stared blankly at him.

"Jessica—we need to leave. And I need your help to do that."

She nodded. "I'm good," she said. "I'm good."

"The keys to the cars. Where are they?"

"Don't know about the Escalade."

"The Porsche?"

"He always leaves them under the seat."

16

Milton dragged the dead bodies out of the way, then pulled the laundry room door shut and twisted the lock on the handle. It was nothing significant, but it might allow them another few seconds in the event that they needed it.

Jessica was already in the back of the Porsche, as he'd instructed her. Milton got into the front, turned the key in the ignition, and the big engine rumbled to life. He pulled the seat belt across his body and clicked it home.

He pressed the button in the car's control panel that lifted the garage door.

"Buckle up."

Jessica did as she was told.

Milton rolled the car out of the garage. Both this garage and the one in the opposite wing were accessed by paved driveways that met in the middle, in a Y shape, and then ran down between the front lawns to the road. The first of the black SUVs had been placed at the end of the drive so that it blocked the way to the road. The second SUV was on the move, and, as Milton watched, the driver turned the wheel and parked nose-to-nose with the first one so that the obstruction was complete.

Milton turned to his right, to the house's open front door, and saw a man there.

The man aimed a suppressed pistol in their direction.

"Down!"

The suppressor deadened the sound of the shot, but did not silence it. Milton flinched as the round punched a hole through his window, passed through the cabin and punched a second hole through the window on the opposite side.

He flung himself upright once more and stomped on the pedal, and the Macan responded, firing forward and sending a spray of gravel up behind it. The force of the acceleration pushed Milton back into the seat. He steered down the driveway and, at the last moment, swung the wheel hard right. The Macan chewed across the lawn, clipped the back of the second SUV, and kept going.

He kept the accelerator pinned to the floor. He roared by his abandoned GTO and raced out of the neighbourhood.

17

"Y̶ou okay?" Milton called back.

Jessica didn't reply; Milton looked into the mirror and saw the young woman sitting up again behind him, her face as white as snow. She had her left arm extended forward, using her hand to brace herself against the back of Milton's seat.

"Hold on."

Milton retraced the route that they had taken to get to the house. He kept his eyes on the rear-view mirror, finally easing his foot off the pedal when they were on the Summerlin Parkway. He waited for his heart to slow down. He had been in situations like this more times than he cared to count; the adrenaline always managed to find him.

"What's happening?" Jessica said. "Those men... my father..."

Milton pushed down on the pedal and picked up speed.

"The blood..." she said. She didn't finish the sentence.

"It looked like there was a struggle," Milton said. "Someone was hurt."

"My father. I don't..." She stifled a sob. "I don't under-stand why that would have happened."

"You said your dad worked for the casinos."

"Yes."

"Would he have any enemies?"

"No," she said. "None."

"Your brother?"

"No. I don't think so."

"He's supposed to be at the airport?"

"Yes. Meeting us there."

"Call him."

Jessica took out her phone, touched the screen and then held it to her ear. She waited, saying nothing, her face in the mirror increasingly concerned. She took the phone away from her ear and shook her head.

"Nothing?" Milton said.

"Straight to voicemail."

"Is that unusual?"

"I don't know... he's not always the easiest to get hold of, but he should be waiting to hear from me."

They were approaching the off-ramp for North and South Rampart Road. Milton checked the mirror. There was nothing behind them. The earpiece he was still wearing—he had forgotten that it was still there—crackled into life, and Milton looked in the mirror again.

"*¿Hola?*"

He recognised the voice: it was the man he had heard before, presumably the man who was in charge.

"Hello."

"*¿Y tú? ¿Quién eres?*"

Milton arranged the in-line mic so that it was just below his chin. "I don't speak Spanish."

"English, then."

"That'll do."

"You are Señor Smith."

It was a statement, not a question, and designed to catch him off-guard. Milton was wise to it.

"You found the bill of sale?"

"It was in your car."

"It was."

Milton watched the mirror. Still nothing. He saw Jessica's face, her expression quizzical. He ignored her.

"You killed three of my men, Señor Smith."

"They shouldn't have pointed their guns at me."

Jessica looked as if she was about to speak. Milton held her gaze and shook his head.

"I would very much like to know who you are."

"And I'd like a date with Jessica Biel. Neither of those things are going to happen."

The man chuckled. *"You're funny, señor."*

"I'm hilarious. What do I call you?"

"My name is Oscar. Shall I call you John?"

"Call me whatever you like."

"You have the woman, John? Jessica Russo?"

Milton could hear the sound of a car's engine behind the man's voice and checked the mirrors again. "That's right."

"How much is she worth to you?"

"What do you mean?"

"How much for you to bring her back?"

Milton looked back again. They were in the middle lane of the three-lane freeway. On their left, four cars back, he saw what looked like an SUV. Its headlights were bright, and although Milton could not identify the make, he could see its size. In the lane to their right, the same distance behind them, he saw the first vehicle's twin. Same size, same shape, same bright lights.

Shit.

"*Ten thousand dollars,*" Oscar said.

Milton watched the cars approach, taking their time as they worked into position. They were patient, not doing anything to attract attention, just slowly reeling them in.

"No," Milton said.

"*Twenty?*"

"I'm not selling her out."

"*Fifty?*"

"You're not paying attention, Oscar. It's not happening."

"*You'll make an enemy out of a man like* me *for the sake of the woman?*"

The two Suburbans pulled closer, getting ready to bracket them. Milton held the Porsche steady, waiting. He wanted to get a feel for what the drivers behind them were doing before he made his decision. He accelerated slightly, then signalled to switch into the left lane. He moved across and checked the mirror. The SUV on their right mirrored his move, changing lanes and moving to the middle.

They wanted to stay close and wide. They weren't going to wait much longer.

Milton looked ahead for a way out. "I'm going to call the police, Oscar."

"*I wouldn't do that. That wouldn't end well for her father.*"

"Doesn't matter if he's already dead."

"*He's not dead.*"

"What about her brother?"

"*What?*"

"Her brother. What about him?"

"*I don't need her brother, señor. I have the father.*"

Milton gave a little push to the accelerator and watched. As the Porsche moved forward, so did both of the SUVs.

"And her father is okay?"

"He is."

"Really? I saw blood at the house."

"Señor Russo did not cooperate. We had to be forceful. But he is alive."

Milton muted the microphone. "You're belted in, Jessica?"

"Yes."

"Next exit. What's it like?"

She squinted. "What do you mean?"

"Just describe the exit and what it takes us to. Downhill? Uphill? Multiple lanes? Busy crossroad?"

"Señor Smith?"

"Downhill, I think," she said. "Two lanes. There's a light at the bottom. You can turn either direction. It's mostly strip malls and a gas station, I think. You should probably be thinking about getting over if we're getting off."

"I will," Milton told her, watching the mirror.

"Señor Smith? Are you still there?"

He unmuted the mic. "I am. And I'm going to say this once. You won't be able to find out who I am, so I wouldn't waste time trying. I don't know Jessica. I just met her today. She's lucky I did. I can't say the same for you. I have a set of rules I live my life by. A series of steps. You could call it a moral code. Do you understand?"

"What does that have to do—"

"I've done some bad things in my life, Oscar, and I'm trying hard to make up for them. That means that I react badly to people like you."

"Is that so?"

The off-ramp raced toward them.

"It really is. You should let her father go and forget this ever happened."

"Is that a threat?"

"It's a suggestion. But you should give it some thought. I'm not the sort of man you want in your life."

There was a pickup in the middle lane just ahead of the first Suburban. The car directly behind the Porsche, sandwiched between them and the second Suburban, was a Nissan sedan.

"You're going to miss it," Jessica said.

Milton gripped the wheel.

"*John!* You're going right past it."

"Hold on."

Milton floored the accelerator and pulled the wheel hard to the right.

18

The pickup jammed on its brakes and Milton flew across the two lanes. They hit the off-ramp at full speed and the Porsche lifted off the ground as it hit the downslope. He watched the rear-view mirror. One of the SUVs was behind them, just reaching the off-ramp, but he didn't see the second.

There was a traffic signal at the bottom of the ramp. Milton lifted his foot from the accelerator. The light was red, but he didn't stop, spinning the wheel hard to the right again, taking the turn. He caught a glimpse of a sedan approaching from the left, screeching to a halt as Milton cut them off.

He stomped on the pedal again and the Porsche responded. They roared forward. He checked the mirror.

The SUV had made the corner, but it was alone.

Good. Maybe the second was stuck on the highway. Evading one pursuer would be far easier than two.

He scanned the road ahead. It was four lanes, two in each direction, with signals every half mile or so. Jessica had been correct. The area was devoted to industrial and retail, with warehouses and stores flying by on both sides. The Porsche continued to pick up speed. The SUV kept pace behind them. Milton knew that the Macan had a horse-power advantage over the Suburban, but he wasn't sure if it would be enough to outrun them. He hit the button on the display to bring up the map and confirmed that that wouldn't work in any event; there wasn't going to be enough road.

It would take a little more than pure speed to get loose.

"Can we get back on the highway?" he asked, his eyes fixed ahead.

Jessica didn't reply.

"Jessica?"

"I'm *thinking*," she said, flustered. "Probably three more lights. Take a right; then it'll be in front of us."

Milton nodded and shifted in his seat, trying to get comfortable as the car barrelled forward at ninety.

The first light was green. Milton swerved around a motorcycle and another sedan, leaving both of them in his wake.

The SUV did the same, veering hard, staying behind them.

There was still no sign of the other SUV.

Milton focused on the next light, watching the rhythm and timing of its changing. He flexed his fingers on the wheel. The light was green, but they were still a good distance away. Milton knew it would be on red when they hit the intersection. He saw cars on both sides of the junc-tion, ready to go just as soon as the light turned in their favour.

"Come on," Milton muttered, standing hard on the accelerator.

Green.

Five hundred metres away.

Ninety-five miles an hour.

Two hundred metres away.

Come on.

Green.

One hundred and five.

Yellow.

"Hold on," Milton said.

Jessica pressed herself back into her seat. "Oh, my God."

They were fifty metres out of the intersection when the light went red.

One hundred and ten.

The car to the left of the junction stayed where it was. Perhaps the driver had seen the speeding Porsche headed in their direction. The car on the right, though—a lime green Volkswagen Jetta—took off as soon as the lights turned.

Milton angled the Porsche slightly to the left. He couldn't afford to brake and he had already committed to getting through. What he needed now was to avoid being sideswiped by the Jetta. He saw the driver's eyes as the Porsche crossed in front of it. It was a young kid with a backwards baseball cap, now furiously pounding his brakes. The Jetta slowed, but not enough, and clipped the back corner of the Porsche.

The front of the Porsche jerked right as the back swung left. Milton kept his foot on the pedal, steering the car into the skid, turning out of the contact. The car wobbled for a moment, righted itself, then kept flying.

Milton exhaled. He checked the mirror.

The Suburban couldn't avoid the Jetta. The two cars slammed together, the impact sending the smaller car spinning. The SUV stopped for a moment, then lurched forward, smoke coming from the tyres as they attempted to catch up.

"You're going to kill us," Jessica said.

"So will they," Milton said, already eyeing the signal up ahead. "If they catch us."

Milton had a bigger lead on the SUV now, but he still wasn't sure that it would be enough.

"This next light," Jessica said. "Go right if you want the freeway again."

"Hold on. This might be rough."

The needle on the speedometer reached one hundred and fifteen. Milton pulled his foot from the accelerator and felt the Porsche slow. He knew he could not take the corner going that hard, no matter how good the car was, but he didn't want to brake, either, and indicate to their pursuers what he was about to do.

The Suburban loomed larger in the rear-view.

"This one," Jessica said, leaning back in her seat, bracing herself. *"This one."*

"Got it," Milton said, then yanked the car hard to the right.

The tyres shrieked beneath them but stuck to the asphalt. The force pulled both of them hard to the left, and Milton had to brace himself against the door as they got around the apex of the corner. The Macan jerked them back to straight, but they were in the wrong lane, with a car coming straight for them.

And Milton immediately recognised it.

A black SUV.

Blinding headlights.

A twin to the one that was still right behind them.

Milton flattened the pedal, taking dead aim at the oncoming vehicle.

"What are you doing?" Jessica cried.

The Suburban in front of them slowed a fraction, just as Milton had hoped it would.

The gap closed between the cars quickly and, a split second before they struck the front of the oncoming vehicle, Milton lurched hard to the right. His driver's mirror caught the side of the second vehicle and snapped off, the debris cartwheeling across the road behind them.

Milton checked the rear-view.

The first Suburban had followed them around the corner and into the opposite lane and was still going full bore as Milton squirted out from in front of the second vehicle. He watched in his rear-view as the drivers veered off in desperate evasion. One Suburban went right and the other careened to the left, both of them leaving the road. Milton heard the crash as one of the cars blasted into a guardrail. The other one bounced down a slope, crashed through a chain-link fence and slid across the asphalt of an empty Walmart parking lot.

Milton turned his attention back to the road. He reached the green light before the underpass, took a wide arc to make the left-hand turn, then put them on the on-ramp. He slowed to a normal rate of speed as they ascended.

He looked back at Jessica. "Are you alright?"

She nodded slowly.

Milton nodded back at her, then began to head back in the direction that they had originally come from.

"Just a cook?" she said.

"Sorry?"

"Who are you?"

"Just a guy."

"Not a race car driver?"

"No, not a race car driver."

"So how does a cook know how to drive like that?"

Milton flexed his fingers on the wheel. "I've had some practice."

19

Milton headed south into Rainbow Park. He turned onto West Sahara Avenue and saw the red and yellow signage for a branch of In-N-Out Burger. He hadn't eaten since the baba ghanoush at the restaurant where he had met Jessica, and he was hungry. He could see that Jessica needed a break, too, and, more than that, he needed to have a conversation with her. He was happy that they had lost their pursuers and was as confident as he could be that it would be safe to stop: it was busy here, and he would be able to hide the Porsche at the back of the parking lot, away from the road.

He turned to her. "Hungry?"

"Not really."

"I am. And we need to work out what to do next. We can stop here for a while."

He indicated and turned off. The restaurant looked as if it had only recently been built, nestled amid a collection of similarly recent-looking businesses. There was a drive-thru lane and a busy parking lot. Milton guided the Porsche into the lot and parked it behind a large pickup that offered extra obstruction in the unlikely event that anyone who was looking for them might happen to drive past.

Milton got out of the car, went around to the passenger side and opened the door. Jessica got out from the back and came to stand behind him. He crouched down and reached his arm inside the front passenger footwell.

"What are you looking for?"

Milton leaned in so that he could look up at the under-side of the console. "The on-board diagnostics port."

"What's that?"

He found what he was looking for just above the footrest. His fingers brushed a block of plastic, and with a single firm tug, he pulled it loose.

"This is a GPS tracker," Milton said. "Modern cars often have them installed. It pings the location of the car back to a monitoring station."

"And you think they could use that to follow us?"

"Probably not," Milton said. "They'd need a password to get at the data, and I doubt they have that. Still, I'd rather be safe than sorry. It won't work now."

Milton didn't mention that getting the password would have been possible, given that their pursuers had her father in their custody. That, at least, didn't matter now; the tracker was inert. He dropped it into the cupholder.

Jessica was looking at him with a mixture of suspicion and curiosity. "Who *are* you?"

"You already asked me that. I'm no one."

"You shot those men," Jessica said, eyeing him closely.

"I told you—I was in the military."

"You said it was years ago. And you shot them like it was *nothing.*"

"I didn't like the alternative," he said.

"You knew how to get us out of the house, and then you

drove like a stunt driver. None of that is normal." She gestured down to the tracker. "And then you knew about that. Who knows stuff like that?"

"People who read the manual?"

"No. Come on. Stop lying to me. What exactly are you?"

"I'm a lot of things," Milton said. "Right now, I'm just trying to figure out if my help is needed. If it's not, you should tell me that it isn't so that we can go our own ways. But if you do want my help, you need to trust me. You need to stop asking about me and start telling me about you. You, your family, everything. That's the only way you'll see your father again."

20

They went into the restaurant. It was a popular hangout and it was Friday night, so there were only a couple of tables free. Milton told Jessica to go and get the table at the back of the room, and went to the counter to place his order.

"What can I get for you, sir?" the server asked him with a bright smile.

Milton looked up at the illuminated menu board on the wall behind the counter. "What's good?"

"You had a Double-Double before?"

"First time I've eaten here."

"Two patties, two cheese slices, lettuce, tomatoes, raw onions and Thousand Island dressing on the bun. You should try it. Seriously. Best burger in town."

Milton was famished and, although Jessica had said she wasn't hungry, he figured she'd change her mind after the adrenalin subsided. "I'll take two."

He added fries and sodas, paid, then picked up his numbered receipt and went to the table while the food was being prepared. Jessica was fretting with a napkin, tearing it into neat strips and then placing the strips one atop the other. Her phone was on the table. The screen was lit.

"You okay?" Milton asked her.

"Not really."

"I know this is hard."

"You think?"

He ignored the snark. "He's alive," he said. "Your father. I'm sure."

"How can you say that?"

"Because the guy on the radio said so."

"What did he say?"

"I told him that I was going to call the police, and he said that wouldn't be good for your father."

"And you believe him?"

"I do. If they were going to kill your father, they would have done it in the house. What would be the point in taking him away? No. They want something from him. That's why they came back for you, too—you're extra leverage to get it from him."

"But what? What do they want?"

"I don't know," Milton said. "I don't think your brother is with them. I asked—he said he wasn't, and there would be no reason to lie."

"So where is he?"

"You should try to call him again."

"I just did," she said, tapping a finger against the lit screen of her phone. "Same thing—voicemail again."

"Keep trying," Milton said.

Two drunken couples took the table next to them. Jessica glanced over at them, then back at Milton.

"This guy," she said, her voice a little lower. "Who is he?"

"He said his name is Oscar. That ring any bells?"

"I don't know anyone called Oscar."

"You're sure about that?"

"I *said* I don't," she snapped. "Jesus."

The server called out Milton's number, and he went up to the counter to collect his tray of food.

"Sorry," Jessica said to him when he returned.

"It's no problem."

She looked down at her phone, as if expecting a message that might clear everything up. "Why has he done this? Taken Dad? What has he ever done to him?"

"That's what we need to work out. You can start by telling me what your father does for a living. You said he worked for the casinos. You said he was in IT?"

"Yes," she said. "Network security."

Milton pushed one of the burgers and a packet of fries towards Jessica, unwrapped his own burger and took a bite. "What does that involve?"

"I don't know. It wasn't like I went and hung out with him. He went to his job; he came home from his job."

Milton took a second bite and then set the burger down on the greaseproof paper. "He must have talked about it, though?"

"Sometimes. But it wasn't like we had these long discussions. I'm not interested in computers, and he was discreet. I think a lot of the stuff he did was sensitive. Talking about it would've got him fired."

"Was there any stress?"

"He never said. Why?"

"I'm trying to work out what might be behind what happened. Maybe it's to do with money."

"Meaning?"

"There is a lot of money in the resorts," Milton said, dancing around the implication. "It might be valuable to the wrong sort of person."

She shook her head vigorously. "No way. Dad's a pretty straightforward, buttoned-down guy. He wouldn't get into anything that wasn't legitimate."

"What about your brother?"

"Like I said—he was a soldier. A straight shooter, just like Dad."

"You said he was discharged?"

"Yes."

"What for?"

She looked down at the table for a moment and then back up at Milton. "Drugs," she said. "He got in with the wrong crowd when he was young, and he joined up to try to go straight. It didn't work out. But if you think this has anything to do with him—no. There's no way."

Milton wasn't quite so ready to come to that conclusion, especially when her brother's location was uncertain, but there was no profit in pushing her now. "Can you think of anything that might explain why those men were there? Anything at all?"

She shook her head, then looked back down at the splayed-open grease paper and Milton's unfinished burger in the middle of it. "No. I have no idea. I wish I did know. It wouldn't be so scary if I knew what was happening, but I don't."

Milton watched her face as she spoke and saw nothing that made him doubt her. She appeared sincere and, as far as he could tell, confused about what had happened.

Jessica opened a packet of ketchup, picked up a handful of fries and dipped them into it. "So what do I do now? Call 911?" She popped her fries into her mouth, then, as though suddenly realising she was starving, unwrapped her burger and took a bite.

Milton leaned back in his seat and took another bite of

his burger. The easy option was to encourage Jessica to call the police, even though that would make things difficult for him. Milton had left three bodies at the Russo house, and any detective worth his or her salt would be able to see that the shots fired had not been simply lucky. Six shots, six hits, and two of those were kill shots from close range. He would have to explain what had happened. They would question where he had learned to shoot. Milton was already constructing a story that he could furnish if need be, but the thought of having to go through the charade made him uncomfortable. He didn't enjoy attention, official or otherwise, and this promised to deliver a whole boatload of it. All that being said, if going to the police was the prudent thing to do, he would have suggested it.

"I don't know if you should," he said.

"Why?"

"Because these men have your father. I'm not suggesting you don't speak to the police, but I think it might be wise to think about it for an hour or two. We need somewhere to stay so we can figure out the best thing to do."

"And you'll help?"

"If you'd like me to."

She cleared her throat. "I don't want to seem ungrateful. You've already helped me so much. But I need to know who you are before we do anything else. You still haven't told me."

Milton knew full well he didn't have to say anything, and he wasn't obliged to be honest with her. He could just get up and go, the way he'd done countless times before. But then he thought about the Steps, and the blood on his conscience, and the chance to do another thing that was right in an attempt to make amends. He couldn't leave her now if she said she wanted his assistance. Selfishness was a symptom of his condition, and he knew that if he allowed himself that luxury, then he would be taking a step along the path to his first drink in years, and he knew where that would lead.

"John?" she pressed. "*Please*. What did you used to do?"

"Special forces," he said. "The SAS."

"Like Delta?"

"Like them," he said. "I did some things after I left the Regiment that I'm not proud of."

"Legal things?"

He smiled without humour. "Legal," he said. "I can't tell you what they were, but I'm trying to make up for them now."

It was a flavour of the truth, enough for Jessica to get a sense of what he meant. She listened intently, and Milton could see that she was weighing up what to say next. She took another bite of her burger, swallowed and, seemingly decided, gave a firm nod of her head.

"Thank you," she said. "I'd like your help."

Milton nodded.

~

MILTON WAITED while Jessica went to the bathroom. He was involved now. The men who had seen him in the house were dead, so at least *they* wouldn't be able to describe him. The only look that Oscar's men would have had at him was through the windows of the GTO and the Porsche; the chances of him being identified from that were practically non-existent. On the other hand, Oscar now had the Pontiac and the documents that were inside it. Milton couldn't say for sure that there was no way back to him through them.

Milton had also exacerbated the situation by speaking to

Oscar and threatening him. Whatever it was that Oscar and his men were after, he knew that he would now be included as part of their problem.

He considered his options. The way he saw it, he had two.

First: he could find a safe place to put Jessica and then leave. But wherever that might be, it would only be safe for so long. She would make an error, Oscar would find her, and whatever Oscar wanted, he would get. It would mean abandoning the girl, and that went against Milton's code.

Second: he could stay and help. That meant finding a spot where they could hunker down in safety so that Milton could get a better handle on the lay of the land.

He had no idea who they were up against. They were professional, well armed, and ruthless enough to have kidnapped a man. That made them dangerous. He had no way of knowing what type of organisation they were and what their reach might be. Oscar had sounded Latino. Mexican? Colombian? Milton had crossed a cartel before and had barely escaped with his life. He would have preferred not to have *traficantes* as enemies again, but he needed to assume the worst. It was possible.

But it didn't really matter who it was, at least not for now. They were serious players. Few places would be safe.

He was going to need help.

21

Beau Baxter stretched out his legs, crossing his right ankle over his left. His snakeskin boots were dusty, and he rubbed the leather against the denim of his jeans to clean it off. What with the swimming pools and the man-made lakes, it was easy to forget sometimes that this crazy-ass town was in the desert.

It was just after eleven at night and the lights beneath the surface of the water threw shimmering reflections up against the sides of the building, where they were muted by the glow from the neon signs that reached up high overhead. The *H* in HOTEL was faulty, flickering on and off, the buzz of the electricity audible over the distant hum of the Strip.

Beau was at the El Cortez at 600 East Fremont. The place had been in Vegas since the forties; it had once been owned by Bugsy Siegel and didn't look as if it had changed much over the intervening seventy years. He had no time for the swanky hotels that had come to dominate the Strip. He had been coming to Vegas for forty years, and he preferred to think of it as it had been: seedy, sinful, sleazy. Full of life. Everything was different now, and the changes were—at least to his eye—not for the better. The corporations with their vast resorts had destroyed the atmosphere that had made the place so special. They had sucked the sap right out of it. It was antiseptic now. Homogenised. The hotels might have looked different from the outside, but they were all the same once you went through the doors. He had stayed in the Bellagio when it opened, dropping top dollar for a suite just to see whether it could possibly have been worth the coin. He had been disappointed then and had promised never to go back. He never had.

This place, though? The El Cortez? He had first stayed here in the late nineties. He had been chasing a felon who had skipped jail in San Francisco in favour of a week of hedonism in Vegas. The man—Beau remembered that his name was Becker—had robbed a bank, and the police had never found out where he had stashed his loot. It turned out that he had given it to his wife, and she had come out to meet him for one last blowout. The man hadn't put any effort into hiding his tracks, and it had taken Beau less than forty-eight hours to find him in one of the high-roller suites at Caesar's. He had collared the man on the roulette wheel just as his bet—fifty large on black—came good. Becker had offered Beau his winnings if he would give him another hour with his wife. Beau wasn't a hard-ass, but a job was a job, and he had taken him in there and then. You give an inch, they take a mile. Beau never gave an inch, but he had taken the man's cash.

The hotel hadn't changed a bit between then and now, and that made Beau as happy as a hog in slop. The slot machines in the casino still ran on real quarters, the carpets hadn't been changed in twenty years, and the wait staff were old and jaded and bitter, tending to the patrons with a sourness that Beau preferred to the megawatt smiles of the pretty young things who worked the main joints downtown.

He had been in the casino all night, taking a place in the weekly hold 'em contest that they had. It was popular with the local hustlers, who figured it was a good chance to feast on the sucker tourists who thought they knew what they were doing. Beau had been playing poker since he was knee-high to a grasshopper, and had stuck around all the way to the final table, placing sixth out of the two hundred who had entered and winning himself five grand into the bargain. The trip was fixing to be a profitable one: he'd add the prize money to the interest he'd claim from the skipper's mom once he ran her errant son to ground.

Beau was reaching over for his beer when his cellphone glowed with an incoming call. He picked it up. "Hello."

"It's John Smith."

Beau put the bottle to his lips and took a sip, washing the dust from his tongue. "Howdy, English. You in town yet?"

"I am," he said. *"And you?"*

"Got in late afternoon. You drive?"

"I did."

"You enjoy it?"

"It had its moments."

"I bet it did." He sipped again and then wiped the cool glass against his brow. "What's up? You need me for something?"

"I do," Milton said. *"Something came up."*

"You got yourself into trouble again?"

"Am I that predictable?"

"What do you need?"

"Somewhere safe to stay. Off Strip. You got any ideas?"

Beau leaned back and glanced at the neon-drenched showgirl sign that flashed on and off overhead.

"Well, then," he said. "Turns out I do."

22

I t was eleven when the two beaten-up Suburbans finally reached the warehouse on East Cartier Avenue. Oscar Delgado looked out of the windshield as Castellanos went to unlock the gate. The warehouse was the last in a line of similar buildings, all of them two storeys tall, brick-built and rendered in neutral tones of beige and white. The building had been occupied by a hoist company until last year. Oscar had rented it and had replaced the signage on the wall with the branding of the front company that they had been using to get the product into the city.

VegasLead imported lead from South America to be turned into ballast that was then sold on to local industry. The ingots came into the country by ship and were transported to Vegas on the backs of trucks, one arriving every week. The cartel had perfected a method whereby the product would be hidden inside steel boxes that were then hidden inside the ingots. The lead couldn't be X-rayed and, thanks to a contact at the port, they knew the maximum length of the drill bits that the customs officials would use should an attempt be made to cut into them. It was an elegant way to deliver the cocaine, and it had already been successful to the tune of eight hundred kilograms safely imported. Oscar's men removed the product before melting down the lead and selling that in the course of the company's legitimate business. The coke was cut and sold to wholesalers across the southwest.

Business had been good and, under normal circumstances, Oscar would have felt the usual buzz of pride at the thought of what he had been able to achieve. But these were not normal circumstances, and he didn't feel that way. Instead, he was angry and frustrated and fearful. And Richard Russo was the source of all of that.

Castellanos was struggling with the padlock.

"What is he waiting for?" Oscar snapped. He lowered the window and called out, "Get it open!"

The outside space and access to the loading bay were guarded by a metal fence with a gate inside it. Castellanos finally unlocked the gate and hauled it back. The Chevrolets followed him as Castellanos jogged to the building and opened the roller door. The two vehicles drove inside the building. Castellanos switched on the overhead lights and then dragged the door down again.

Oscar got out. He gestured to Russo. "Put him in the office," he snapped. "I'm gonna take a piss and then he's gonna tell me where he's put the money he stole."

～

THERE WAS a restroom next to the loading bay. Oscar went inside and locked the door, then went to the mirror and stared at his reflection. He thought that he had managed to hold it together. The last few days had been the worst since he had left Mazatlán to come and run the business in Las

Vegas. The cartel's bookkeeper had discovered the discrepancy in the ledger. Someone had been siphoning cash—a *lot* of cash—from the VegasLead account. It had taken no time at all to conclude that Russo was responsible.

Delgado had recriminated with himself already. If he had stayed within the limits of his assignment, then none of this would have happened. But Russo had come to him with a proposal. He had large medical bills to pay and the urgency of his predicament had led him to consider illegal means of making the money he needed. His proposal promised outsized profits for minimal risk. The scam was neat, and Delgado had been unable to resist it. The cartel paid him well, but no one had said anything about him being unable to develop alternative sources of income. He knew of others back home who had done the same thing and, provided La Bruja received a cut, there was never a problem with it.

But Delgado had been careless and Russo had been greedy. Oscar knew that his failure to notice would be held against him when the inevitable investigation was completed. He knew that his only chance to save his skin was to recover the money that had been taken and to punish those who had been so stupid as to steal from them.

Tonight had taken things to another level. He had lost three men and had been embarrassed in front of the others. He didn't want to think about what would happen if La Bruja learned about what had happened. An example would have to be made of everyone who had been foolish enough to cross the cartel. *Everyone.*

Oscar would start with Russo. Then the girl. The other man—Smith, whoever he was—well, he would vent the bulk of his fury and frustration on him.

Oscar ran the tap, cupped his hands and filled them with

water and then dunked his face. He looked up again, the beads of water rolling down his cheeks and forehead. There was fear in his eyes. He couldn't afford to let any of the others see that.

He reached for a paper towel from the dispenser and wiped his face. He thought back to earlier. Russo had been easy enough to collect. He had put up a fight, driven by the fear of what he must have known was about to happen to him, but they had subdued him without any significant effort.

As they had driven him away, Oscar had recognised the girl in the oncoming car as the old man's daughter. Having her would have been useful. The question of her well-being would have been another threat to hold over her father. But, of course, that had not turned out the way he had planned.

Oscar found his thoughts snagging on the stranger once again. They knew his name was Smith from the paperwork in his car. Clearly, he was a problem. He had killed Pérez, Lòpez and Morazán and then escaped from both SUVs on the freeway. Oscar had no idea who he was or why he was with the girl, but he was going to have to find out.

23

M
ilton kept the Porsche comfortably under the speed limit as he drove through Harry Levy Gardens and Marble Manor, heading due east. The rear of the car was dented, there was a bullet hole in the windshield and one of the wing mirrors had been torn off. The Macan was already conspicuous, and he didn't want to draw any additional attention to it.

She looked over at him. "So you're basically Steven Seagal."

"Sorry?"

"*Under Siege?*"

He shrugged. "What? The film?"

"Yes, the film."

"I only remember the girl in the birthday cake."

"He's a soldier pretending to be a cook."

"Right," Milton said. "And you think I'm pretending?"

She waited for him to answer his own question.

"No, Jessica. I really *am* a cook."

He kept a regular watch in the rear-view mirror, but it stayed clear. The two Suburbans would have been damaged,

but he couldn't discount the possibility that the occupants—
or others in their group—had access to fresh vehicles and
might be trawling the main arteries into and out of the city
in the hope of a lucky hit. Right now, he didn't see anything
or anyone else that they needed to be on guard for. They
were free of them, at least for the moment.

On the other hand, it was obvious that their pursuers
were professionals and that they would not stop coming.

The best ones never did.

He glanced over at his passenger. Jessica was slumped
against the door, staring out at the blur of lights as they
made their way into town. Her eyes were glazed over; she
was somewhere else.

Milton checked the mirrors again.

Still clear.

The glittering neon lights of the Strip shone in the
distance up ahead. The lights ahead of them glowed
brighter as they approached, the hotels rising into the sky
like temples to audacity and flamboyance, each trying to
outdo the next.

"Are we going to the Strip?" Jessica asked, pushing
herself off the door.

"No," Milton said. "I don't think that's safe."

"So?"

"North of the Strip."

"Fremont?"

"Near there."

Milton came off the expressway at the exit for downtown
and followed Las Vegas Boulevard to East Ogden and then
East Fremont. The El Cortez was ahead of them. He parked
the car at the rear of the hotel lot and stepped out. He stood
for a moment and looked around at his surroundings. East
Fremont was just five miles from the Strip, but it might as

well have been five hundred. The buildings around and about had none of the glitz and glamour that could be found in the chic resorts. The streets were narrower and traffic was lighter, especially at this time of night.

The hotel was large, but modest in comparison to the behemoths with which it was forced to compete. A sign on the awning above the entrance advertised $5 Patron Margaritas and 24/7 drinking. Milton felt the familiar stirrings of temptation and started to wonder whether he was going to have to find a meeting if he was forced to stay in the city for longer than he had planned. He knew that he would benefit from an hour's peace, and it wouldn't hurt to have his defences buttressed. There was temptation here, and plenty of it.

Jessica got out of the car. She looked exhausted.

"Coming?" he said.

She nodded and followed him toward the hotel's entrance.

Milton led the way into the reception. If the place looked dowdy from the outside, it was obvious that effort had been expended on making the interior a little more pleasing to the eye. There was a 1948 Cadillac in the lobby, the paintwork polished up to a high sheen, and the walls were adorned with cartoons of mobsters and their Rat Pack acolytes. The PA played classic Sinatra and, as Milton gazed around, it wasn't hard to imagine that this might have been the sort of place that Ol' Blue Eyes would have frequented. The casino was off to the left, the usual collection of green baize tables, roulette wheels and slots. The clientele had none of the well-heeled swank that one would expect at a higher-end resort. The atmosphere was more relaxed, but the clamour—the buzz and rattle of the slots, the constant music and the hum of conversation—was just the same.

Beau Baxter was waiting for them next to the check-in counters. He was sitting down at a low table, a margarita in his hand.

"English," Beau said, getting up.

"Beau," Milton said.

They shook hands.

"You okay?" Beau asked him.

"I'm good," he said. "Thanks for this. I appreciate it."

Beau waved that off. "It's nothing," he said, and grinned. "Just a couple of hotel rooms. I just made the reservations—you're paying."

"It's kind of a thank-you in advance," Milton corrected him. "For the favours I'm going to ask you."

"And which I will gladly provide. What do you need?"

Milton angled his head behind him to where Jessica was waiting. "Can we talk later?"

Beau nodded his understanding. "Sure."

Milton took the older man over to Jessica so that he could introduce them both.

"This is Jessica Russo," he said.

"Good evening," Beau said to her, shaking her by the hand. "How are you?"

"I've been better."

"And this is Beau Baxter," Milton added. "He's a friend."

"Good to meet you," Beau said to her. "Whatever's ailing you, you've ended up in a safe pair of hands."

"I'm grateful, really, but I don't really know who he is"—she inclined her head at Milton—"and I don't know who you are, either."

If Beau was offended by her brusqueness, he didn't show it. "I've booked you in up on the second floor. Two rooms, one opposite the other. You look cooked."

"I am," she said.

"So go get yourself some sleep. They serve breakfast in the restaurant between seven and ten. I've eaten a few Vegas breakfasts in my time, but none of them are as good as the grits they got here. You come down then, and if there's anything I can do to help, you just got to ask."

"Why would you do that?" she said, still abrupt. "You don't even know me. Why would you help someone you've never met?"

Beau nodded over at Milton. "He helped me out of a sticky situation not that long ago. A friend of his is a friend of mine. It'll be a pleasure to help get whatever's bothering you squared away."

She looked as if she was about to speak, but bit her lip and looked away. "I'm sorry," she said. "I know I sound like an ungrateful bitch. It's just... it's just that it's been a long day and I don't know what to think anymore."

"No need to apologise," Beau said, smiling. "Whatever it is, it'll look better in the morning."

She smiled wanly and started toward the elevators.

"What time are you up tomorrow?" Milton asked.

"I'll catch a couple of hours," Beau said. "Seems I need less and less sleep the older I get."

"See you down here for breakfast?"

"I'll see you then. I mean it about those grits."

24

M ilton went up to the second floor and followed the signs for the rooms between 200 and 250. Beau had made reservations for room 205 and, on the opposite side of the corridor, room 206. Milton went into his room first. The hotel literature described it as 'Vintage Queen' and, although it was of a decent size, the fixtures and fittings looked old and tired. The bed came with a heavy wooden headboard, the carpets had a mildly hallucinogenic swirl to them, and the bathroom, when he investigated, was very basic. But Milton was satisfied: discretion was more important than amenities. He went to his window and looked outside. They were two blocks from the insanity of Fremont Street, with enough distance between them to offer a little peace and quiet. That, of course, was comparative; this was serene by *Vegas* standards.

He went back out to the corridor, knocked on the door for 206 and waited for Jessica to open it.

"You alright?" Milton asked.

She stared at him, her eyes tired and red. "No. Not really."

"Sorry," Milton said. "Not my best ever question."

He stepped inside and went over to the minibar. He opened it, ignored the temptation offered by the array of miniatures, and took out two bottles of water. He tossed one over to Jessica and took the other to the window.

"We need to talk," he said. He watched Jessica's reflection in the glass.

She looked up, with—perhaps—a flicker of concern. "What?"

He turned back to face her directly. "We can speak more freely now."

"About what?"

"What did you take?"

"Take? What does that mean?"

"From the house."

"I didn't take anything."

"You're not a very good liar."

"Why would you think I took something?" she asked, not looking at him.

"I saw you, Jessica. In the bedroom. You reached around the back of the bed. It wasn't to do with a gun. What did you take?"

"I didn't."

"Okay," Milton said. He started for the door.

Jessica looked at him. "What are you doing?"

Milton opened the door. "I'm going."

Jessica leapt to her feet. "*Wait!*"

"I can't help if you lie to me."

"Wait."

Milton held the door open, but turned back to her. "This is your last chance. If you want my help, be honest. If I ask you a question, answer it. If you don't, I'm gone. You can deal with those people on your own."

Jessica bit down on her lip. Milton could see that she was wrestling with something.

"Do you understand me?" Milton pressed. "I mean it. You'll never see me again."

She swallowed. "I'm sorry."

Milton let go of the door. It closed as he came back into the room. He took the chair from the desk and turned it around so that he could sit and watch Jessica. The young woman, for her part, put her bottle of water back in the fridge and grabbed a beer instead. She popped the top with the opener she found on the desk and took a long draught.

"Well?" Milton said.

25

J essica slumped back down onto the bed.

"Dad called me." She scrubbed the heel of her hand against her eyes. "It was a week ago. That was weird enough—he never calls. I remember, I was just coming back from the gym. He said he needed to talk to me and that it was important. I remember what he said: 'This is going to sound crazy, and I don't want you to worry, but if anything happens to me, I need you to know what to do next.' The first thing I thought was that he must've been sick. You know—the cancer. I asked him and he said he wasn't, that it was nothing to do with that, that he was doing okay."

"So? What was it?"

"I didn't press him. I decided to wait until I saw him."

"But he told you what you'd have to do?"

She nodded. "He said that he'd rented a storage unit out in North Vegas. He said that if anything happened to him, I had to go up there. He told me that he had taped a key behind the bed. I looked tonight. And this was there."

Jessica reached into her pocket and took out a small

silver key and a swipe card. She handed it over. The key was marked with a brand name—American Lock—and looked like it might be the sort that would open a padlock. The swipe card was a plain oblong of plastic with a black magstripe down one side and a number to call in the event that the card was found.

"Where's the unit?"

Jessica reached into her pocket and took out her phone. She tapped the screen to wake it and then navigated to a note that she had taken.

"I wrote it down. Cheyenne Storage Depot," she read, "8650 West Cheyenne."

"And did he say what was inside the unit?"

"No," Jessica said. "He didn't say anything."

"You have no idea? None at all?"

Jessica shrugged helplessly. "None."

Milton stared at her. "This is one of those moments where I need you to be completely honest with me."

"I don't know, John, I swear. I was going to speak to him about it tonight."

Milton swigged down a mouthful of water. The situation had just become a little more complicated. He considered all the information that he had: a man had been abducted from his home by armed men. Those same men had given chase in an attempt, he assumed, to secure the daughter, too. The father was seemingly in fear for his life, and he had a storage locker with contents important enough that the daughter was told to go and get them in the event that he was no longer able to do so.

What was in the unit? It must have been what Oscar was looking for.

"What do we do now?" Jessica asked him.

"I'm not sure."

"I should go and look in the locker—right?"

Milton exhaled. "No," he said. "Not you. We have no idea what we might find there. You need to stay."

"Who, then?"

"Me," he said. "I'll go."

26

Oscar stepped into the office. Sacca and Abellán were lounging against the wall, both smoking cigarettes. Richard Russo was sitting in a chair in the middle of the room, his wrists and ankles secured to its arms and legs with cable ties. His face was bruised from where Pérez had struck him, and his scalp was matted with dried blood from when they had subdued him at the house.

Oscar took off his jacket and draped it over his desk. He made a show of unbuttoning his shirt and then folded it neatly, placing it atop the jacket. He took off the Rolex Submariner that he had bought from the store at the Wynn with the commission that he had earned after his first month in the city. He had found the watch heavy in the first few days of wearing it, but he had grown accustomed to it now. He had also grown accustomed to what it represented —his hard-won success, the distance between his beginning in the slums of Mazatlán and where he found himself now —and he wanted more. He was not about to let this *cabrón* ruin everything.

He turned and walked over until he was right in front of

the old man. He crouched down so that he could look into his eyes. "Do you think I am a fool?"

"No, Oscar. Of course not."

"But you must think I am a fool. Why else would you think that I would miss your thieving?"

"What are you talking about?"

"Please," he said.

"I don't know what you're talking about."

Oscar stood up and took a quarter-turn so that he could look over at Sacca and Abellán. "He says he doesn't know what I'm talking about."

"I don't—"

Oscar wheeled around, bringing the back of his hand across Russo's face. It was a hard, stiff slap, the knuckles catching against the old man's cheek. Russo's head snapped around, and blood splashed from his nose onto his top lip.

Oscar grabbed him by the chin and turned his head, tilting it up so that he could look down into his face. "*¡Que te jodan!* Where is my money?"

There was a pause; Oscar's angry denunciation rang around the room, faded, and was replaced by Russo's ragged breathing.

"I'm not afraid of you," he said at last.

"No?" Oscar laughed. "You should be."

"I have cancer, Oscar. You know I do. I have months to live. A year if I'm lucky. I'm not scared of death. I've made my peace with it."

"It is not death you should be afraid of," Oscar suggested. "I will make you beg for it. What you should be afraid of is what I will do to your children. Your son is Mason, no? A soldier, dishonourably discharged from the army, lives here in Las Vegas. *Sí?* And your daughter, Jessica, lives in Los Angeles. We know her address. We know where she works. I can have them both brought here like this." He snapped his fingers.

Russo's head drooped; Oscar held it more firmly, squeezing his chin.

"What do you say? Perhaps we take a chainsaw to your son? Perhaps we cut his limbs off one by one. And Jessica? Perhaps we ship her back to Juárez in a crate. A pretty girl like her? She would be taken to one of the kitchens in the jungle. I have been to the places where they are kept. She would be tied to a stake, and men would come whenever they wanted, do whatever they pleased."

Russo closed his eyes; the life drained out of them, all of the fight gone. He didn't speak.

"What do you say? You tell me where I can find my money and perhaps your children can continue with their lives. If not..." He shrugged. "If not? Well, what happens to them if not is your fault."

∾

OSCAR PUT his shirt back on and slipped the Rolex onto his wrist again, snapping the clasp shut. Russo wasn't watching; he had slumped forward in the chair, held upright by the cuffs that secured his wrists to the arms. Oscar was a little annoyed that Russo had folded so quickly. He was full of frustration and he had anticipated taking it out on the man responsible for it. He would wait, though. It was a case of delayed gratification. He knew that Russo was telling the truth, but he wanted him alive until the moment the money was returned.

But then?

He would get what was coming to him.

Him and his children and the *pendejo* who was helping.

Oscar went outside to where Ellacuria and Higuaín were waiting.

"There is a storage facility," he said. "He says he has been keeping the money there."

Ellacuria dropped his cigarette to the floor and ground it out. "Where?"

Oscar took the piece of paper from his pocket and handed it to him. He had written down the address and the number of the storage unit.

Ellacuria looked down at it. "West Cheyenne Avenue."

"Go now."

"The key?"

"At his house. You missed it."

"A key, boss. How could we be expected to find—"

"Enough excuses! I am *sick* of them." He went to the rack of tools that they used on the shipments and selected a pair of long-handled bolt cutters. He tossed them over; Ellacuria fumbled them and they clattered against the concrete floor. "Use those. And do not come back unless you have my fucking money!"

Milton made sure that Jessica understood how important it was that she stay in the hotel room while he was away. She asked how long he would be gone, and Milton replied that he would be back as soon as he was able. There were a few things that he needed to do, and it was difficult to know how much time he would need.

He went back to his room and took out the pistol that he had taken from the man in Russo's garage earlier. He popped the magazine to confirm that his count of how many rounds were remaining was correct—it was—and then slipped the weapon into the waistband of his trousers, arranging his shirt to hide it.

Milton decided that he would leave the Macan in the lot. It was a distinctive car even without the damage that it had suffered, and the last thing he wanted to do was to draw attention to himself. He called Beau again and asked if he had something that he could borrow. Beau had hired a rental from the airport and said that Milton was free to use it; he told him where to find it and that he would leave the keys on reception for him to collect.

≈

THE HOTEL HAD a small gift store in the lobby that was open twenty-four hours a day. Milton picked out a ball cap with WELCOME TO LAS VEGAS emblazoned across the front and added a T-shirt that featured a drawing of dogs playing poker. He bought both items, changed into the T-shirt in the restroom and then went outside to the lot. Beau had hired a Denali Yukon, a big and powerful SUV with a four-wheel-drive configuration.

Milton started the engine and tapped the details of the storage facility into the satnav. The unit reported a twenty-five-minute drive, following the Las Vegas Freeway and then Route 95.

He pulled out and started on his way.

≈

THE STORAGE DEPOT was advertised by way of a tall sign at the side of West Cheyenne Avenue. It was set within a typically sprawling retail property that also included a McDonald's and a Burger King. Milton flicked the turn signal and turned into the quiet parking lot. There was a roller gate to one side of the building that offered access to a series of outside storage units. The main facility was constructed out of plain blocks of concrete, with miserly windows at ground level and nothing above.

Milton parked the Yukon. He put the cap on his head, pulling it down so that the brim was low over his forehead. He got out, locked the SUV and went up to the door of the facility. The window offered a glimpse inside, and it looked as if the desk was not manned at this late hour. That was fortunate; Milton had wondered whether he might have to spin a lie to get inside.

The building was accessed by way of a swipe card. Milton reached into his pocket for the card that Jessica had given him and ran it through the reader. The machine chirped, the lock buzzed, and the door opened. Milton kept his head down and went inside.

The reception was quiet, with lights flicking on as his presence was detected by a motion sensor somewhere nearby. He glimpsed a security camera on the other side of the room, pointing down at the door, and turned away from it, confident that the cap would shield his face. He went to the door that led to the storage area, used his elbow to push the handle down, and then shouldered his way inside.

A series of corridors bisected the warehouse. Storage units were arranged on either side of these, and each unit was secured by substantial metal roller doors. Strip lights provided the illumination, their harsh glare glinting off the doors and the polished epoxy floor. Hisco security cameras were placed at regular intervals. Milton didn't like the look of them, but he was hopeful that they were up high enough that they would be defeated by the cap; he pulled it down a little more to be sure.

He found the unit that he wanted, knelt down and inserted the key into the padlock that fastened the door to the metal bracket on the floor. The lock turned easily and the clasp popped open. Milton hauled the door up enough to allow him to duck inside.

The unit was dark. Milton used the flashlight on his phone to find the light switch and flicked it. A single over-head light flickered on and he looked around.

The space was reasonably sized—perhaps five feet by ten—and would have been big enough for small pieces of furniture or several large storage boxes. Despite that, the only item stored inside was a single briefcase. Milton crouched down beside it and examined it. It looked expensive: leather, with metal clasps and two combination locks that secured the lid. He picked it up and hefted it. It wasn't heavy.

He was about to open it when he heard the sound of breaking glass.

Someone was forcing their way into the building.

Milton took the case and, as quietly as he could, stepped out of the unit and lowered the door so that it was down to the ground. He slipped the padlock through the clasp and locked it, then made his way swiftly and silently along the corridor to the first junction. He waited there for a moment, holding his breath, until he heard the sound of approaching footsteps. He reached around for the pistol, holding it in a loose grip and slipping his finger through the trigger guard.

He heard a voice and then another. Spanish? It was difficult to be sure. Two men, he thought. Relaxed, perhaps even a little bored. That was good.

The footsteps approached and then stopped. It was difficult to judge, but Milton guessed that the two men were now next to the unit that he had just been in. He heard the rattle of the padlock against the clasp and then a frustrated invocation.

"*¡Ábrelo!*"

"*Estoy haciendo mi mejor esfuerzo.*"

Milton stayed stock-still. He heard the sound of something metallic clanging against the concrete floor, a grunt of effort and then a metallic popping sound as, he guessed, the padlock was forced with a pair of cutters. The roller door rattled as it was pushed up, and there came the sound of a click; a flashlight, perhaps.

Milton waited.

"Esta vacio."

"Puedo ver eso. Oscar va a estar enojado."

Milton's Spanish wasn't good enough to translate what was said, but he could tell that the men were irritated. He could guess at what they were discussing: the unit was empty and Oscar was going to be mad.

Milton waited.

The first man muttered an angry *"Bastardo!"* and the door was lowered again, the handle ringing as it crashed back to the concrete. Milton heard the men's footsteps moving away from where he was standing and back to the main door. He gave a moment's thought to whether he should follow and take them out. There was eventually going to be a confrontation after what had happened tonight, and thinning out Oscar's complement of muscle a little more would be helpful. He dismissed it; the men had no idea that he was here; his car was an anonymous rental that they likely would not even notice, and killing in cold blood was not something that he relished. There was no need.

He waited for the sound of the exterior door as it opened and closed, the lock automatically fastening again, and then took another thirty seconds until he thought he could hear the sound of a car engine from outside.

He pulled the cap down again and walked carefully to the door. He reached the reception just as it was raked by the headlights of the car that was pulling out of the lot. He couldn't make out the details save that it was a big Lexus, the engine rumbling as the driver hit the gas and accelerated away.

28

M ilton parked the Yukon in the empty parking lot of Angelina's Pizzeria on West Cheyenne. He collected the briefcase from the back seat and put it on his lap, switched on the vanity light and examined it. The case was obviously expensive, with a logo that identified it as made by Aspinal of London. It was fronted with calf leather in a dark brown pebble texture, with a soft and supple feel to it. The tactile materials, the precise contrast stitching, the chrome fixtures, and the sturdy handle all suggested luxury. The case was sealed with reasonably substantial clasps. The clasps were held in two locks, one on either side of the case, each lock secured by a combination.

Milton wondered whether he should take the case straight back to the hotel. It wasn't his, after all, and he should leave it up to Jessica as to what to do with it. On the other hand, he still felt that he was operating in the dark. The girl had been unable to provide any suggestion as to why her father might have been abducted, and she had been sparing in what she had told him until he'd threatened to abandon her to her fate. He needed to know more. He would give her the case and whatever was inside it, but only after he had examined it himself.

Unlocking the case was a simple enough trick. Milton turned it around so that it was positioned vertically on his lap, and then angled it backwards so that he was able to look down at the sides of the combination locks. There were three dials on each. Milton started with the left-hand lock. He thumbed its rightmost dial around until he had found the small bumps beneath one of the numbers. Then, working one twist of the dial at a time, he turned it in a clockwise direction before trying the lock. It took six attempts, but, eventually, the lock opened and the clasp popped free. Milton repeated the trick on the left-hand dial, popped the lock and opened the case.

The lid opened to reveal a generous leather-lined compartment. The main pocket contained a large collection of American banknotes. Milton thumbed through six thick wads, each fastened with a rubber band. The notes were all of high denominations—fifties and hundreds—and Milton guessed that there must have been a hundred thousand in total, maybe more.

Milton put the money back and turned his attention to the pockets in the lid, each closed with a snap. There were three slots: one for a phone, another for business cards and a third for pens. Milton opened the phone pouch and took out a phone. It was a simple TracFone LG with a flip design. It looked new. Milton fired it up, but it required a password to proceed. He powered it down and put it back into the case.

He opened the next section and took out two USB drives. They were identical: white, marked with the logo of the manufacturer—SanDisk—and with a capacity of 64 GB each. There was nothing that gave a hint of what might be contained on them.

Milton turned the drives around in his fingers and looked down at the cash.

Oscar's pursuit of Richard Russo suddenly made a lot more sense.

29

Milton arrived back at the El Cortez at two in the morning and went directly to the twenty-four-hour business centre. There was a table with four old-fashioned PC terminals together with a printer. He went to the terminal that was farthest from the door and tapped the keyboard to wake the screen. He took the first USB drive out, plugged it into the port in the tower, waited for the computer to detect it, and then clicked the icon when it appeared on the screen.

A box popped up asking for a password. Milton had no idea what that might be, and closed it down. He swapped the first drive for the second and, this time, the directory showed four files that were ready to be opened: two Word documents, an MP4 file and an Excel spreadsheet.

Milton opened the spreadsheet. The various tabs were a maze of accounting figures. Deposits, withdrawals, and interest calculations. The numbers were detailed, but the information that accompanied them was not. There were initials here and there, and a few random notes typed into the documents, but he was not able to untangle where the numbers were from or what they meant.

He closed it down and clicked the first Word document. The program fired up and, after a pause as the old PC struggled to open the file, several paragraphs of text appeared on the screen. Richard Russo had composed a draft email and had saved it onto one of the sticks.

Milton read:

My name is Richard Russo. I am head of network security at the Stardust hotel in Las Vegas. I recently found myself in significant debt after paying for cancer treatment for which I was not insured. I was introduced to a man called Oscar Delgado, who lent me the money to clear those debts. His offer did not come without obligations, and, as a result, I have been forced to work for him in the operation of a sophisticated scam.

Señor Delgado hired me to identify customers in the hotel database with perfect credit scores. I was responsible for hacking the identities of those individuals and, using their names and addresses and social security numbers, I assisted him in opening credit accounts with a number of other Las Vegas casinos. The accounts were provided with large initial deposits to foster the illusion that the individuals were liquid and to encourage the casinos to extend lines of credit.

Señor Delgado then recruited a number of credible gamblers to pretend to be these people. He continued to top up the accounts and paid down the markers. The players looked like high rollers and the casinos were happy to increase their credit lines.

It is at this point that the scam is operated. The gamblers lay large bets of ten or twenty thousand dollars. Most of those bets lose, but some do not, and when they are successful, hundreds of thousands can be won. The gamblers cash out the accounts, usually leaving large debts behind. The casinos pursue the individuals who

had their identities stolen, and quickly find that they have no recom-
pense against them. They have lost tens of thousands of dollars, and
the individuals I targeted have their credit ratings ruined.

You will find evidence of Señor Delgado's fraud in the finan-
cial documents that are attached to this email. These are the bets
that he laid and the amounts that were won and lost.

Milton rubbed his tired eyes. He had suspected that
there were depths to the mess that he had stumbled into,
but not how far those depths might extend.

He opened the second draft email.

Further to the financial crimes that I have detailed in my
previous note, I can also prove that Señor Delgado is responsible
for the murder of those who have stood up to him. I am aware of
at least three such homicides. I will set out details below.

Oliver and Christoph Lindermann were German brothers
who worked for Señor Delgado in 2015. Oliver had a particular
skill at counting cards, and Christoph was his chaperone. They
threatened to expose Señor Delgado unless he agreed to pay them
$500,000. Their bodies were found burning at the side of the road
in Yermo, California. Señor Delgado told me that he was respon-
sible for their killings, in an attempt, I am sure, to win my
continued cooperation by putting me in fear of my life.

Joseph Singleton worked in The Dunes as an account
manager. He was brought into the operation in order to help me
identify possible targets with pre-existing credit histories at that
resort. He was arrested by the Las Vegas police on an unconnected
matter, and, in an attempt to reduce the charges against him, he
offered to give evidence against Señor Delgado. He was murdered
at Delgado's commercial property in Sunrise Manor. I understand
that his body was dumped near Needles, California. I am aware
of television reports of unidentified human remains that were
found there, and believe that they belong to Singleton. I am sure a
DNA check would prove that I am right.

Whereas I can offer only circumstantial evidence of Señor Delgado's involvement in the murder of the Lindermann brothers, I have concrete proof that he murdered Singleton. I had previously installed a Trojan on his computer in order that I might capture some of the financial evidence against him that I have provided under separate email cover. Using this, I captured an audio recording of Singleton's torture and murder. I attach that evidence to this email.

Milton closed down the draft email and navigated back to the drive's file menu. The MP4 was labelled with a single word: SINGLETON.

Milton checked that the room was empty and the volume was down low. He pressed play.

The recording wasn't clear—it sounded as if the microphone was in a different room to the voices it had captured —but the content was still audible. There were two distinct voices: the first was angry and threatening, the second apologetic, almost pleading. Milton caught several phrases from the louder of the two speakers—"you betrayed me!" and "how could you be so fucking stupid!"—and then the sound of a blow, of something thudding into flesh. He heard mewling, then a plea—more desperate this time—and then another blow, and another, and another. This went on for a minute, and then two. Milton listened intently, inured to what he was hearing, recognising it from his own experience. There came another blow, a pause, and then the crack of a single gunshot.

The conversation stopped, but the recording still had another thirty seconds to run.

Milton let it play.

"*¿Qué dijo el?*" a new voice said. It was clearer than before, as if the speaker was in the same room as the microphone.

"*Nada.*"

"¿Qué quieres que haga?"

"Llevarlo al desierto," he said. *"Los coyotes pueden tenerlo."*

Milton leaned back in the chair and scrubbed his hand through his hair. It had been obvious that the man with whom he had spoken—Oscar Delgado—was dangerous, but he now knew Delgado was more than that.

He was a killer.

30

M ilton awoke at six after three hours' sleep. He felt sluggish and knew that he would benefit from a little exercise. He went down to the store in the lobby and found a rail with a small selection of swimming shorts. They were as garish as the T-shirt that he had purchased here last night, and, with little in the way of choice, he made do with a pair in a lurid lime green with 'Vegas' printed across the back.

He changed in a restroom, went to the pool and grabbed a towel from the stack that had been left next to the line of loungers. The atmosphere was very different to how it had been last night; instead of the light glowing from beneath the water and the neon from the signs overhead, everything was bright and sharp. There had been an edge of Vegas glamour here before, but now that the darkness was gone, it all felt a little tacky and jaded.

He dove into the pool, swam a few strokes under the water, surfaced and then stretched out into a front crawl. Milton was a strong swimmer and the pool was just fifteen metres long; he reached the end in ten strokes, rolled through a tumble turn and kicked back in the opposite direction. He stroked out again, churning quickly through the water and settling into a steady pace. The strokes became repetitive and he quickly drifted into the meditative state that he always tried to find when he was working out. It was purer even than the peace that he found in meetings: just the water, the rhythm of his strokes, the burn that was somewhere between pain and pleasure that he felt in his shoulders and quads.

He lost track of time and, eventually remembering that he had a lot to do today, he slowed his strokes and cruised to the wall. He looked up at a pair of legs and, as he shielded his eyes against the sun, he saw that Jessica was standing there.

"Morning," she said.

"Morning."

"That was impressive."

"You been there long?"

"Long enough."

Milton put his hands on the side of the pool and boosted himself out of the water. He stood next to her, a head taller, the water running off his body. She looked at him, her eyes a little wider. He could guess why that was: she was looking at the tattoos on his body and the scars from the times that he had been injured in the course of his work.

"You've got a lot of ink," she said.

He turned to grab the towel and heard her exclamation of surprise. "What?"

"On your back," she said. "The angel."

She meant the tattoo of the angel wings across his shoulders.

"Where'd you get that done?"

"South America," he said.

"That must've hurt."

"I was drunk."

He dried himself down and tossed the towel onto the nearest lounger.

"You didn't wake me last night," she said.

"I didn't get back until late. I thought you needed sleep."

"But—"

"Nothing was going to happen that couldn't wait until today," he said, cutting her off.

"What about now?"

"Give me a couple of hours," he said. "I have an errand to run first. Do you need anything? Clothes? Toiletries?"

"That would be great," she said. "I left my case in the car."

"What do you need?"

"Shampoo, soap, deodorant. Maybe nail clippers and tweezers. Toothpaste, toothbrush, razor."

"Clothes?"

"There's a store in reception. I'll go there. I'll get the rest of what I need at the airport when..."

"When we get your father," Milton finished for her. "Okay. I'll pick those things up."

"And then?"

"Knock on my door. We need to talk."

31

Milton went back to his room. He changed into yesterday's clothes, collected the briefcase and took it with him into the corridor. The business centre had been quiet last night, but it might not be like that now. He and Jessica were going to have a frank conversation that had the potential to be upsetting, and the last thing he wanted to do was to conduct it in front of an audience. Jessica had been subjected to a nightmarish day yesterday, and now the context that he was about to provide was going to make it much worse. He would rather have said nothing, but he couldn't do that. Apart from the fact that it would have been patronising, she had the right to know what her father had been doing, and what was happening to her because of it.

He went down to the bellhop and asked for directions to the nearest electronics store. The man at the stand told him there was a pawnshop on East Charleston that would be open, and gave him directions.

Milton exited the hotel, turned onto Fremont and walked to Fifteenth Street. It was a mile to the store, and

Milton covered it in twenty minutes. The place was in a strip mall, between a store that identified itself as Dawg Traffic Ticket Law Office and a branch of Intermex. Milton went inside, pointed to a cheap fifteen-inch used MacBook that was displayed with other equipment inside a large metal cage, and paid cash.

There was a CVS on the way back. Milton went inside and picked up the toiletries that Jessica had requested, together with a stick of deodorant, a toothbrush and toothpaste for himself, too. His bag had been lost along with the GTO, and the thought of his misfortune prompted him to reach back and pat the back pocket where he kept his passport. He tried to keep that on his person and had been rewarded for his foresight on more than one occasion even before this. His modest collection of clothes was lost, though, so he picked up a couple of fresh T-shirts and underwear from a branch of J.Crew.

He went back to his room, unpacked the small rectangular box and pulled the silver computer out. He unwrapped the plastic and tape from the charging cord and inserted it into the machine. He popped up the screen, and the computer booted up immediately. After a few setup steps, it was ready to go.

He opened the briefcase, took out the unprotected USB drive and plugged it in. The files appeared on the screen and he copied them across to the desktop, ejected the drive and put it back in the case.

～

HE HEARD a soft knocking on the door.

He went over to open it. Jessica was standing outside.

"Come in," he said.

She did. She looked pensive, which wasn't surprising.

"Have you heard from your brother?"

"No," she said.

"You've tried?"

"Yes. A dozen times. Voicemail."

"He must know something is wrong. You weren't at the airport."

"Mason is..." She paused. "*Unreliable*. He has a problem with drugs, like I said. There have been times when he's been impossible to reach."

"You think he might be on a bender now?"

"Like I said, it wouldn't be the first time. It's the only reason I can think of why I can't get him."

"Keep trying."

The briefcase was on the bed. Milton went over to it and tapped his finger against the leather.

"What's that?" she asked.

"Have you seen it before?"

"No."

"It was in the storage facility. I'm guessing that it belongs to your father."

"I suppose it must. What's in it?"

Milton popped the clasps, opened the lid and stood back so that she could look inside. Her eyes widened as she saw the money.

"Jesus," she said.

"They're all high-denomination bills," Milton said. "Fifties and hundreds. I counted it. There's a hundred and fifty thousand dollars there. Your father never mentioned it?"

"Never. Why would he have that much cash?"

"I was hoping you might be able to tell me that."

She shrugged. "I have no idea." She paused. "Do you think that's why…"

"Why he's been taken?" Milton finished for her. "I think it's very likely."

There were two chairs in the bedroom: the slim armchair next to the bed and the wooden chair that was pushed underneath the desk. Milton brought the armchair across, put it down next to the desk and indicated that Jessica should sit. She did, and Milton pulled out the desk chair and sat down in front of the laptop. The girl was close to him, close enough for him to feel the heat from her arm on his, close enough to smell the citrus scent that she used.

He opened the laptop screen and tapped a key to wake it up.

"Your father has been kidnapped," he began. "He has this money hidden in a storage unit. The two things are linked."

"I can't explain it."

"Can I ask you something else? About the house?"

She nodded.

"It's expensive. How much? Two million? More?"

"Two point five," she corrected him.

"So—"

"I know what you're going to say," she cut him off. "There's no way that he could've afforded that on the wage the casino pays. And that would be true—he couldn't. But my grandfather was rich. The house belonged to him. He passed it on to Dad when he died. They didn't get on when he was alive. Dad said it was an attempt to say sorry."

"The cars? Neither of them would've been cheap."

"The same," she said. "And the same for my Tesla. My grandfather left the money for it in his will."

Milton reached over and took the two USB drives out of the case.

"What are they?" she asked.

"They were inside the briefcase, too. This one"—he held it up—"is password protected. Do you have any idea what he might have used?"

"No idea," she said.

"Think about it," he said. He put the stick down and picked up the second one. "This one isn't protected. I've copied the data on it to the laptop. Look, here—you need to see it."

He dragged the cursor to the folder that he had created for Jessica. He double-clicked it, selected the first of the Word documents, and opened it. He turned the screen so that she could scroll down herself, and then sat back while she read.

"This can't be true," she said when she had finished reading the first email.

"Why?"

"Why? Because my father isn't a criminal."

"Those are his words," Milton said, tapping his finger against the top of the screen. "This is his insurance policy. If something happens to him, he wants to have something that he can hold over the people he suspects will have been responsible. This"—he tapped the stick—"is your father's loaded gun. He's laid out everything that the police would need to go after the man he says he's been working for."

"Oscar Delgado," she said.

"That's right. Him and whoever else he has working for him."

"I've never even heard that name before."

"Why would you? He's not likely to admit to his daughter what he's been doing. He's probably ashamed."

She shook her head. "No. I don't see it. That's not my dad."

Milton opened the spreadsheet.

She looked at the screen. "What are these?"

"Financial statements. I don't know for sure, but it looks like a series of payments made from a number of casino accounts to a series of secondary accounts. It won't be easy for us to get any more detail—that'll be a job for the police. I suspect we'll find that these numbers match the money that Delgado's gamblers took from the casinos."

She moused over to the second statement. "What's this?"

"Read it."

She clicked and the document opened. Milton watched her face carefully as she read. Her mouth fell open.

"You okay?" he asked her.

"Delgado is a murderer?"

"Yes," Milton said.

"And Dad has evidence?"

"There's an audio file," Milton said. "You don't have to listen to it."

"But you did?"

He nodded. "It sounds just as he says."

"You're serious? Dad recorded Delgado killing someone?"

"That's what it sounded like."

She closed her eyes. Her bottom lip quivered.

Milton shut the laptop. He laid it over the money in the briefcase and closed the lid.

"Here's what I think has happened," he said. "I'm not making any judgements; I'm just telling you what looks most likely. Okay?"

She opened her eyes. She looked troubled, but nodded.

"Oscar Delgado is a criminal who has been operating a

financial sting in Las Vegas for the last year. Your father has been working for him. Everything on that data stick is there to make sure that Delgado doesn't make a move against him. Or against you or your brother."

"But now we're saying that didn't work out as he thought it would."

"That's what we're saying. Your father has been helping Delgado to run his scam—finding suitable targets, setting up large credit lines at the casinos, then cashing out the accounts when whoever uses the credit to lay bets has been successful. It's a very neat, very tidy scheme."

She pointed at the cash. "And all that money?"

"I think he stole it from Delgado."

"But you said he was dangerous."

"He is dangerous. Very. But your father has cancer. Maybe his diagnosis changed his perspective. Maybe he doesn't care about the consequences anymore. What are they going to do to him that's worse than what's already happened? That's a lot of money. A lot. More than enough to make a difference over his last few months. Maybe he used some of it to buy those cars. Maybe he used some to fund the trip you were going on. Did he pay for the tickets?"

She nodded.

"So maybe that's where the money came from. Or maybe he decided that he wants to leave you and your brother a tidy sum when he passes on. It doesn't matter. It's a lot, like I said, more than enough for Delgado to have the motive to do what he did yesterday. I think he's got your father because he knows what he's done, and he wants to get the money back."

"So what do we do?"

"I'd like to know a little bit more about Delgado first," Milton said.

"How?"

"My friend Beau, the man you met last night, has contacts in the Las Vegas police. I'll ask him to ask around and see what he can find out."

"Do we tell the police what's happened?"

"We could," Milton said. "That's your decision to make."

"What do you think?"

"I think it would be risky. Delgado might decide that the money isn't worth the aggravation."

"And..." She didn't finish the sentence; the catch in her throat told Milton she knew what would happen if Delgado decided to stop fishing and cut bait.

"Yes," Milton said. "It's dangerous."

"So we offer Delgado the money—right?"

Milton stood. "That's what I'd do."

32

It was nine by the time that Milton and Jessica were finished. Milton took out his phone and sent a message to Beau, saying that he needed to speak to him. A message bounced back in return: Beau was in the restaurant having breakfast and Milton should come down and join him. Milton told Jessica that he would come and get her when he had worked out how best to proceed, and made his way down to the ground floor.

Beau was sitting at a table in the middle of the large restaurant. He saw Milton and raised his hand.

"English," he said as Milton arrived next to him, "you okay?"

"I'm fine."

"You sleep?"

"A little. I needed to check some things out. They couldn't wait."

Beau gestured to the waiter and pointed down at the pot of coffee on the table. The waiter nodded his understanding and made his way to the serving station to collect a fresh one.

Milton sat. "Thanks, Beau. I appreciate your help in this."

Beau waved it off. "Ain't nothing."

"I'm going to have to ask for more."

"That's what I figured."

The waiter came over to the table with a second pot of coffee. He poured out a mug for Milton and refreshed Beau's.

"What can I get you for breakfast?" the man asked.

"Get the grits," Beau said. "You like shrimp, English?"

Milton said that he did.

Beau looked up at the waiter. "He'll have the shrimp and grits."

The waiter took down the order and Milton's room number and went back to the kitchen.

Beau took a sip of his coffee. "Where's the girl?"

"In her room."

"You want to tell me what's going on?"

Milton explained. He told Beau everything: how he had run into Jessica at the truck stop on the way to Vegas, how she had told him she needed to get home, that her car had broken down. Beau made a joke about how a man could get in trouble offering help to a pretty girl, but Milton shut him down with a shake of his head. He explained how he had driven her to the big house in Summerlin and how it had quickly become obvious that her father had been abducted. He told him about the men who had come to the house, about how he had taken three of them out, and then how they had eventually put distance between the rest of them on the highway.

"And then you called me?" Beau said.

"I did. And we came here." He sipped the coffee. "You know Vegas, right?"

"Been coming here for years. Professionally and socially. I guess I know it about as well as anyone."

"And?"

"They say Vegas is cleaned up, but you don't want to believe a word of it. There's still a lot of dirty money here, and that brings the bad actors. It's like blood in the water. Always gonna attract the sharks."

"That's what I need to talk to you about," he said.

"The sharks? You got one in particular?"

"You heard of Oscar Delgado?"

"Can't say that I have. That don't mean I can't find out about him. What you got?"

Milton put his coffee mug down. "I noticed Jessica taking a key from the house before we got out. I confronted her about it—she says her father told her that if anything ever happened to him, she needed to pick up the key and then take it to a storage facility in North Vegas. I went up there to check it out. There was a briefcase there. I opened it."

"And?"

"There was a lot of money. One hundred and fifty thousand."

Beau whistled. "Beaucoup bucks. Enough to get someone into a lot of trouble."

"That's what I thought," Milton said. "There were USB drives, too. I went through the data on the one I could open. It lays everything out. It looks like Jessica's father was involved with Delgado. Some kind of credit scam—he was setting up accounts at the casinos, making them look like they were on the level, increasing the credit line and then ripping them off."

The waiter returned with Milton's breakfast and set the plate down: there was a generous portion of seared shrimp, roasted tomatoes, Virginia ham, red onions and grits. It smelled good, and Milton remembered how hungry he was. He started to eat.

"So the old man had his fingers in the till?" Beau said.

"Yes," Milton said. "And I think he was worried he was going to get found out. He put together evidence to use against Delgado. There are financial reports—probably a record of the payments that he made to and from the casinos. Draft email confessions."

"And?"

Milton laid his cutlery down and lowered his voice. "And an audio recording of what Russo says was the torture and murder of someone who was trying to blackmail Delgado."

"Authentic?"

"I'd say so," Milton said.

"And he ripped this guy off?" Beau said. "Sounds like he loaded the wrong wagon, English."

The waiter returned with a jug of orange juice. He filled Milton's glass and gestured down to Milton's plate. "Is everything all right, sir?"

"It's delicious," Milton said. "Thank you."

The man walked off again.

Beau tapped his fingers against the tabletop. "So last night? They went after him to get the cash?"

"Seems most likely." Milton laid down the cutlery again. "You're sure you've never heard the name?"

"I haven't. You know my contacts—they tend to be Italian, and the mob hasn't been big in Vegas since the sixties. Howard Hughes went after them, then the Feebies. The wise guys got out or got locked up." He emptied his coffee and put the mug back down on the table. "I mean, there are still a few old-timers here, but they don't have the connections like they used to. That all being said, I do still have a police contact who'll have a better idea of what's going down out here than I do. Want me to ask him?"

"Who is it?"

"Name's Louis Salazar."

"He's on the level?"

"Let's just say there are a lot of nooses in his family tree. He's helping with the skipper I'm here to take back."

"Because you're paying him?"

"Cops don't earn much, and he's just making sure I can deliver the skipper so justice can be done. I don't see the harm in it." He shrugged. "You want me to ask him or not?"

"That would be helpful," Milton said.

"I'll get right on it."

33

M ilton went to his room and lay down on the bed for an hour, his eyes closed. He slept lightly, waking to the sound of his phone vibrating on the nightstand. He picked it up and looked at the message. Beau said that he had spoken to his police contact, and that the officer was down by the pool now.

~

MILTON STEPPED out the door to the pool. It was hot now, and the sun glared off the water. Beau and a second man were sitting at the tiki bar. The newcomer was in his late middle age, with a spreading gut and hair that was thinning on top. He was dressed in a rumpled suit, and his brown leather brogues were scuffed and dusty. He was wearing a pair of mirrored Aviators and had a toothpick in the corner of his mouth.

Milton joined them, taking a seat where he could face away from the sun.

Beau nodded in acknowledgement. "This is Sergeant Louis Salazar," he said. "Louis—this is John Smith."

Milton offered his hand and Salazar took it. "You're Vegas police?"

"That's right," Salazar said. "Homicide."

"I think Louis has something you might be interested in hearing," Beau told Milton.

"Beau tells me you're interested in Oscar Delgado," Salazar began.

"I am."

"And he tells me not to ask why."

"I can't say right now."

"That's fine by me," he said. "You got trouble with Delgado, I'm not sure that's something I'd *want* to know about."

"So you know who he is?"

"You know anything about La Frontera?"

Milton glanced over at Beau and, for a brief moment, they shared a look. The two of them had met when they had both been involved with La Frontera in Juárez, Mexico. Beau had taken mafia money to kill or catch Santa Muerta, the bloodthirsty son of the man who ran the cartel's operations on the border. Milton had helped Beau to bring the son in, and Milton had taken out the old man.

"I know enough," Milton said.

"They've been fighting among themselves for the last couple of years after the Don got offed in the mountains," Salazar said. "We think Delgado represents the faction that took over."

"And the cartel has a presence in Vegas?"

"Some. Drug distribution, car theft, prostitution, fraud. I was working a homicide last year—the vic was this young Salvadoran, Arturo Napoleón-Romero. He was shot up like

Swiss cheese and dumped in the desert. We charged three Mexicans for it. The vic was from MS-13, part of their effort to push into Vegas. One of the Mexican brothels got hit. The beaners didn't like that, not a bit. Made an example out of this guy, a warning for the Salvadorans to think again about their plans."

"And how does that tie in with Delgado?"

"He was brought in for questioning as a part of the investigation. We had a witness who said that he was responsible for the hit—not just responsible, but that he was the triggerman. We were ready to charge Delgado when the witness disappeared. The three guys who got charged, they swore blind that they'd never even seen Delgado before, even though there was strong circumstantial evidence that they'd been friends since forever. Those guys went down for it, but not one of them has so much as mentioned his name, even when we offered to shave time off their sentences if they gave him up."

Milton exhaled.

"Tell me about it," Salazar said. "You need to tread carefully if you've got an interest in him. Guys like him play for keeps."

"I know the type," Milton said.

Salazar stood. "That's all I got."

"Thank you. It's very helpful."

"I'm serious. Be careful. Whatever it is you're involved in, it can't end up good."

"I hear you."

Salazar turned to Beau. "When you want to pick up Anwar?"

"I was thinking tomorrow?"

"Not a problem. I know where he's at—he's not gonna be

hard to find. Give me a call when you're ready and we'll go get him."

Milton and Beau thanked the detective and watched him make his way around the pool to the door.

"Shit," Milton said.

"Your day just took a turn for the worse, English."

Milton leaned his elbows on the bar, suddenly dog-tired.

"You think her old man would try to rip off people like that?"

"What else could it be?"

"He'd have to be as dumb as dirt," Beau said.

"He works for them; there's cash in his lock-up; he goes missing…"

Beau shrugged. "Yep—evidence surely points that way. I just can't get to figuring out why he'd do something so reckless."

"He has cancer," Milton said. "Maybe he thinks he has nothing to lose."

"Getting eaten alive by the worst cancer would be like a walk in the park compared to what the narcos do to people who steal from them."

"You don't have to tell me that," Milton said.

"I know I don't." Beau nodded up to the rooms above them. "You think she has any idea how bad her daddy has fucked up?"

"No," Milton said. "I don't think so."

"Then she's gonna get the mother of all shocks when you tell her."

34

M ilton went back to Jessica's room and knocked on the door.

She opened it.

"Can I come in?"

She went inside and Milton followed. The bedsheets were bunched up at the foot of the bed and the window was open, the blinds blowing in the gentle breeze that eased inside. She went to the coffee machine and switched it on.

"Want one?"

"Thanks," he said.

She put a capsule into the machine, put a cup beneath the nozzle and pushed the button.

"What is it?" she asked him.

"I spoke to Beau's contact in the police."

She handed him the coffee. "And?"

"Delgado works for La Frontera."

"I've never heard of them."

"It's a Mexican cartel. They're involved in various criminal activities in Vegas, including fraud."

She shook her head and, for a moment, he wondered

whether she was about to cry. She laid her hand to her cheek, blinked several times, then backed up, sitting down on the edge of the bed again.

"Jessica," he began.

She put her head in her hands and her shoulders started to shake.

Milton reached for her, paused, then stepped back. He didn't know what to say. He knew that everything that she had learned was going to be hard to process. But he was also concerned that they did not have time on their side. Her father... Milton thought that he would still be alive, but his position would be precarious.

Milton took the cup of coffee from the machine. "Here."

She looked up at him, her eyes heavy with tears. She wiped them away with the back of her hand. "I'm sorry."

He handed her the coffee. "Forget it," he said. "It's a lot to take in."

The tears had streaked her mascara. "What do I do?"

"Your options haven't changed. You can go to the police, or we can try to work a deal with Delgado."

"And what do you think?"

"The same as before. Knowing who Delgado is makes no difference to the equation."

"I don't know," she said after another long pause. "I can't believe that my father..." There was a catch in her voice. She paused and swallowed. "I can't believe that he would be involved in something like this. With people like that. I just can't believe it."

"Jessica," Milton said, "look at me."

She turned.

"I *know* this is a shock. You'll need time to get your thoughts together. But that has to come later. You don't have time now. More to the point, your father doesn't have time.

Delgado is dangerous. He wants his money back. I didn't tell you this—when I went to the lock-up last night, two men arrived just after me."

"And how would they have known..."

"Because Delgado threatened your father until he told him what he wanted to know."

"But if he sent men to the storage place..."

Milton picked up the thread. "That's right. Your father told him. And now he knows what's happened there, that the place was empty—he'll probably have guessed that you have the money. It's not about leverage anymore. We've balanced things out."

"And we're safe here? They won't find us?"

"For now," Milton said. "But he'll find us eventually. We can't just wait it out, apart from what that would mean for your father." He paused. "I know it's hard, but you have to make a decision. I need to know what you want to do."

"How can you be so calm? It's not *normal*. A normal person reacts like me. They freak out. You know—they *panic*. They don't know what to do." Her face quivered and tears gathered in her eyes again. "And they're scared to death."

Milton let her cry.

She wiped her eyes for a second time.

Milton sat down beside her. "What do you want to do?"

She swallowed, regained her composure. "We can't go to the police."

"That would be dangerous."

"So I give him what he wants. An exchange, like you said. I give him the money; he gives me my father." She frowned. "But how can we trust him?"

"We can't. But there are ways to make sure both parties behave themselves during an exchange."

"How?"

Milton had already thought about that. He was going to have to ask Beau for another favour, a very big favour. "You can leave that to me."

"Is that what you'd do? The exchange?"

"It is."

She looked down at the floor for a moment. "And you'll help me?" she finally asked.

"If you want me to."

Jessica stood. "All right. That's what we'll do."

35

M ilton left Jessica in the room with the same instructions he'd given her before: don't answer the door, don't make any calls, stay put. He told her that he would be back in an hour.

He walked to East Charleston Boulevard, putting a mile between himself and the hotel. He found the branch of T-Mobile that he had seen online, went inside and bought two pay-as-you-go phones. He went back outside and crossed over to Esmeralda's Café, a quiet joint at the end of a strip mall with the spire of the Stratosphere Tower visible behind it. He ordered a coffee and a Danish and took a table in the corner where he wouldn't be overheard. He took the phone that he had confiscated from the first man he had shot in Richard Russo's garage and switched it on. He noted down the most frequently dialled numbers and then switched the phone off again.

"Here you go, sir."

The waitress put the coffee and Danish on the table. Milton thanked her, waited until she was back at the counter, and then started to call the numbers that he had written down.

The first went to voicemail.

"Hello, Oscar," Milton said. "I have your money. Call me back."

He took a pen and scored a line through the first number. He took a bite of the pastry and washed it down with a mouthful of coffee. He was about to dial the second number when the phone vibrated in his hand. He took a breath, pressed answer and put the phone to his ear.

"That was quick," he said.

"Such an intriguing message."

It was the same man. The same English, spoken with a heavy South American accent.

"I know who you are, Señor Smith."

"And I know who you are, Señor Delgado."

"Then we are even."

"I know who you work for, too."

"Really?"

"Some criminals down in Colombia."

He chuckled. *"Yet you still have these cojones."*

"Because it doesn't frighten me."

"Is that so?"

"I don't scare easily."

"That is a simple thing to say when you are on the telephone. It is something else when you are face to face."

"It won't change. Don't waste your breath."

Delgado didn't answer at once. Milton let the silence extend, taking a sip of the coffee and watching a pickup reverse into a space in the parking lot outside the window.

Delgado broke first. *"What do you want?"*

"You know what I want. Richard Russo. Is he still alive?"

"*He is a little—how do you say—the worse for wear. But alive? Yes, he is alive.*"

"Prove it."

"*You don't tell me what to do.*"

"Then you don't get your money."

Milton left another pause and, again, Delgado broke first.

"*I will send you a video.*"

"Send it to this number. Make sure there's something to prove it's current." Milton took a chance: he ended the call.

"Get you anything else?" the waitress asked him.

"No, thanks," Milton said. "I'm good."

He looked at his watch: it was just past midday.

He finished the pastry and pulled out a paper napkin from the chrome dispenser on the table. He wiped his fingers.

He checked his watch: three minutes past midday.

His phone buzzed with an incoming message. He took it out of his pocket and saw that the number was the same as the one that he had used to contact Oscar. He tapped the screen to open the message and saw that a video had been attached. He hit the video and watched. It was a short ten-second clip, the camera showing a man whom Milton recognised as Jessica's father. Richard Russo was holding up a copy of the *Las Vegas Review-Journal* that bore today's date. He had clearly been beaten up; his face was bruised and bloodied, with contusions around both eyes and a purply-black bruise across his right cheek. His eyebrow had been cut and blood had crusted around it. He did not speak in the video, but the fear in his eyes was eloquent.

The phone buzzed with a call.

"*If you put the phone down on me again—*"

"Shut up, Oscar. I told you—I'm not scared of you."

"You have your proof. What about my money?"

"I've got it."

"And what do you propose that we do?"

"Make a deal."

"You think that you are in a position to do that?"

"I do. You have Russo. I have the money. We each have what the other wants—it should be easy."

Delgado chuckled. *"Who are you, Smith?"*

"You said you knew."

"I know that you bought your car in Oakland."

"That was easy. What else?"

"We could ask the man who sold it to you for a description."

"You could, but I'm not all that remarkable to look at."

"We'll know more soon."

"Let me save you the effort. I'm bad news. I'm someone you don't want as an enemy."

"Such big talk."

"You've had three chances to take me out. Three swings, three misses. Three men came at me in that house. What happened to them?"

"They were sloppy. They got what they deserved."

"We can agree on that, at least. But I can handle you, too, Oscar. Just the same."

Milton sipped his coffee, letting the silence extend again.

"So?" Delgado said. *"We meet? I give you the old man; you give me my money. As simple as that?"*

Milton switched the phone from his left hand to his right. "It really is. You won't get a better offer. And I won't make it twice."

"What if I say no?"

"You wouldn't be foolish enough to do that. I know what they'll say about failure in Mazatlán. You're already worried how they'll react when they realise you've been fooled by a gringo. I doubt you've told them yet, have you? Too frightened."

It was a calculated escalation. Milton sensed that the man would not enjoy his *cojones* being questioned, and the sharp exhalation of breath that greeted his rejoinder was confirmation of that.

"Is that so?"

"Yes," Milton said. "And there's something else. The fact that you have the girl's father is the only thing that's stopping me from coming after you. You sent men after me. That's bad manners. I don't appreciate bad manners."

Milton left another pause. He could hear the sound of conversation on the line, but it was muffled, as if Delgado had cupped his hand over the phone. Milton took another sip of coffee while he waited.

"Fine," Delgado said at last. *"We will meet. The money for Russo."*

"Watch your phone. I'll send a message with the details."

Milton hung up.

36

Oscar Delgado was still angry. An hour had passed since the Englishman had called him, and all he could think about was putting his pistol in the gringo's mouth and pulling the trigger. No one spoke to him like that. *No one*. The Englishman was infuriating. He had shown no fear of him, despite apparently knowing who it was he represented in Vegas. He took a breath and told himself to relax. Smith had been bluffing. If he had known about the cartel—really known—then he could not possibly have been so sanguine about the insults that he had so casually dispensed. Oscar would correct his behaviour. He would educate him about the cartel, and about what happened to those men and women who were foolish enough to cross it.

He was standing outside the entrance to the Wynn. He looked up at the vast curve of the hotel's main building, the glass glittering like gold in the bright sunlight. The resort staff were attending to new arrivals, removing their luggage from the trunks of the limousines that had ferried them here from the airport. This was one of the more expensive hotels on the Strip, attracting a moneyed clientele from all around the world. Oscar had grown up dirt poor on the streets of Mazatlán and had dragged himself through the ranks of the cartel to a position where he controlled the business that was conducted here, in this vulgar city. He looked at a young couple getting into their high-end Uber Lux and wondered whether the supply lines that he oversaw would lead to a purchase that they might make. A line of his cocaine, snorted through a rolled-up fifty on the top of a marble cistern in a hotel suite that cost five grand a night.

Maybe.

El Patrón had justified his vast business as a means of attacking the imperialist dogs who persecuted him. He extracted billions of dollars from their economy while poisoning the blood of American youth with cocaine. El Patrón might have been killed, but his reasoning was still sound. He had seen himself as a *bandito*, a soldier working for the glory of Mexico. Oscar saw himself in the same way.

He straightened out his jacket and made his way to the entrance. He glanced up again at the building looming overhead and thought about one of those five-thousand-dollar suites, this one up on the thirty-eighth floor. He thought about the man who was inside it—Héctor del Pozo, La Bruja's emissary from Juárez—and felt the fear that he wanted Smith to feel.

37

M ilton walked back to the hotel. He took his time, paying close attention to the cars that were parked at the side of the road and the pedestrians who were making their way to and from their businesses. He didn't see anything that was out of the ordinary, but he was still careful and would remain that way.

He went inside and took the elevator to the second floor. He knocked on Jessica's door and waited for her to open it.

"Well?" she said.

Milton came inside and closed the door behind him. "I spoke to Delgado."

"And?"

"The money in exchange for your father. That's the deal."

"How do we know that he's okay?"

Milton took out his phone and opened the video that he had received from Oscar. He handed the phone to Jessica and watched her face as the footage played. The blood drained from her cheeks and she swallowed hard.

"They've hurt him," she said.

"A little."

"His face..."

"It looks worse than it is. He's alive. He's lucky."

"He's not... tricking us?"

"Your father is all Delgado has to bargain with if he wants his money back. He's no good to him if he's..."

"If he's dead," she finished.

"If he's dead," Milton said. "But he's not."

She went to the window and stared out. "I'm nervous."

"I'd be surprised if you weren't."

"You're not?"

"A little," he said. "That's natural."

"That doesn't make me feel any better."

"If we plan carefully, there's no reason why it won't work as we want it to."

She ran her fingers through her hair. "Where is this going to happen?"

"I'm going to speak to Beau," he said. "He knows Vegas better than I do."

"In town, though?"

He chewed his lip. "Probably not. There are going to be weapons on both sides. It's not the kind of thing we want the police to find out about."

"Weapons?"

"I'm not going to go and meet someone like Delgado without a weapon, Jessica."

"But having witnesses would help, wouldn't it? Delgado won't be able to do anything."

"He wouldn't agree to do it here," Milton said. "It has to be somewhere quiet. But *we* choose the place and *we* control it. It happens on *our* terms."

Milton collected the phone from her and put it back in his pocket.

"What do we do now?" she said.

"We need to get ready. I'll speak to Beau, and then I'll go and scout the location."

"And then?"

"Then I'll call Delgado and set it up."

"For when?"

"Tonight."

38

Oscar looked at his reflection in the mirrored wall of the elevator. He looked nervous. He had been summoned to the Wynn for a meeting with Héctor del Pozo, the cartel's go-between and his main point of contact with La Bruja. Delgado did not like del Pozo, and he knew that del Pozo did not like him. Del Pozo was critical and had no problem with speaking his mind. During their previous transactions, he had never failed to point out the shortcomings in the way that Delgado organised the business. That would have been irritating enough, but, as del Pozo was the eyes and ears of La Bruja, his disapproval was potentially dangerous.

Del Pozo was based in the States, shuttling to and from the cartel's stronghold in Juárez as necessary. The cartel kept its business strictly compartmentalised, meaning that Delgado did not know how many other cartel businesses del Pozo oversaw, save that he operated across the west coast and inland. Los Angeles, San Diego, Vegas and who knew where else. It was usually the case that weeks would pass between visits. The fact that he had been in Vegas for the last week, and had rented a suite at the Wynn for the fore-seeable future, was not something that filled Oscar with joy.

He knew what it meant: La Bruja was concerned about the operation that Delgado was running, and del Pozo had been assigned to keep an eye on him. A bad report would not just lead to the termination of his employment. It would be much worse than that.

The elevator reached the thirty-eighth floor and the door opened. Delgado made his way along the quiet corridor, the walls and carpet in the same dark chocolate hue, until he reached room 3801.

He knocked on the door and stood back. The door was opened by a man with tattoos on his bare arms and a dead-eyed stare. Oscar hadn't seen him before, but assumed that he was the muscle who had been sent to guard del Pozo while he was in Vegas.

"I'm here to see Héctor," Oscar said.

The bodyguard stepped aside and nodded with his head that Oscar should go inside.

The foyer opened into a large living area with two full-size couches, a mirrored ceiling, a bar, a dining room table that could seat six, and a bureau. A large flat-screen TV was set into the wall, and the far side of the room was all windows, with a stunning view of the city, the desert and the mountains beyond.

Del Pozo was standing at the window, looking out at the view.

"Héctor," Oscar said, forcing a smile.

Del Pozo turned to face him. The greeting was not returned. "I hope you have good news."

"We have made progress."

"What does that mean? You have the money?"

"Not yet."

"Disappointing."

Del Pozo took a glass of water from the bureau and sat down on the sofa. Oscar noticed that he didn't offer him a drink, leaving him to stand like a fool in the middle of the room.

"This progress, then—what is it?"

"We have Russo."

"Where is he now?"

"At the warehouse."

"And the money?"

Oscar took a breath and swallowed on a dry throat. "He didn't have it."

"I wouldn't expect him to be stupid enough to have it at his home. I'm sure he told you where it was, though."

"He said that he had stored it in a unit in Silver Spur. I sent a man to collect it, but it appears that we were too late."

"It 'appears'? It was there or it was not there. Which is it?"

"It wasn't there."

"Failure after failure, Oscar. I would say that I was surprised, but that would be a lie."

Del Pozo was watching him with a contempt that he did not even attempt to conceal. Oscar was not used to people talking to him in that way, and would have liked nothing better than to toss him through the window; del Pozo would have enough time before he fell to earth to have considered the good sense of showing him a little respect. But that was impossible, of course. The bodyguard watching from the side of the room would be armed, and would have no compunction in putting a bullet into his head, even here. And Del Pozo was the representative of La Bruja; to show him disrespect would be seen as disrespecting the cartel. That would mean Oscar's own death, and it would not be a death that would be pleasant or quick.

He took a breath. "Russo's daughter went to his house just after we had taken him. She was with a man. We turned around and went back to get her, but it didn't go well. The man appears to be working with her. He was capable. He shot three of my men and escaped with her before we could take them."

"This man," del Pozo said, "who is he?"

"His name is John Smith."

"And?"

"We are working to find out more."

"Do you have *anything* else?"

"His car."

"You have searched it?"

"Yes."

"Fingerprints?"

"Sorry?"

"Do you have his fingerprints? He must have left his fingerprints in his car."

He swallowed. "No, Héctor."

"He left no fingerprints, or you haven't checked?"

"We haven't checked."

"Where is the car?"

"The warehouse."

"Leave it there. I will send a man. He will do your job for you."

"Of course, Héctor."

"And the money?"

"The daughter must have known where it was kept. The lock-up was empty when we got to it. Smith called me this morning. He says he has it. He wants to propose an exchange—the money for Russo."

"And Russo is in a position to be exchanged?"

"We roughed him up a little." Oscar shrugged. "Other than that, he's fine."

"Get the money, Oscar. This man Smith—we will deal with him. The Russos, too."

Del Pozo stood and crossed the living room to the panoramic windows. He put his hands behind his back as he gazed out onto the wide vista of the Strip.

"Is there anything else you need, Héctor?"

Del Pozo did not turn back. "I am not impressed," he said. "This whole situation has been badly managed. You should never have put yourself into a situation where someone was able to steal so much of our money. That is unprofessional, and professionalism is the minimum required if you want to work for the cartel. La Bruja shares my disappointment."

"Tell her I'm—"

Del Pozo cut him off. "You can tell her yourself. Fix this mess. When it is done, you will travel to Casa Victor. She wants to speak to you. You are going to have to persuade her that you're still the right man to run this operation."

Oscar wanted to protest, but he knew it would be pointless. You did not negotiate with people like Héctor, far less La Bruja. He knew that he was in a perilous position and that the only way he would be able to extricate himself was to demonstrate that he could resolve this situation and then show that he was able to continue to generate revenue for the cartel.

"Is there anything else?" Oscar said.

"No," Héctor said. "We are done. Tell me when this has been resolved."

Oscar said that he would, and made his way to the door. He looked back; Héctor was still looking out of the window.

The bodyguard opened the door and Oscar stepped out into the serenity of the corridor. He set off toward the elevator, waiting for his pulse to slow. He felt a riot of emotion: anger at being spoken to like the shit on Héctor's shoe, frustration that there was nothing that he could do about it and, most of all, fear.

Fear of La Bruja, and of what she would do to him if the situation was not resolved to his satisfaction.

39

Héctor del Pozo waited for Delgado to leave the suite. The conversation had been irritating. His job was to ensure that the business of the cartel was conducted smoothly and securely, and, when he was presented with evidence that it was not, to take steps to improve it. Delgado had overseen the operation here for several months and, in that time, he had made a considerable sum of money. He had built an efficient network for the distribution of the cartel's products—cocaine, meth, women —and, until recently, there had been little to suggest that there was a reason for concern. His proposal that he open a new business stealing the casino's money had been checked and approved, and the results had been everything that he had promised. Millions of dollars had been siphoned from the vaults of the corporations that ran the legitimate businesses on the Strip, and there had been no indication that the authorities were close to discovering who was responsible. It had been an impressive operation, and Delgado's stock had—until recently—been high.

His report that money had been stolen by the man he

had employed to administer his scheme had been concerning. La Bruja had dispatched Héctor to investigate and to take whatever steps were necessary.

He had been here a week and had found, to his annoyance, that Delgado had allowed standards to slip. His men were lazy and unimpressive. The heavy metals business that had been established to receive the product did not look particularly impressive and would not have stood up to scrutiny if the police ever paid it any attention. Delgado himself had allowed his own standards to slip; Héctor had discovered that he helped himself to the cartel's cocaine. That was an egregious flouting of the rules. A man who liked the product too much was prone to making errors. Delgado needed to be sharp, and Héctor had seen too much evidence that he was not.

He went to the bar and made himself a vodka tonic, then returned to the window and sipped at it as he watched a jet descend into McCarran. The view was undeniably impressive and one of the reasons the hotel was able to charge so much for the suite, but he wasn't really paying attention to it. Instead, he ran back over the conversation for anything that might suggest that the course of action he had been considering might have been premature. He had decided several days ago that Delgado was incompetent and that his continued management of the operation here would be unwise. He had called him to the suite for a chance to demonstrate that his conclusion was incorrect.

He knew now that it was not.

Delgado had said nothing that had changed his mind, and Héctor had no time for second chances. Just like Delgado, his own continued employment depended upon the efficient execution of his duties. La Bruja would not allow *him* the benefit of the doubt if he made a mistake; likewise, he himself would not have been able to forgive Oscar even if he was minded to, and he was not.

He took another sip of the vodka tonic and put it down on the bar. He took his phone from his pocket and opened the encrypted messaging app that he used when he needed to speak with the cartel. He opened a fresh message and typed.

Situation is not promising.

He pressed send, waited for the phone to indicate that the message had been delivered, and then put it back in his pocket again. He collected his drink and walked back to the window. The first jet had landed, and another was already in the latter stages of its descent. That was the thing about Vegas. It never slowed down; new potential customers were continually arriving. It might not have been on the vast scale of Los Angeles, but it was awash with money, and he was sure that he was right: they could not continue to entrust those opportunities to someone as lackadaisical as Oscar Delgado.

Another jet would arrive soon, and it would deliver a *sicario* to correct the errors that had been made.

It was time for a change.

40

M ilton called Beau and arranged to meet him down by the pool. 'Maniac' by Michael Sembello was playing loudly over a PA and, as Milton came outside, he saw that there was some sort of exercise session taking place. A buff instructor wearing Lycra and a microphone was facing a line of elderly men and women as they followed his instructions in the water. The music and his overenthusiastic exhortations were amplified by a small speaker that he had set up at the edge of the pool.

Beau was waiting and, as Milton joined him, he nodded down at the curious display. "Progress," he observed. "Ain't it grand."

Milton led the way to a spare table and sat down.

Beau sat opposite. "So?"

"I called Delgado," Milton said.

Beau cocked an eyebrow. "And how'd that go?"

"He was full of bluster."

"Bluster he can probably back up."

"Maybe," Milton said. "But I've heard it all before."

"Does he still have the old man?"

"He does. Beaten up a little, but I think he's still alive."

"Lucky for him."

The track changed to 'Livin' La Vida Loca.' The instructor somehow found even more enthusiasm.

"I suggested a swap," Milton said. "The money for Russo."

"And Delgado's good with that?"

"Said that he'd do it."

"You can't trust him to play it straight. Man like that'll be as crooked as a barrel of fish hooks."

"I know that. But it might be something that we can manage without getting everyone shot to pieces."

"You give any thought to where you might wanna do that?"

"That's what I wanted to talk to you about. Somewhere quiet where I can control the environment. You got any ideas?"

Beau stroked his whiskers. "I can think of one," he said. "There was this one skipper I went after six months ago. Skinny little tweaker, ornery as all hell, jumped bail and went down to his daddy's place outside Goodsprings. There's an old gas station just outside the town. Been out of action for years. They were cooking meth in back. I went in with a shotgun."

"Describe it."

Beau closed his eyes. "So you got the gas station, the store alongside, and then nothing anywhere near it. It's in the middle of nowhere. You'll get the odd car now and again, but that's it."

"And at night?"

"Only living things out there will be coyotes and snakes."

"Sounds perfect."

"You want to check it out before?"

"I would."

"Now?"

"Sure."

Beau got up and stretched. He looked over Milton's shoulder and gave a nod. Milton turned and saw that Jessica was walking toward them.

"Afternoon," Beau said.

She smiled tightly and turned to Milton. "What's happening?"

"Beau has suggested a place that might be suitable for the exchange. We're just going to go and see it."

"I want to come," she said.

"No," Milton said.

"I want to be there when you meet them."

"No," Milton repeated. "Absolutely not."

"How many of you are there? Just the two of you?"

Milton realised that he hadn't even asked Beau whether he would be prepared to help. He glanced over at him and saw a nod of assent.

"That's right," he said.

"And Delgado will have more than two?"

"Probably."

"I know how to shoot. My father used to take Mason and me out to the range when we were younger. I was good."

"I'm sure you were," he said, "but this isn't going to the range. These are dangerous people. And your father will be there."

"That's why I'm coming," she insisted. "What happens if they get the jump on you? They'll kill you, right? And then they'll kill him."

"I don't think that's a good idea."

She put her hand on his shoulder. "I'm grateful," she

said. "I'm grateful for everything you've done, and I'm incredibly grateful that you'd even think about doing this for me. I'm grateful to both of you—you don't even know me or my family, and I know it's dangerous. But—and please don't think I'm being disrespectful—this isn't your decision to make. You can't stop me from coming."

"I can call it off," Milton said.

"And my father will be killed."

Milton couldn't disagree with that.

"Is this because I'm a woman?"

"No," Milton said. "It's because this is dangerous."

"It'll be more dangerous for you if you're outnumbered. You need someone else who can fire a weapon. I can. I'm good. I can help."

"They'll have more than two of 'em," Beau said. "Can't say those are odds I'm all that fond of."

Milton exhaled. On the one hand, the idea of taking Jessica seemed like the greatest folly. It would be perilous; he had no idea whether she was being truthful about her ability with a weapon; and, worst of all, she was emotionally involved given that it was her father they were going to bring back. On the other hand, he knew that she and Beau were right. Delgado would bring more than two gunmen with him. An exchange in those circumstances was possible— Milton had pulled off swaps like that before—but it would have presented the kind of situation that involved razor-thin margins, the kind of circumstance that could go one way or the other. Much as he was loath to admit it, there was some sense in what she was suggesting.

He turned back to Jessica. "You would have to do everything that we say. *Everything*. If you make a mistake, we all get killed—your father, too. Understand?"

"Yes," she said. "Is that a yes, then? I can come?"

"You can come with us now to take a look at where Beau thinks we might be able to do it," he said. "I want to see you shoot."

"Fine."

"That's not a yes, Jessica. I haven't made up my mind about later. I need to think about it."

"I can live with that," she said.

They took Beau's rental and headed south out of the city. The satnav directed them onto the Las Vegas Freeway, paralleling the Strip for the first couple of miles before they cut through the traffic and picked up I-15. Beau was driving with Milton alongside. Jessica sat quietly in the back, lost in thought. No one had very much to say, so Milton turned on the radio and skipped to KCYE. It was a country music station, and a song that Milton didn't recognise was playing.

"This your kind of music, English?"

"Not really," Milton said. "I thought—"

"You thought it was the kind of thing the old redneck would be into?"

Milton smiled and gave a helpless shrug. "Just trying to be thoughtful."

"His taste is much worse," Jessica piped up from the back.

"That so?"

"All this British stuff from the sixties."

"Classics," Milton corrected.

"Whatever," she said, and as he looked up in the mirror, he saw that she was grinning at him.

The road was clear and Beau put his foot down.

∽

BEAU TURNED off the interstate at Jean and headed west, following the signs toward Goodsprings. They drove on for another ten minutes before he slowed the car and pointed.

"Over there," he said.

Milton saw the shapes of the buildings ahead: the canopy of the gas station, the pumps long since removed; the outline of the attached store; power lines that ran along poles that had been planted in the desert beyond it. There was no sign of anything that might have suggested that the building was occupied.

Beau hit the brakes and turned the wheel, bumping the car off the road and onto the rough track that had once served drivers stopping for fuel and provisions. He drove onto the forecourt, passed between the concrete piers that would have mounted the pumps, and continued around to the rear of the building. They were sheltered from the road here, the remains of the store blocking them from anyone who might be passing along the quiet road to Vegas.

Milton opened the door of the Yukon and stepped out. The cabin was cool from the air conditioning, but the mid-afternoon heat quickly overwhelmed it. It was a dry heat, without humidity, and Milton would not have liked to have been outside in it without protection for too long. He shielded his eyes with his hand as he moved away from the car and started to check out the immediate vicinity. The desert surrounded them on all sides, split by the highway and prickled by a single row of utility poles. The landscape ascended to the north, the desert rising into the low foothills of the Sierra Nevada mountains.

Jessica got out of the back of the car and walked over to the station, sheltering in the shadow cast by the building.

Beau came over to stand next to Milton. "What do you think?"

"How close are we to a town?"

Beau pointed to the southeast. "You saw Jean when we turned off," he said. He turned and pointed to the northwest. "You got Goodsprings there. We're a good mile away from anyone. Nothing else. What you think?"

"I think it'll do," Milton said.

"How you gonna play it? You don't want them knowing where we're gonna do the swap in advance, do you?"

Milton had been considering that. "We passed a gas station at Jean. We'll arrange to meet them there; then they can follow us out here. We park up behind the building, like now, keep them at a distance—over there—and then we get them to bring Russo out. We give them the money and then we get out that way."

He pointed to a dusty set of tracks that led around the other side of the building, back to the road. A set of motorcycle tracks was still visible; someone had turned their bikes off the highway here to ride out in the desert.

Beau nodded his approval. "Nice and quiet. Shielded from traffic. What about practicalities?" He gestured out to the open plain. "Would sure be nice to have a shooter out there."

"You got a rifle?" Milton said.

"No."

"Me neither. And we haven't got time to sort that out."

Beau squinted into the bright sunlight. "So?"

Milton looked out onto the plains, too. There was nothing there. "Are you still sure you want to do this, Beau?"

"I don't *want* to," he said, "but I'll do it. You'll get shot to shit if you come out here on your own."

He knew that Beau was right. There would be no chance of getting out alive without at least another gun as backup.

"I'm going to owe you," he said.

"Damn straight you are."

"What about a firearm? What do you have?"

Beau reached into his jacket and took out a pistol. He handed it to Milton. "Springfield XD-M."

Milton hefted the weapon. It was the competition model, with the 5.25-inch barrel that offered good sight radius and made the pistol easier to shoot at longer ranges. Nineteen-round capacity. He handed it back to Beau.

"What do you have?"

Milton took the Ruger from the waistband of his jeans. "Took it from one of the bad guys at the Russo house," he said. "Could do with a few more rounds, though."

"What is it?"

"The Security. Takes nine-millimetre parabellum."

"I got some you can have."

Milton pushed the Ruger back into his waistband. "You got a backup weapon?"

Beau grinned. "Does the Pope shit in the woods?"

He bent down, reached his hand to his boot and hiked up his trouser leg. He was wearing an ankle holster with a second weapon. He pulled out the little snub-nosed revolver and handed it to Milton. It was a Colt Detective Special, a classic concealed-carry weapon. Milton opened it up and spun the cylinder, revealing six .38 Specials. It was a good weapon and Beau had kept it in excellent condition. Milton ran his finger across the brass, then snapped it closed.

"Mind if I let her take a look at it?" he said.

"Be my guest."

Milton turned to Jessica. She had wandered away from the building, about twenty metres into the desert. She was looking back at them, framed against the spectacular backdrop behind her.

"Can you come over here for a moment?" Milton called over to her.

She made her way back to them, her feet slipping on the loose dirt and scree.

"You want to show me how good you are with this?"

"Little piece like that?" she said. "Easy."

She put out her hand and Milton gave her the Colt. She hefted it, opened the swing-out cylinder and checked it out, then snapped it closed once again.

"What do you want me to hit?"

Milton pointed at the stump of a long-since-dead Joshua tree out in the desert. It was around ten metres away and on the same level as them. "How about that?"

"No problem," she said.

"Just point and shoot," he said. "Be ready for the recoil. Nice and re—"

Jessica thumbed the hammer back, took aim, and fired. The impact of the round was marked by a puff of dust in the old trunk. Milton was about to congratulate her when she fired again, hitting the target in almost the same spot.

"I can do this all day," she said with a grin.

Beau gave a whoop. "Where'd you say you learned to shoot?"

"My dad," she said. "We used to go to ranges all the time. I had a Taurus PT111 back then. I must have sent a thousand rounds downrange, one way or another. I got to be pretty good."

"I can see that," Milton said, his natural caution preventing him from being too effusive in his praise. "But shooting a tree is one thing. Shooting a man is another."

"I know," she said. "I've never shot anyone before. I don't ever want to. But if my dad is in danger, and there's no other choice, I will. You don't need to worry about me."

"You'd follow my instructions," Milton said.

"You open fire," Beau added, "and the lead isn't going to be going just one way. They'll fire back."

"Does that mean I can come?" she said, handing the gun back to Beau.

"I'll think about it," Milton said.

They needed every gun they could get, and she had demonstrated that she was able. He was reluctant to involve her more than she was already involved, but, on balance, perhaps there was more good to be had by having her with them than the harm that would be caused by going up against cartel shooters at a numerical disadvantage.

He would consider it.

42

It was six in the evening when Beau parked the Yukon into the hotel lot and killed the engine.

"What do we do now?" Jessica said.

"I'd try to relax for a bit," Milton said. "Go and get something to eat, maybe."

"What about you?" Jessica said.

"I'm going to set this up."

"You need me?"

"No," Milton said. "I've got it."

Beau nodded and swung around so that he could look back at Jessica. "There's a nice pizza restaurant down the way. We could go and order some pies."

"Sure," she said.

Beau turned to Milton. "What do you like?"

"Whatever's good," he said.

"Come over when you're done. It's called Evel Pie. As in Evel Knievel."

"What?" Jessica said.

"*Who*," Beau corrected. "He used to ride motorbikes."

She shook her head, perplexed. "Never heard of him."

"Kids," Beau observed with an exaggerated roll of the eyes.

Milton smiled. "I'll see you in there."

They got out. Milton watched as Beau and Jessica walked to Fremont Street, turned the corner and disappeared. He reached into his jacket pocket for his burner phone and held down the button to power it up. He gave a moment's thought to what he was going to say and then tapped the number for Oscar Delgado.

The call connected after just four rings.

"Señor Smith," Delgado said.

"Are you ready?"

"I am. Are you?"

"Yes."

"So when will it be?"

"Tonight. Ten o'clock. We'll meet you in the gas station on I-15, just after Jean."

"That's forty minutes away. Let's do it closer to Vegas."

"We do it where and when I say we'll do it or not at all."

"All right."

"You'll need to follow me."

"To where?"

"The place I have in mind is out of the way and quiet. We won't be disturbed."

"You expect me to trust you?"

"I know who you work for, Oscar. I know what happens if this goes wrong. Your organisation's reputation is your insurance. All we want is for you to get your money and for the girl to see her father again. That's it."

"What then? We go our separate ways?"

Milton heard the sarcasm in the flippant suggestion. "That's right. We each get what we want. Everyone's happy."

Delgado chuckled. *"You are either very naïve or very stupid —I can't work out which."*

"Yes or no?"

There was a long pause; Milton clutched the phone tightly.

"Ten o'clock. We will be there."

"There are a couple of other requirements," Milton said. "You come with a driver and no one else."

"I'll come with whoever I want."

"If I feel like we're outnumbered, we're not going to stick around. It'll be a waste of everyone's time."

Delgado grunted; it might have been assent, it might not. *"Bring my money."*

"Bring Russo."

He ended the call.

43

Evel Pie was more than simply inspired by the famous stuntman; it was more like a shrine to him. A life-size bronze statue had been erected on the sidewalk in front of the restaurant and, as Milton went inside, he saw that the large room had been stuffed full of memorabilia. Photos of the stuntman had been hung along one long wall, including one that showed him jumping over the fountains at Caesar's Palace in the sixties. A Knievel-branded kid's bike was suspended from the ceiling and a vintage 'Stunt Cycle' arcade game blared out from next to the restrooms.

Beau and Jessica were at a table near the bar and waved him over.

"What does Evel Knievel have to do with pizza?" Milton asked as he sat down.

"Who knows?" Beau said with a grin. "It's Vegas. There's an Eiffel Tower and a pyramid. It don't have to make sense."

Milton poured himself a glass of water and drank it down in one draught.

"What did he say?" Jessica asked.

"It's on," Milton said. "We'll meet at ten and lead them to the meet."

"All right, then. We need to be out of here by eight thirty at the latest. We got a couple of hours to kill."

"I'm going to eat and then get an hour's sleep," Milton said. He turned to Jessica. "You should probably do the same."

Beau stood. "I need to use the little boys' room." He crossed the restaurant to the restroom.

Milton poured out another glass of water.

"You thought about what I said?" Jessica asked him.

"About?"

"About me coming."

"I'm reluctant," he said. "Delgado is dangerous. I don't need to be worrying about you *and* your father *and* him."

"Don't patronise me," she said. "I can shoot. You saw."

"I'm not saying you can't," Milton said, on the back foot. "I'm just saying..."

"What? What are you saying?"

Milton started to speak, then stopped. He realised that she was right: he *was* patronising her.

"Look," she said, her tone a little more mollifying. "You said it yourself—he's dangerous. Right?"

Milton nodded.

"You don't know how many people he's going to bring with him, but you know it won't just be him. Right?"

"Yes."

"And it's you and the old guy. I don't mean to be rude— I'm grateful for what he's done for me, and all—but he's pretty old."

Milton allowed himself a smile as he thought how Beau would react to his age being used to diminish him. He *was* old—that much was right—but he was as tough as old boots and still more capable than many of the operators whom Milton had worked with, especially in an environment that he knew and understood. He'd thought Beau's competence was obvious, but perhaps he was allowing his past experiences to colour his view. Jessica did not have those same experiences.

"All I'm saying," she said, "is that I can help even out the numbers. I'm good with a weapon. You need me there. It doesn't make sense for me to sit on my hands here."

Milton leaned back, feeling all the kinks and aches in his joints and muscles. He bit down on his lip, thinking. He needed Beau to be on board before he committed to anything.

He stood. "I need to speak to him about it. Wait here."

Beau was just returning from the restroom, and Milton intercepted him by the serving station.

"What's up?"

"She still wants to come," Milton said. "You okay with that?"

"Delgado's serious. Some guys, they're all hat and no cattle. Not him."

"I know," Milton said.

"So?"

"So she insisted. She made a persuasive case and, the more I thought about it, the more it made sense. She knows her way around a handgun. And, if she doesn't go, it's just me and you up against however many people Delgado brings along. She's an extra gun to point at them."

Beau sucked his teeth. "Devil's advocate? I can see why you might think that, but you don't know her. You don't know how she'll react if she starts feeling shaky, and it's her old man we're going to get. She'll be as jumpy as spit on a hot skillet—might not be the most predictable, in the circumstances." He paused, sucking his teeth. "That all being said, having an extra gun's no bad thing. It's your call. If you think she should come, I'm good with it."

Milton nodded and led the way back to the table. Jessica had been watching their conversation, and now there was an expectant expression on her face.

"So?"

"You can come," he said. "But no freelancing."

"No freelancing?"

"You stay back at the car and let me and Beau deal with Delgado."

"Understood."

The waitress came over with their pizzas. They were served on Evel Knievel plates and came with cutters that also bore the stuntman's signature. She laid them down on the table.

"We got the World-Famous Snake River Special with rattlesnake jalapeño sausage, the Balls to the Wall with meatballs and Sunday gravy, and the Super Kick-Ass Combo with pepperoni, sausage, ham, mushrooms, onions and peppers. You folks enjoy your pies."

She put down a beer for Beau and went over to clear the adjacent table.

The pizzas were vast. Milton took one of the cutters and sliced up the pie that had been put down for him. He picked a slice and took a bite; it was delicious.

44

They walked back to the hotel together. Beau said that he was going to play a hand or two of poker and that he would see them in the parking lot at eight thirty. Milton and Jessica climbed the stairs to the second floor. He went to his door and opened it.

"Can I come in?" she asked him.

He stepped aside to let her through and then followed. She went to the minibar and took out a bottle of beer.

"You want one?"

"Not for me," Milton said.

She popped the top and took a long draught. Milton went and sat on the edge of the bed. He had presumed that she wanted to talk to him about what might happen later that night, but, to his surprise, she took another slug of beer, put the bottle down and then came and sat next to him.

"I haven't thanked you yet," she said. "This isn't your problem. I don't understand why you're helping me."

Milton shrugged. "Because you need it," he said. "And because I can. You should go and lie down for an hour. The rest will help."

"I could stay here," she said and, before he could do anything to stop her, she held a hand up against his cheek, turned his face toward her, and leaned in to kiss him on the lips.

Milton let her kiss him. Her lips were warm and full and her citrus scent was sweet, reminding him of the time he had spent in Rio not so long ago. She put her other hand against his chest and pushed, trying to get him to lie down on the bed. He realised what that might mean and stopped her, disengaging from her embrace and standing up.

"No," he said. "It's not like that."

She stood. "Like what?"

"Like what you said when I picked you up."

"That you were doing it because you thought you might get laid?"

"Yes," he said awkwardly.

"I don't want to sleep with you to say thanks. I want to sleep with you because I find you attractive."

"No," he said again.

"You don't find me attractive?"

"Of course I do. But I don't think it's a very good idea."

Her cheeks flushed red. "Suit yourself."

She stepped around him and made for the door.

"Jessica—"

"I'll knock for you at eight thirty," she said as she left the room.

45

Milton managed to sleep for an hour and felt a little fresher when he woke at eight fifteen. He took a quick shower, dressed and then spent five minutes field-stripping the Ruger. Beau had provided him with extra ammunition; Milton loaded the magazine to full capacity and shoved two extra magazines into his jacket pocket. He pulled on his boots, pushed the Ruger into the back of his jeans and zipped up the jacket.

Jessica came out of her room at the same time as Milton.

She smiled awkwardly at him. "Sorry."

"Forget it," Milton said. "It's not that I don't... It's..."

He didn't know how to finish the sentence.

"I shouldn't have. It's my fault. But we're good?"

"We're fine," Milton said. "Nothing has changed."

They set off down the corridor together.

"Are you okay?" Milton asked her.

"Nervous."

"You still want to come? You don't have to."

"I'm coming."

"Nerves are fine. They mean you'll be sharp. Just remember—"

"Do what you tell me to do," she finished for him. "I know. I'm not going to do anything stupid."

Milton led the way down to the parking lot. Beau was waiting for them next to the Yukon.

"We good to go?" Beau said.

Milton nodded. He checked his watch: it was twenty-five minutes past eight.

"Let's do it," he said.

∽

BEAU DROVE. Milton sat up front, with Jessica in the back. Beau had given her the little Colt, and she had it in her lap, her fingers tracing a pattern over the blued grip. Beau had regaled them with the story of the skipper he had picked up in the gas station. Jessica had admitted that she didn't understand how a bail bondsman went about his business, and Beau—never one reluctant to tell a story—was indulging her.

"Let's say you've been arrested for a crime. You break into a house. You get brought before a judge, and maybe he'll agree to bail you. He's gonna set your bail—the money you have to lay down if you want to be let out before you have to come back to court—at a set amount. Let's say it's twenty grand. You get the twenty back if you show up at court when you're supposed to. You lose it if you don't."

"And what does that have to do with you?"

"Most defendants don't have twenty grand lying around. If they want to get out, they have to turn to someone like me. You'll usually get the perp's mom or wife or girlfriend coming in to explain what's happened and how much they need. I guarantee the full amount of the bail money to the court and charge the defendant a ten per cent fee. If the defendant skips, I'm liable to pay the court the entire bail amount—that's when I go track them down."

The conversation was a way to fill the time and distract from the nerves that they were all feeling. Milton was half-listening to it, the rest of his attention focused on what might happen when they got to the rendezvous. They would be mobile at that point and would be able to get away in the event that he decided that Delgado was playing them.

Milton visualised the meeting point: a wide-open space, desert on both sides, nowhere to hide. Delgado would not be able to drive south without being seen, and that should mean that he would only be able to bring one vehicle. Milton assumed that he would be in one of the big Suburbans that his men had used at the house. Milton had checked online and had confirmed that the 2019 model had seating for seven passengers. One of those spaces would be taken by Richard Russo, leaving six spaces for Delgado's muscle. Would he come out heavy despite Milton's stipulation that he should not? Hard to say. Probably.

Milton would assume the worst and hope for the best.

The conversation tapered out into an anxious silence.

They passed beyond the city limits. Milton looked out to the side mirrors and watched as the stupendous neon glow of the casinos slowly faded into the enveloping mantle of the desert night.

46

They followed I-15 until they saw the turn-off for Jean. Beau took them off and they looped around, running west for fifteen seconds until they saw the lights of the businesses that had gathered around a Chevron gas station. A huge Stars and Stripes marked the entrance. The road was dusty and the surface uneven, and the Yukon bounced over it and approached a run-off that led to the forecourt.

A black Chevrolet Suburban was parked up there.

"That's them," Milton said.

The windows of the Suburban were smoked, and there was no way to see inside. Milton looked around, scanning carefully and thoroughly. There was a white panel van next to a building with a series of advertisements plastered to the wall—he saw ads for Coca-Cola, Red Bull, White Castle—and a pickup was getting gas. There was nothing else, and nothing that made Milton think that Delgado had brought more than the Suburban with him. That did not mean that he was prepared to take any chances.

"Flash your lights," Milton said.

Beau flicked the stem forward and back, the high beams reflecting off the paintwork of the Chevrolet. Milton lowered his window, heard the engine of the other vehicle rev and then watched as it rolled out. He couldn't hear anything else.

"Okay," Milton said. "Let's go."

〰

THEY CONTINUED WEST TOWARDS GOODSPRINGS. Beau drove at fifty, allowing the Suburban to follow without needing to race. Milton kept his eye on the mirrors, looking for any sign that another car might be following. The road was empty and, out here in the desert, he was able to see for several miles. He wasn't ready to discount the possibility that Delgado might have another vehicle close at hand. There was cellphone coverage here, and it would have been a simple enough thing for him to have a second vehicle with more muscle, ready to be directed in once their final destination was revealed. But, even with that, Milton was sanguine; the landscape was too flat and open for a second car to approach without giving itself away a good minute or two before it arrived. If he was alert—and he was always alert—it was going to be difficult to get the drop on them.

The atmosphere in the Yukon had changed. There had been moments of levity during the drive, but those were all gone now. Beau was staring forward, his eyes on the road, occasionally glancing up into the rear-view mirror to make sure that the Suburban was still behind them. Jessica was rubbing her left index finger up and down the barrel of the Colt, her right hand resting on the door handle. Milton scanned for additional vehicles or any suggestion that their control over the exchange might be challenged.

"Here it is," Beau said.

Milton checked the mirrors again; the only lights behind them belonged to the Suburban.

"Indicate," he told him. "Give them plenty of notice."

Milton reached for the Ruger.

The buildings of the gas station were lit up by the Yukon's high beams. Beau reduced their speed and turned the wheel.

47

Milton directed Beau around the back of the derelict store, just as they had discussed during their reconnaissance that afternoon. Beau turned the Yukon around so that it was facing back to the Suburban, the lights from the two vehicles crossing on the wall of the store. Milton saw the track that he had identified earlier; it would offer a secondary way back to the road in the event that they needed to bug out quickly.

"Stay back by the car," Milton said to Jessica.

"I got it," she said.

He turned to Beau. "Ready?"

Beau's usual sour humour was gone. He was stone-faced. He nodded. "I'm good."

Milton opened the door of the car and stepped out. The store was to his left, fifteen feet away. The Suburban was twenty feet from him. Both vehicles were angled toward the store so as to avoid dazzling one another with their lights. Both engines were running. Beau opened the driver's side door and got out; Milton saw the pistol in his hand. Jessica opened the rear door and got out, shielding herself behind it just as Milton had instructed. She, too, was holding her firearm.

The Suburban stayed where it was, big and black and malignant, the engine rumbling. Milton couldn't see inside.

"Come out," he called.

There was still no movement from the Suburban. The engine revved once and then twice.

Milton reached down into the cabin and brought out the briefcase. He held it up.

"This is what you want," he yelled.

The passenger door of the Suburban opened and a figure stepped out. It was a man. The light was dim and he couldn't make out much beyond the man's silhouette.

"Señor Smith," the man called out.

Milton recognised the voice: it was Delgado.

"Where's Russo?"

"Where's my money?"

Milton held the case aloft in his left hand; his right hand held the Ruger down at his side.

"Bring him out."

The Mexican paused. Milton saw that he had a rifle attached to a sling that he had hung around his neck. It looked like an AR-15, and he had his right hand down by the receiver as his left rested on the sill of the open door. He turned his head and said something to someone inside the Suburban and, a moment later, the door behind him opened and another man emerged. The visibility, once more, was too poor for Milton to make out any detail save that the man was hunched over and it appeared that he had been hooded.

"I want to see his face," Milton called.

A third man disembarked from the car and went up to stand behind the second man. He reached down and yanked off the hood. The man was still in darkness; Milton couldn't see much at all.

Milton didn't take his eyes off the men in front of him.

"Is that him?" Milton called back to Jessica.

"I think so."

"You need to be sure."

"It's dark…"

"Send him into the light," Milton called out.

Delgado said something to the third man. Milton watched as the man who had been wearing the hood was shoved forward, stumbling into the glow around the edges of the high beams. Milton didn't look at him, aware that he would be compromising them all if he allowed the lights to affect his vision. Jessica, though, did not share the same consideration. Milton heard as she gave a little gasp.

"That's Dad," she said.

"Happy, Señor Smith?"

"I am."

"So bring me my money."

"We'll meet in the middle. Bring Russo."

Milton took a step away from the Yukon.

"Careful, English," Beau warned. "He's slicker than a boiled onion."

"I know," Milton said, "but this is the only way this is getting done. Cover me."

elgado had a flashlight attached to the barrel of his rifle. It looked as if it was fitted with a remote tape switch that had been fixed to the rail; he reached down and pressed the switch and the light flicked on.

It took Milton fifteen paces to reach the middle of the space between the two vehicles. He took a route that meant that he could avoid looking into the Suburban's lights, and saw, to his irritation, that Delgado was thinking the same way. The Mexican approached with care, holding his rifle with both hands and prodding Russo in the back with the muzzle to chivvy him on. The light shone around the older man's body, casting him in the deepest of blacks.

Milton assessed: Delgado had the AR, and the man who had brought Russo out of the car had a handgun. He was considering the state of the odds against them when a fourth man stepped outside, this one also toting a carbine. The driver stayed inside the car, the engine still running.

Three hostiles out of the car and a fourth inside, likely

all armed, two of them with rifles. The bad guys would be able to lay down a barrage if things went south.

Facing them were Milton and Beau with 9mms and Jessica with a Saturday Night Special.

Not good odds. He was going to have to play this expertly.

Milton could see Russo properly now. The old man had been given a serious beating: both eyes were bruised, with the left swollen so much that it had closed; there were scabs of dried blood in his brows and down his nose; the side of his face was florid with a wide purple contusion. He walked slowly, hunched forward and with a pronounced limp.

Delgado was five paces away when he reached out and grabbed Russo and brought him to a halt. The Mexican was wily; he had the older man between himself and Milton, Beau and Jessica. He was dressed in black, save for a pair of white alligator-skin cowboy boots. He wore a chunky gold necklace, and there were heavy rings on the fingers of both hands.

"On your knees," Delgado said to Russo.

The old man did not protest, slumping down as if relieved to take the weight off his legs. Delgado stayed behind him. Milton looked back at the Suburban and saw the third man had levelled his own AR-15, aiming across the space at the Yukon.

"Give me my money," Delgado said.

Milton held out the briefcase. "It's in here."

"Throw it over."

Milton swung his arm and let go of the handle. The case thudded down into the sand between the two of them.

"Pick it up for me," Delgado said to Russo.

Delgado stood back and shone the light down onto the case. Russo crawled over on hands and knees and popped the clasps, opening the lid and turning it around so that Delgado could see into it.

"Empty it."

Russo did as he asked, taking out the bricks of notes one at a time and laying them down on the sand. Milton looked up at the two men back at the Suburban, their weapons raised and aimed, ready to fire. He felt a knot of tension in his gut. This was it. The exchange would either go ahead or it would not, and, if it didn't, he was standing in range of two AR-15s and a beefy hand cannon. He had backup behind him, but they didn't have rifles, and he wasn't sure how Jessica would react *in extremis*. Her father was here, in the same crossfire.

Would she even be able to pull the trigger?

"There," Russo said.

Delgado shone the light into the case.

"Where is it?"

"Where is what?" Milton said.

"You want to mess around with me?" he spat. "Are you out of your fucking mind?"

"Calm down," Milton said. "I don't know what you're talking about."

"Where's the data stick?"

Milton was confused.

"The data stick. The Bitcoin." He kicked out, sending the nearest stack of notes flying. "*Where is it?*"

Milton swallowed. An icy knot of fear expanded and filled his gut as he realised what might have happened. He remembered the second stick, the one with the password protecting its data. What if the banknotes were not all of the proceeds of Richard Russo's theft? Delgado wasn't interested in the hundred and fifty thousand. What if the real theft had been more?

The data sticks were back at the hotel. Milton had kept them, assuming that he might need the insurance.

"Where is it, *pendejo?*"

He knew that he was losing control of the situation quickly. Delgado would see this as a double-cross. They were out in the desert: no witnesses, guns aimed at each other, tempers high. All it would take was one spark and they were all done for.

"Take it easy," Milton said.

"'Take it easy'?"

"I didn't know about any Bitcoin, Delgado. How much are you expecting?"

"How *much?*" Delgado shook his head. Before Milton could move, the Mexican raised his boot and drove it into Russo's back. The old man jerked forward, his chest and face sliding through the sand and grit. Delgado aimed the AR between Russo's shoulder blades, the flashlight lighting him up. "You tell him, old man. How much did you steal from me?"

Russo muttered something.

Delgado shouted, "How much, *pendejo?*"

The old man looked up. To Milton's astonishment, he saw that he was grinning.

"Five million," he said more clearly. "I stole five million from you, you dumb fuck, and you'll never see a red cent of it ever again."

Delgado hugged the butt of the carbine into his shoulder and aimed down at Russo's body.

"Don't do it," Milton called. He raised the pistol, his finger through the guard, the trigger pressed into the joint.

"Back it up," Beau called out. "We can figure this out."

"No," Delgado said. "We can't. We—"

The top of Delgado's head exploded. Milton felt a fine spray wash across his face.

A loud boom echoed out across the desert a moment later.

Milton hadn't fired. Neither had Beau or Jessica.

The shot had come from his right, from out of the darkness, somewhere amid the dunes.

The Mexican nearest the Suburban opened fire with the AR-15, the rifle rattling as the first few rounds fired out.

Milton dropped to the sand, bullets flying overhead.

49

Mason Russo didn't even watch Delgado fall. He had already nudged his rifle through ten degrees and sighted on the Suburban. He had watched the car through his night-vision goggles. He knew that Delgado had brought four men with him: three of them were outside; the driver was still at the wheel.

His sniping trench was two hundred yards from his target. He was a good shot, and he had arrived in the desert in plenty of time to make sure that his calculations were accurate. Elevation was minimal at this range and the air was still, with no windage to take into account. The weapon fired .338 Lapua rounds; those were notorious for drop-off, but again, it wasn't really an issue at this range. He was close enough that spindrift was a minimal concern, too, but he had aimed just an inch or so to Delgado's left to account for the bullet's right-hand spin. There would be no time for such precision with the subsequent shots, but he was confident that that wouldn't be necessary.

The rifle was a Sako TRG M10. It was expensive—nearly ten grand from Northwest Arms—but money was not an issue, certainly not when his father's and sister's lives were concerned. It was an excellent weapon, and Mason had spent three hours at the range in Clark County making sure that he was as familiar with it as he needed to be. He had fired thousands of rounds before that, ever since his father had introduced him and his sister to the range when they had been in their teens.

He squeezed the trigger once, and then twice, and then a third time.

50

Milton heard the boom of the rifle—one, two, three—and saw the man with the second carbine fall. His head jerked to the right as if he had been punched, and he fell to the side, dropping out of sight behind the car door. The second shot clanged as it slammed into the wing, and the third blew a hole through the windshield. The man with the handgun dropped down behind the door; Milton's boots slid through the scree as he scrambled to the left, opening up the angle so that he could see around the man's cover. He was crouched down, back pressed against the side of the car, gun clasped in a two-handed grip, the muzzle pointing straight up.

Milton pressed himself against the earth, extended his arms, held the Ruger in both hands and drew a bead on his target. He fired twice. The first shot missed, but the second did not. The round punched the man in the gut. He fell to his knees and Milton shot him again.

The booming echoes from the rifle shots rolled over the landscape.

Milton saw movement through the driver's door. Beau fired, six shots ringing out. An airbag detonated; the rear windshield was punctured; a round blew straight through the roof.

The gunfire stopped.

Milton stared at the car, looking for any sign of movement. He dared not get up for fear of opening himself up as a target to whomever had taken out Delgado and the man with the second AR.

He had no idea what had just happened. His tactical assessment was in tatters.

He called out, "Beau?"

"I'm all right."

He stared at the Suburban: still no sign of movement.

"Jessica?"

There was no reply.

Milton stayed low, the Ruger still aimed at the car.

"Jessica?"

Nothing.

"Beau—where is she?"

Beau didn't answer.

Milton risked a look over his shoulder.

"Stay there," Jessica called out.

"John," Beau said. His tone was all wrong.

Beau had his arms above his head. Jessica was behind him, her arm outstretched, the little pistol aimed into his back.

"We've got a problem," Beau said.

Milton gaped. "Jessica?"

"Stay down!" she barked, her voice full of steel that he had never heard from her before. "Throw the gun away."

"What are you *doing?*"

"The gun—toss it."

He had no choice; he flicked his arm, throwing the Ruger away.

"Hands behind your head."

Milton put his hands behind his head and laced his fingers, then rested his cheek against the ground so that he could look over at where Beau and Jessica were approaching. Milton could see his friend's face in the glow of the headlamps; he was angry, his eyes flashing and his lips pinched and white. Jessica brought him over to where her father was picking himself up.

"Dad," she said, "are you okay?"

"I'm fine," he said.

Milton stayed low.

"Get over there," Jessica said to Beau, gesturing in Milton's direction. "On your knees."

"What are you doing?" Milton repeated.

"It's my family," she said. "I'm sorry. I couldn't take the chance. You would've done the same."

51

Milton looked out and saw that someone was walking toward them. The figure gradually grew clearer as it passed into the penumbra cast out by the headlamps. Milton was able to make out that it was a man and that he was aiming a long-barrelled weapon in the direction of the Suburban. The man drew closer, and Milton saw that what he had first taken as shadow across his face was, in fact, a slathering of camouflage paint.

Milton kept his eye on the man as he spoke to Jessica. "What's going on?"

"Be quiet." She continued to aim the pistol in their direction. "Dad," she said, "can you get up?"

Russo put his hands in the dirt and pushed himself to his knees and then to his feet. "I'm okay," he said. "Probably looks worse than it is. They just roughed me up a little bit."

The man with the rifle reached them. The gun was on a sling; he moved it around so that it hung vertically and, now that his right hand was free, he took a pistol out of a belted holster and aimed it at the nearest of Delgado's men. It was the man whom Beau had shot; he had been drilled in the gut, but he was still alive, trying to crawl away in the vain hope that he might not be noticed. The man stood over him, aimed down with the pistol, and fired a shot into his head. The man's body twitched and then lay still.

He turned to Jessica and her father. "You both okay?"

"We're good."

"Got the money?"

"In my pocket," Jessica said.

"What about that?" the man said, pointing to the banknotes that Oscar had scattered just before he had been shot.

"We won't be able to take that much with us," Jessica said. "And it's small change compared to the rest."

"And we have to get moving," her father added.

The younger man chuckled. "You're right. I'm getting greedy."

Milton looked at him. It was difficult to see much of his face beneath the paint, but Milton guessed he was in his mid-twenties, with bright white teeth—American straight—and, as he took off the woollen beanie that he wore on his head, Milton saw that his hair was worn down at his scalp, razor short. He was tall, not large, but he looked lithe and muscular. He looked like a soldier. Mason Russo had been in the military. That would have accounted for the accurate sniping and the ability to select a shooting position that none of the participants at the exchange—Milton included —had been able to see.

Jessica's father looked over at Milton. "What's your name?"

"John Smith."

"He's been helping me," Jessica said.

"I don't think your daughter has been completely honest with me."

"What choice did I have?" Jessica said. "I didn't mean to trick you, but you wouldn't have helped me otherwise, would you?"

"No," Milton said. "I wouldn't."

Mason came closer to him. "What you say your name was again?"

"John."

"John. I'm sorry about this, John."

He aimed the pistol down at Milton's head.

"Don't!" Jessica called out.

"What?"

"He doesn't deserve that."

"He's seen all of us, Jessie. They *both* have. It doesn't matter what they deserve. They can ID us. We got no choice."

Milton closed his eyes. This wasn't how he'd imagined he was going to go out, but tonight had been surprising in many ways.

"No, Mason," Jessica said. "If he hadn't been at the house, Delgado would have taken me, too. He got me out; he kept me safe. He got the case from the storage. We're not shooting him. That's *not* happening."

Milton raised his head a little, just enough so that he could see Mason's feet. He was standing close to him and, from the sound of his voice and the smudged prints that he had left in the dirt, Milton thought that he had turned slightly away.

Beau spoke up. "You kids need to have a think about what you're doing," he said. "I've dealt with men like Delgado before. It's not him you need to worry about, it's who they'll send out here to figure out what's gone down.

That's who you need to worry about. You know much about the narcos? If it were me, doing what you've done, to people like that? Well, it'd make me as nervous as a fly in a glue pot."

"It's not you, though, is it?"

Milton knew what Beau was doing: he was distracting them, giving Milton a chance to take Mason out. Milton was face down in the dirt and couldn't be sure, but he thought it was more likely than not that the man was looking away. If that was right, and if he moved quickly, he might be able to hook his legs and topple him. If he could do that, he was confident that he would be able, at the very least, to take his pistol away from him.

If he was wrong, though... Mason was close and he wouldn't be able to miss.

"We gotta go," Russo said.

"We're going," Mason said. "But if we don't shoot them dead, we'd better give them something else to think about instead."

Milton released his hands and readied himself to hook Mason's legs, but, just as he was ready to reach out, Mason took four quick strides away from him. Milton got his head up in time to see him aim the pistol at Beau.

Shit.

The pistol barked, the report echoing back at them from the side of the derelict building. Beau grunted in pain.

Milton got to his hands and knees.

Mason fired another shot. Grit flew at Milton from the impact just a few inches from his head.

"I swear to God I'll kill you if you don't stay down."

Beau dropped to his knees, his hand pressed to his gut.

Milton caught Jessica's eye for a moment and saw a flash of regret, but it didn't last; she helped her father to the

Yukon and got him inside. Mason covered Milton, the gun on him as he backed up and slid into the cabin through the open driver's side door.

"Beau," Milton called.

The Yukon's engine roared. The tyres slipped through the loose scree, sending a rooster tail of stones and sand out behind the vehicle before the rubber bit and the SUV bolted toward them.

Milton scurried over to where Beau was kneeling.

"Beau—I'm here."

"Gut shot," he grunted through clenched teeth.

Milton looked up as the vehicle rushed by. Mason Russo was driving, his eyes on the way ahead. Richard Russo was in the passenger seat, his eyes also fixed out front; Jessica Russo was in the back, looking out at Milton and Beau, her face blank.

"They did us," Beau said. He took his hand away from his gut; his palm was slicked with blood. "Look at that, John. They made us look stupid."

Milton looked over at Delgado's shot-up Suburban.

"Come on," he said. "I'm going to get you to a hospital."

PART III

52

M ason bounced the Yukon over the pitted road that led away from the gas station. He drove carefully, but with purpose; damaging the vehicle before they even made it back to the highway would be dangerous, yet that had to be balanced against the need to put distance between them and the gas station as quickly as they could.

Jessica glanced back and saw Smith kneeling down in the dust, taking off his shirt and pressing it down against Beau's stomach. The Yukon reached the end of the access road and bounced over onto the smoother asphalt. Mason straightened the wheel and pressed down on the gas.

Their father reclined the seat a little so that he could stretch out his legs. "Who were they?"

"John's the English one," Jessica said. "John Smith. The old guy is Beau. Friend of John."

"'John'?" Mason said, shaking his head. "What is this? First-name terms?"

She shook her head. "Fuck off, Mason."

"I'm just saying—"

"I played the helpless woman. He swallowed it up."

"What else do you know about him?" her father asked.

"He said he used to be a soldier. SAS."

"Special forces?"

She nodded. "He went face-to-face with Delgado, didn't flinch. Took out three of his guys at the house, too. Made it look easy."

"Where did you find him?" her father asked.

"My car broke down on the way to Vegas."

"The Tesla?"

"Yes."

"I *told* you electric cars were shit," Mason said.

"And I told you I'd ask when I wanted your opinion," Jessica shot back.

Their father cut through the sniping. "So he picked you up?"

"I was at the Mad Greek and the car wouldn't start. I sold him the story about us all going travelling, and he said he'd drive me. We got to the house and I saw what had happened. We were still in there when Delgado came back. John took the guys out and got us away. It was only when we got to the hotel that I got the chance to call Mason."

"I went straight over," Mason said.

"We figured out what to do." Mason paused, tapping his fingers on the wheel. "We should've shot them *both*. He's seen your face. He's seen all of us. Does he know who you are?"

"He knows my name."

"You told him?"

"What else was I going to do?"

"Make one up?"

"Why would I do that? I didn't know what had happened to Dad when he picked me up. He read the documents Dad wrote, the ones on the stick. How'd you think it would've gone down if I'd made up some name and the emails contradicted me?"

"You did the right thing," their father said. "What else does he know?"

"Nothing. Not a thing."

"We still should've shot him," Mason persisted. "They're loose ends. Leaving them is a mistake."

She banged her palm against the back of his seat. "Shut up, Mason. You want to know what a stupid mistake looks like? It's leaving Dad in the house on his own so he can get jumped by Delgado."

"I was gone for three hours. Three hours, Jessie. That's it."

"Stop it," their father said. "Enough—enough of the bickering. You're behaving like kids."

Jessica looked out of the window, staring through her own pale reflection at the darkened dunes that were racing by.

There was a moment of uncomfortable silence that persisted until their father spoke again.

"What happened with the case?" he said.

"I was going to go up there myself," she said. "But Smith saw me get the key, and I couldn't think of how I could get away from him without giving it all away. I figured I'd be able to persuade him that I didn't know what was in the case —make it look like I didn't know what you'd been doing."

"And the Bitcoin?"

Jessica reached into her pocket and took out the USB stick. "I got it."

"And Smith didn't figure it out?"

"Why would he? He saw the cash in the case—he thought that was what you'd taken. He couldn't unlock the stick."

"Well done," Russo said. "What about tonight?"

"I came out here with the two of them this afternoon. I saw what they had in mind and told Mason."

Her twin took over. "I bought the rifle, drove out to Goodsprings and walked back. Dug a trench as soon as it was dark and stayed out of sight. Waited for five hours."

"Well done," their father said again. "Both of you. It was well handled. I'm impressed."

Mason brightened at their father's praise; it had always been like that, ever since they were children. It was as if he had a fundamental need for approval, and still did. Jessica knew that part of it was to do with their late mother, cold-hearted and caustic until the end. Praise from her had been as rare as hen's teeth. Jessica had learned to live with that, but her brother had not. It had bred his insecurities, and age had not smoothed those rough edges.

"We need to think about how we're going to get out," their father said.

"I've got the tickets," Jessica said.

He shook his head. "Can't use them. It would've been fine, but not now."

"Why not? Delgado's dead. Smith doesn't know anything."

"We can't take the risk. We need to change it up."

"How?"

"We'll drive," he said. "We'll need to change this car. We'll go up to Crystal Springs and rent one there."

"Drive to where?"

"Vancouver," he said.

Jessica exhaled, long and hard.

"Relax," Richard said. "We're clear. This time tomorrow, we'll be out of the country and we won't have to think about any of this ever again."

53

M ilton took off his shirt, leaving his T-shirt on, and held it against Beau's stomach. He had seen plenty of gut shots in his time, and he knew that unless it was treated, Beau would bleed out. If there was any positive to the situation, it was that it could take an hour for that to happen provided that the wound was properly compressed.

"Hold that down," he said, indicating the bunched-up shirt.

Beau grunted. "I got it."

"We need to get you to hospital."

"Shot me," he said, shaking his head. "Right in the gut."

"I'm sorry, Beau. She tricked me."

"Fooled me too." He grunted with pain. "I'll say this about her—she's mighty convincing."

Milton got up and looked around. He would have liked to investigate the hiding place from which Mason Russo had taken his shots, but he didn't have time to go wandering into the desert. Instead, he hurried over to the Suburban, stepping over the bodies of the dead men on his way. Delgado was lying face down, his arms outflung as if he had been caught in flight. Milton took the AR-15 and a magazine that he found in the man's pocket.

The windshield of the Chevrolet had been perforated in two places when Beau had opened fire on it, but the safety glass had stayed in one piece. The doors were still open and, as Milton approached, he levelled the AR and aimed it into the cabin. He pulled the driver's side door all the way open. The driver was still in his seat, slumped forward, his head resting on the wheel. He had been shot in the torso; blood was still running down the side of his body. Milton grabbed him, dragged him out of the car and dumped him on the sand.

He climbed up into the seat, put the vehicle into drive and pulled it across the gravel until it was next to Beau. He got out and crouched down beside him. "I'm going to get you out of here. Where's the nearest hospital?"

There was sweat on Beau's brow. "Vegas," he hissed.

Milton gritted his teeth.

He didn't know whether Beau had enough time left to get back to the city.

"All right," he said.

Milton crouched down and snagged a bundle of banknotes, stuffing them into his pocket. He helped Beau to his feet, then draped the older man's arm over his shoulders and helped him into the back of the car. He glanced down at Beau's shirt; it had just looked dark in the blackness of the desert, but now that the cabin's lights were shining down on it, Milton could see that it was a deep, dark red. It wasn't bright enough to signal that the blood was arterial; Beau *might* have been fortunate. If the aorta had been hit, he would have been dead in two minutes. The vena cava might have allowed him four, the other large vessels leading to an organ perhaps ten. The intestines would be the best that he could hope for; Milton had seen a man take three hours to die that way. Sepsis would take him eventually, but, while that was painful, at least it was a slow way to go.

Maybe they had a chance.

Maybe.

Milton closed the doors, got back inside and turned the Suburban around.

"The guy who shot me," Beau said, his voice a rasp. "Who was he?"

"The brother. Mason Russo."

"She say anything about him?"

"That he was in the army."

"He knew what he was doing. He must've been laid up there in the dunes."

Milton tried to work out what might have happened. He thought back to the first time that he and Jessica had met. She had told him that her car had broken down; that must have been true. She had been upset and wary of him at first, understandably, but had become friendly and cheerful as they had completed the trip to Summerlin. Milton might not have counted empathy amongst his strengths, but he had always believed himself a good judge of character, and he had detected nothing that gave him any suggestion that she was aware of what she would discover when they had arrived. That impression continued as he remembered her reaction to finding the house empty, and then discovering the evidence that her father had been taken from the property by force. She had been frightened. Surprised. Neither response had been faked. She hadn't known in advance what had happened to her father.

From that point on, though... No, he decided. *That* had been different, and the ease with which she had tricked him caused him to doubt the conclusions that he had drawn about her earlier behaviour. She had taken the key for the storage unit from its hiding place in the bedroom and might not have mentioned it had Milton not noticed. She had told him that she didn't know what would be found in the locker. Yet, when Milton collected the briefcase and delivered it to her, she had recognised whatever it was that Oscar Delgado was *really* looking for. It wasn't the banknotes. He'd wanted the data sticks.

Milton wondered now whether she had sent him to collect the briefcase because she knew that it would be dangerous for her to go, that he would be distracted by the cash that he would see when he opened the case, and that he wouldn't recognise the significance of everything else that he would find.

The Bitcoin.

How much had Russo said they had taken?

Five million dollars?

"Her coming out with us this afternoon," Beau said, the words tight and clipped and heavy with pain. "That was her doing a recon, wasn't it?"

"She needed to know where the meet was happening so she could tell her brother. She was scoping it out. She gets back; she tells him; he goes straight up there and waits."

Beau coughed.

"I was focused on Delgado," Milton said. "It didn't even cross my mind that I should have been worrying about her."

"Don't beat yourself up. She fooled me, too."

Milton thought back to her attempt to seduce him. Was that her trying to guarantee his cooperation? She'd needed him to help with Delgado. She'd needed him to set up the meeting, to take her to the rendezvous, and to point a weapon in the Mexican's face while her brother picked his moment. The twins wouldn't have been able to get their father back on their own.

Milton thought of what she had said in the hotel room, her hand on his cheek, the awkward kiss. He clenched his jaw and tried to keep the anger down. He wasn't done with the Russos, but he was going to need a clear head.

"Your contact in the police," he said.

"Salazar?"

"Will he talk to me?"

"Sure. Why?"

"I want to find out what they have on that family."

"You proposing to go after them?"

"He shot you," he said. "I can't let that stand."

Beau started to speak, but another grunt of pain forestalled it.

"Hold on," Milton said.

"English—I ain't proposing on going anywhere tonight, but, if it is my time, you got to do me a favour."

"Of course."

"My wife—I'd want you to go and tell her what happened. You remember the office?"

"I do."

"You go on by there and you ask my fool son to put you in touch with Debbie. His mother. And then you tell her how much I loved her, all right?"

"You can tell her yourself," Milton said. "You're not going to die."

"Promise me," Beau said, a little more strength in his words.

"I promise," Milton said, looking up in the mirror at him.

"Thank you," Beau said. "You're a good man."

Milton ignored that.

He didn't feel like that at all.

54

The *sicario* raised the blind and watched as American Airlines flight 1368 began its final approach to McCarran airport. It had been a long few days. He had been in Bogotá to take care of a problem with the supply chain that was responsible for the steady flow of product from Colombia to Mexico. A politician who had lubricated the process had demanded more money for his continued compliance, and had threatened to change his allegiance if his terms were not met. That was a questionable decision, and the *sicario* had been sent to put an end to the irritation.

That done, he had been provided with a ticket on the American flight to Miami and had then transited onto the connecting flight to Vegas. He had flown business, using the ten-hour flight time to stock up on his sleep. He suspected that he would be busy once he reached Las Vegas, and he couldn't be sure of when he would next be able to relax.

He watched out of the window as the twinkling lights of the streets and avenues that comprised the city became clearer. He closed his eyes and waited for the plane to land.

~

IT WAS JUST after midnight when the *sicario* reached the terminal. Flying business had its benefits, and chief among them—at least as far as he was concerned—was being able to process through the airport formalities before everyone else on the flight. Discretion and efficiency were valuable assets in his line of work and well worth the surcharge.

The airport was not busy at this late hour. The *sicario* collected his checked luggage as soon as it slid down onto the carousel, and made his way into the arrivals hall. He had been to Vegas on three separate occasions, all for work, and he recognised the interminable ringing and buzzing of the slot machines as the soundtrack of the place. He found the city to be in the worst possible taste. Only in America could you find a city like this: billion-dollar casinos thrown up in the middle of a desert, receptacles into which had been poured the worst impulses of a crass and tasteless people.

Never mind. He would not be here for long.

He made his way out of the terminal and followed the signs for the long-term car park.

55

Beau's condition worsened as they raced north back to Las Vegas. He became quieter, and his breathing rattled a little, as if there was an obstruction in his lungs. He was pale and drawn, with a sheen of sweat glistening on his brow whenever they passed through the lights that marked the smaller towns and hamlets on the road.

The nearest ER was at Green Valley Ranch, on the south-eastern fringe of the city. The satnav suggested that it would take twenty-three minutes, but Milton covered it in twenty. The ER looked as if it had been newly constructed, a plain white block of a building that had been dropped down in a wide space at the side of the road. Milton turned right, passing a digital sign that suggested that the ER waiting time was two minutes.

"We're here," Milton said.

There was no answer.

"Beau," he repeated, fearing the worst.

The older man cleared his throat. "I'm still here," he said, but his voice was weak.

Milton spun the wheel to the right once again and accelerated across the empty parking lot to the entrance.

"Hold on," he said. "I'm going to get you inside."

He opened the door and leaned in to help Beau get out. The scene in the back was much worse than it had appeared from the front of the car. It was like an abattoir. Beau must have bled out several pints of blood. His lap was a sticky pool of it; it had soaked into the denim of his jeans, onto the leather seats, and his shirt—once white, now the deepest claret—was sopping with it.

Milton slid his hands beneath Beau's shoulders. He tried to be gentle, but there was no way of getting him out without manhandling him a little. Beau grimaced, then clenched his jaw, but was unable to prevent a cry of pain as Milton dragged him out of the car.

"You got to get away," Beau said. "They're gonna want to know what happened, and you don't want to have your name anywhere near this."

"Forget it."

"I'm serious," he said between shallow breaths. "They'll have CCTV. You don't want that. Just get me to the door and sound the horn. I'll take it from there."

"What are you going to say?"

"What we agreed."

"All right."

"And Salazar will be here soon. He'll straighten it out."

Beau had given Milton the detective's telephone number on the way, and Milton had called to tell him what had happened. He had already determined that he would call Salazar again as soon as Beau was safely inside the ER.

Milton put Beau's left arm over his shoulders and hoisted him up, helping him as they made their way from the car to a wheelchair that had been left outside the entrance.

"I'm sorry," Milton said.

"Don't talk crazy."

"This happened because I dropped the ball."

"Shut up, English."

Milton took Beau to the wheelchair and carefully settled him into it.

"I'll see you later," Milton said.

"You will."

Milton returned to the car and slipped back into the driver's seat. He opened the window to try to get rid of the cloying stink of blood and then held his hand against the horn for five seconds. He saw activity inside, and, after waiting for the automatic doors to slide open and a nurse to come outside to investigate, he put the car into drive and pulled away. He looked back in the rear-view mirror as the nurse knelt down next to Beau. The woman assessed him, went around so that she was behind the chair, and pushed him into the ER.

He drove away.

56

The long-term garage was next to Terminal One. The *sicario* checked the message that had appeared on his phone when he turned it on in the terminal. There was a picture of a plain Chevrolet Malibu and an annotation that said that the car could be found on the first level. The *sicario* reached the garage and walked the aisles until he saw the jet-black vehicle. He checked to ensure that he was not being watched, and then took his case around to the trunk. He knelt down next to the rear right wheel and felt up into the wheel arch. The key had been attached to the chassis with a length of tape. He tore it free and pressed the button to pop the trunk.

There was a grey rucksack inside the compartment. It was large, with shoulder straps and a number of pouches and pockets that opened with paracord ties. He would check it later. He deposited his luggage in the trunk, closed the lid and went around to the driver's side door.

He checked the details that del Pozo had sent him and tapped the destination into the GPS. The Highland Inn was at 8025 Dean Martin Drive.

It took the *sicario* twelve minutes to drive there, enjoying roads that were much quieter now than they would be later in the day. He pulled into the generous parking lot that surrounded the building. The motel was three storeys tall, with bright white lights set along the ceilings of the outside corridors. The *sicario* had arranged for del Pozo to book a room for him here. It could not have been farther removed from the glamour of the casinos on the Strip, but the *sicario* did not care about that. This was off the beaten track and much more discreet, and the greater privacy would allow him to set about his task while minimising the possibility that he might be discovered.

He parked next to the reception building and went inside. It was late and the night clerk was dozing in his chair. The *sicario* cleared his throat and then, when that didn't work, he tapped the bell.

"Good evening," he said when the clerk awoke with a start.

"Yeah?"

"I'd like to check in, please."

"You got a reservation?"

"I have."

He took out the printed sheet of paper that del Pozo had given him and laid it flat on the counter. The man squinted down at it.

"Quince," the man said.

"That's right," he said pleasantly, taking out his fake passport and a credit card in the same name.

The clerk ran through the mundanities, running the credit card to cover any incidentals.

"We got breakfast in the restaurant between six and ten," the man said, handing over a key card. "The pool's open from eight. You got an ice machine outside the room. You need anything else?"

"That's all," the *sicario* said. "Thank you."

～

HE PARKED the car in an empty space next to a cheap-looking statue of a prancing horse and got out. He had been given room 14, a ground-level room accessed by a door that faced onto the parking lot. He went to the door, held the key card against the reader, waited for it to go green, then opened the door and went inside.

The room was not pleasant: a chequered bedspread featuring squares of brown and grey, a brownish carpet, cheap furniture that looked as if it was held together by glue, a white fridge that still had the manufacturer's bright-yellow installation label affixed to the front. The bathroom was tiny, with just enough room for the toilet and a small bath with a shower attachment fitted to the taps. It was clean, though, and, more importantly, it was not the sort of place where one would attract attention. The *sicario* was satisfied with it.

He went back out to the car and popped the trunk. He took out his luggage and the rucksack, shut the lid, and transferred both items to the room. He shut the door, closed the curtains, and hefted the bag up onto the bed.

He started with the top pocket, unzipping it and noting that it had been packed to capacity. The mesh pockets included a pair of gloves, a bandana, a trauma kit and a pair of ballistic glasses. The main compartment of the bag included a BCM Recce AR-15, broken down into its constituent parts, a pistol belt with a holster containing a Ruger SR1911 .45 and extra magazines in the mag pouches.

Finally, he saw a Condor plate carrier with the plates inserted, together with additional mags for the AR and the Ruger in the pouches.

He would check out the equipment later, but for now, he was happy.

He looked at his watch.

One thirty.

He would get started in the morning.

57

M ilton drove south, out of Vegas, and back towards Jean. He saw a track that led into the scrub of the desert and followed it until he reached a depression that would partially obscure the Suburban from passing traffic. He texted Salazar to tell him where he was and got out of the vehicle. He knew that he would have to abandon the SUV; it was a miracle that he hadn't already been pulled over, given the obvious damage that had been done to it during the shoot-out, and he would not have been able to provide a satisfactory answer that could explain the bloodbath in the back.

His prints would be all over the vehicle, of course, but at least he was able to do something about that. He went to the front and removed the license plate, then went to the back and removed that one, too. He lifted the door to access the load space and took out the jerry can that he had noticed earlier. He unscrewed the cap and took a sniff: gasoline. He poured the gas into the back seat, then went to the front and sloshed it over the seats there, too. He poured it out—into the footwells, over the dash, over the leather steering wheel, over the AR-15—until the can was empty. He took the manual out of the glove compartment, tore out a handful of pages, and used his lighter to set them on fire. He tossed the burning paper onto the gas-soaked driver's seat and stepped back as the flames quickly spread and took hold.

Milton turned and trudged back to the road. He looked at his watch. It was a quarter past one. He found his thoughts drifting back to what had happened at the gas station. Should he have anticipated what Jessica had done? He was prepared to give himself a hard time about it, but, as he ran back over the events of the last day and a half again, he still wasn't sure that he *had* missed any signs. She was an accomplished and convincing liar. His only mistake had been to assume that the money that Richard Russo had stolen was just the hundred and fifty thousand that he had found in the case and, even then, it was a reasonable mistake to make. That was a *lot* of money, even to a cartel; besides, Milton suspected, they would have reacted in the same way if the amount had been one-tenth of what had been there. The fact that Richard Russo had the temerity to steal from the Mexicans at all would have prompted the same response; how was Milton to know that the amount that he had taken was many multiples more?

He knew that was all true, but still he found that he blamed himself.

His phone buzzed. He took it out and saw that Salazar was calling.

"Where are you?"

"On the side of I-15," Milton said. "About a mile south of Seven Hills."

Milton saw headlights piercing the darkness ahead.

"That glow I can see to the southwest?" Salazar said.

"Yeah," Milton replied. "That's me."

58

Milton got into Salazar's car and rubbed his tired eyes as the detective swung the car around and set off back towards Vegas.

"How is he?" Milton asked him.

"They're operating," Salazar said.

"What are his chances?"

"They wouldn't say. He'd already be dead if the bullet had hit anything important, so he got lucky there. On the other hand, he's lost a lot of blood."

"What a mess."

"You got that right."

Salazar had pouches under his eyes that suggested he could do with more sleep. His cheeks were heavy with stubble, and his skin looked sallow in the artificial glow of the dashboard lights. He was wearing jeans and a sports jacket.

"You want to tell me what in God's name happened out there?"

"The woman that I was helping wasn't who I thought she was."

"That so? You never told me her name."

"Jessica Russo. Her father is Richard and her brother is Mason. They're all involved."

"And this is to do with Delgado?"

"Looks like Richard ripped him off."

"How much?"

"More than five million."

Salazar gawped across the cabin of the car at him. "Seriously?"

Milton told him about the briefcase, the evidence that had been left on the thumb drive, and the Bitcoin.

"They *do* know who Delgado represents, right?"

"They do," Milton said. "And they did it anyway. He has cancer—he might not care anymore."

"But his kids?"

"They were all planning on leaving the country. Delgado got to Richard just before they did. And they're resourceful—Jessica fooled me, and Mason is cunning. They make a good team. And, right now, they've got away with it."

"You wanna tell me what happened?"

Milton went over the events in the desert. He explained how Jessica had led them all into a trap, and how Mason had closed it. He told him how Mason had been determined to shoot both him and Beau, and how Jessica had persuaded him against it. He described Mason's compromise— shooting Beau in an effort to prevent their pursuit—and how Milton had taken Delgado's vehicle and driven Beau back to the city.

Salazar shook his head with weary resignation. "So you're telling me we're gonna find dead Mexicans out in the desert?"

"Four of them," Milton said. "Delgado and three others."

"Shit," Salazar said. "That's gonna generate some heat.

Staff at the ER said Beau told them he'd been shot by a hitch-hiker."

"We agreed that would be the best story," Milton said.

"And you don't want to be involved?"

"Not if we can help it."

"And what'll Beau say about him being out there after midnight?"

"He'll say he was chasing a lead to a skipper out near Jean, but that it didn't go anywhere. He was driving back to the city when he saw the woman. He pulled over; he got shot. He was picked up by another driver who was passing and he took him to the ER."

"The Good Samaritan."

Milton nodded.

"But he left him outside?"

"Because he didn't want to be involved with the police. The story won't stand up to too much scrutiny. It'd be helpful if you could move it in the right direction."

"Keep you out of it, you mean?"

"Is that possible?"

"Yeah," he said. "I can probably do that."

"Thank you."

"The fire back there—that was you torching your wheels?"

"Yes," Milton said. "That was the car Delgado came to the meet in. I don't want my forensics in it."

Salazar gave a nod. "All right, then," he said. "If that's what you both want to say, that's what we'll go with. I'll call my partner and get her to go take his statement as soon as he comes around. She'll probably send a car out to the desert to have a look. Will they see anything?"

"Not until light," Milton said. "And, even then, it's round

the back of the gas station. The bodies might not be visible from the road."

"We'll just have to play that by ear," Salazar said. "I can't tip her off—I can't know that the bodies are there. If they get found, they get found. Odds are, though, the coyotes and the vultures will get to them first. We'll deal with the scraps they leave behind."

"There's something else I'm going to need you to do," Milton said. "I need you to see if you have anything on the Russos. We know that Richard was working with Delgado. Maybe there's something on him. Mason was a Marine, but he got discharged. I wouldn't mind knowing why. Anything would be helpful."

"Why?"

"Because I want to find them," he said.

"And then?"

"I haven't decided yet."

"I'll ask."

They raced past the sign that welcomed drivers to fabulous Las Vegas. Milton looked at it sourly. All he had wanted to do was enjoy a road trip, but, just like always, he had allowed himself to be dragged down into a mess. Regardless, he couldn't walk away from it now. Beau had been shot. There would be a reckoning for that.

59

S alazar dropped Milton at the El Cortez and said that he would go back to the hospital to keep an eye on Beau.

The casino was busy as Milton passed through it to the elevators. He went up to his room, took a moment to listen out of an abundance of caution and then, satisfied that he could hear nothing that might suggest someone was inside, he opened the door and went in.

He had blood on his clothes. He undressed and showered, washing Beau's blood from his skin, waiting until the water ran clear. He dressed in clean clothes, took the dirty ones and disposed of them in the trash. He moved quickly, collecting the MacBook and double-checking that he hadn't left anything behind, and then went back into the corridor and across to Jessica's door. There was a paper room service menu that had been left on a tray on the floor next to the door. Milton took it, folded it in half and then in half again, and slid it into the gap between the door and the doorframe. He slid the paper down and applied pressure on the striker until the lock retracted. It had taken him less than ten seconds and was a reminder—not that Milton needed one —that a door wedge was a wise investment when travelling.

He opened the door and went inside.

The room was empty. Jessica had abandoned her luggage in the back of her beached Tesla and had brought nothing with her. She had taken her phone with her to the gas station rendezvous and left nothing else behind, either.

Milton left the room and made his way back down to the casino and then into the lot outside. The Porsche was still in the same spot. He unlocked it and got inside, started the engine and reversed out of the space. He took out his phone, opened the map and tapped in his destination: the Mad Greek Café outside Baker, California. There was no traffic to contend with at this time of the morning, and the phone app reported that it would take Milton ninety minutes to get there.

That, though, was at lawful speeds.

Milton was going to drive a little faster this time.

60

Milton made excellent time, pushing the car up to a hundred on the quieter stretches of the interstate when he was confident that he wouldn't attract the attention of the highway patrol. The Mad Greek was still open, catering to refugees fleeing their disappointments in Vegas. He pulled into the parking lot and saw that Jessica's Tesla was still there. He had suspected that it would be—he doubted she could have had time to arrange for it to be collected in the chaos of the last two days —but it was still a relief to see it in the same spot.

Milton got out of the Porsche and went into the restaurant. He took a seat at the window where he was able to watch the car. The waitress came up to the table.

"What can I get you?"

"Coffee, please," he said.

"What you having to eat?"

"I'll have a cheeseburger."

"You want fries with that?"

"Please."

The restaurant was quiet. Milton watched as the waitress

made her way back to the open kitchen and passed his order on to the chef. He thought back to his first visit here, looking over to the table where he had seen Jessica crying to herself. If he had known then what he knew now, he would have ignored her and made his way back to his GTO and continued on his drive to Vegas. He would still have his car, Beau would not have been shot, and he would not have found himself caught up in a conspiracy that he knew was going to prove difficult to unravel. He allowed himself a moment of wry introspection. Remembering his own fallibility was useful; grandiosity was a symptom of his alcoholism, and perhaps it was not such a bad thing for him to be reminded that he made mistakes.

The waitress returned with a pot of coffee and a mug.

"What you doing on the road tonight?" she asked him as she filled the mug.

"Driving to LA," he said.

"Been gambling?"

"Luck wasn't on my side."

"I heard that before," she said, smiling at him. "I'll be back with your burger in a minute."

61

Milton finished his meal, laid a twenty on the table to cover it, and nodded his thanks to the waitress as he made his way back to the Porsche. He climbed in, opened its glove compartment and took out the LifeHammer that he had seen earlier, a small tool with a double-sided carbon steel hammer head that was designed for breaking through car windows in the case of an emergency.

He stepped outside. A truck was just pulling out of the lot, but, apart from that, there was no one. The Tesla was a decent distance away from the windows of the restaurant; it was visible, but not so close that he would be easily seen, especially if he was careful. He approached, watching carefully for anyone who might have emerged from the parked trucks or the restaurant. He went around to the side that faced away from the restaurant and, with a sharp swing of the hammer, smashed the passenger-side window. The glass fractured around the point of impact and fell into the car. Milton wrapped his hand in the sleeve of his jacket, swept the remains of the glass out of the frame and reached inside to open the door.

He brushed the glass from the seat into the footwell and slid into the cabin. He opened the glovebox and took out the car's documentation, flicking through it quickly before disregarding it. Nothing. There was a bottle of water in the cupholder and a half-finished Twinkie next to it, but nothing else of interest.

Milton slithered between the seats into the back. He unlatched the rear seat and lowered it so that he could look into the trunk. There was a medium-sized suitcase and a small leather shoulder bag. Milton took them both, swept the space with his phone's flashlight to make sure that he hadn't missed anything, and stepped outside. He took the luggage and made his way back to the Macan.

There was still no one else in the lot. Milton got back into his car, started the engine and drove out. He made his way north for two minutes before turning off the road and rolling to a stop in a run-off area.

Milton stepped out and went around to the trunk. He took out the suitcase and opened it, removing the contents one by one. There were several tops, underwear, a light jacket, a wrap, a pair of walking shoes and a pair of sneakers, several sundresses, sunglasses and a hat. There was a washbag with toiletries and anti-nausea medicine. Nothing useful. He felt around the lining of the suitcase in the event that something had been secreted inside it, but found nothing there, either.

He unzipped the shoulder bag and tipped it out. The contents looked as if they had been chosen to be taken on board during a flight. There was a clean T-shirt and underwear, an inhaler, a pair of wireless earbuds and a book: *Tuscany for the*

Shameless Hedonist: Florence and Tuscany Travel Guide. He flipped through the pages. It was well thumbed, and several pages had been marked with loops of red ink. Milton skimmed the entries, seeing restaurant recommendations and beaches, all of them apparently in the vicinity of Siena. He flicked to the end and was rewarded with a folded piece of foolscap. He opened it and found a printed itinerary from a travel agency based in Los Angeles. Jessica had booked three tickets on Air Canada flight 585 from San Diego to Portland, connecting there onto Condor flight DE 291 to Frankfurt. The itinerary called for an overnight layover before picking up Lufthansa flight LH 238 to Leonardo da Vinci International Airport in Florence.

Milton stared at the piece of paper.

The San Diego flight was scheduled to depart at twelve thirty this afternoon.

He checked the time: it was two thirty.

He swiped to his phone's map and typed in San Diego. The phone processed his request and then displayed the best route: it would take him five hours and fourteen minutes to cover the three hundred and seven miles.

He could be there by eight.

Plenty of time.

∾

MILTON RACED SOUTH. He couldn't stop thinking about what he would do if he was able to intercept Jessica and her family before they left the country. He doubted that he would be able to stop them at a busy public airport, and the alternative—retribution in return for what they had done to Beau—was not something that he was prepared to contemplate. They were criminals, that much was certain, but Milton had no wish to add their names to his overflowing ledger. His struggle since leaving Group Fifteen had been to bring balance to his debits and credits, and spilling more blood would not help with that.

He would find another way.

He took out his phone and called Salazar.

"Hello?"

"It's John Smith. How is he?"

"It'll take more than that to put that old bastard down. The doctors have X-rayed him. They say he's gonna be all right."

"You said they were going to operate."

"They're waiting. The bullet passed right through him, front to back. Lord knows how it missed everything on its way, but it looks like it did."

"Are you still at the ER?"

"I am. Just waiting for my partner to get over here. Where are you?"

Milton looked up. "On the interstate, coming up to Beacon Station."

"You wanna tell me why?"

"Jessica Russo left her car at the Mad Greek in Baker. It's where I met her—the car broke down. I thought it was worth coming down to take a look, and it was. I think I know where they're going."

"Go on."

"I found an itinerary. They've booked flights out of San Diego."

"Going where?"

"Italy," Milton said.

"When?"

"The flight leaves at twelve thirty. I can get there by eight at the latest—in plenty of time before the flight leaves."

"And when you get there, assuming they show?"

"Can you have them arrested?"

"*I can call San Diego PD,*" he said. "*They could send someone down there.*"

"They'd do that? I'm a civilian?"

"*I'm owed a favour. We can say you're a private investigator with an interest in the Russos. It's unusual, but it'll wash.*"

"Thanks," Milton said.

"*I'll do it as soon as we're done.*"

Milton approached a sharp left-hand turn and dabbed the brakes. "Have you got anything on the family yet?"

"*Not yet. I've put a request in.*"

"Let me know if you get anything."

"*You too.*"

Milton ended the call. He exited the turn, pressed down on the gas and raced to the south.

Sergeant Shannon Shepherd parked her Crown Vic in the lot outside the ER and made her way inside. It was four o'clock in the morning. Salazar had buzzed her an hour ago to tell her that there had been a hijacking out in the desert, that a man had been shot and that he had been delivered to the hospital at Green Valley Ranch. Shepherd was tired and grouchy and had been looking forward to getting home; that, though, would have to wait until she had spoken with Salazar and decided whether there was anything for them to do or whether they could pass it on to the day shift.

It was cold as she stepped out of the car. She grabbed her jacket from the back and jogged across the lot. Salazar was waiting for her in the reception area.

"Shep," he said.

"What've you got?"

"I got a mess," he said. "You want a coffee?"

"Sure."

He went to the machine, ordered two coffees and paid for them with his card.

"So?"

The first cup was dispensed. Salazar took it from the machine and handed it to her.

"I got a call from a friend of mine just after midnight. He's a bail bondsman, chasing down a skipper down near Goodsprings. He struck out and was coming back to Vegas when he saw a female hitch-hiker on the side of the road."

"At midnight?"

"Exactly. Cold, too. He pulled over to give her a ride, but instead of getting in, she pulled a piece, told him to get out and shot him. Stole the car and left him there."

Shepherd sighed. "Jesus. The guy's name?"

Salazar took the second cup from the machine and sipped it. "Beau Baxter."

"And how is he?"

"He's going to be okay. They imaged him when he came in. The bullet went in through his stomach and passed out through his back. No major damage."

"He got lucky."

"If you call having your car stolen and getting shot lucky, then yeah, I guess he did."

"Can we talk to him now?"

"I spoke to the doctor. He says we can—I was just waiting for you."

~

SHEPHERD AND SALAZAR waited in the corridor while a doctor went into the room to tell the patient that the police were there to speak to him. She could see into the room through the window: the hospital bed was surrounded by a collection of equipment and IV stands, wires and probes attached to the body of a man who was semi-reclining. She guessed that he was in his late sixties. He wasn't frail, though; quite the opposite. The man had a solid build that was evident beneath the hospital-issue pyjamas that he was wearing.

The doctor came outside. "He's happy to speak to you."

"Thank you."

They went inside.

"Hey, Beau," Salazar said.

"Louis."

"This is my partner—Detective Shepherd. You okay to speak to her?"

"Sure," he said. "What do you need?"

Shepherd sat down on the chair next to the bed. There were a pair of snakeskin boots next to the chair and she moved them aside.

"How are you feeling?" she asked.

"Sore," Baxter said. "Like I just got shot in the gut."

Shepherd took out her notebook and a pen. "You want to tell me about last night?"

"Louis probably told you—I'm a bail bondsman."

"He did. You were going after someone who skipped out on you."

"That's right—this tweaker, guy by the name of Otis Williams. I heard that he was shacked up with his wife down by Goodsprings. I went down and checked, but I struck out. I was headed back when I saw a woman on the side of the road."

"Describe her?"

"Young. Mid-twenties. Blonde hair, down to her shoulders. Pretty."

"What was she doing?"

"Waving her hands around. Looked like she was panicking about something."

"What did you do?"

Baxter shrugged. "What anyone would do. Pulled over. Wound down the window and asked her what the problem was. She pulled a piece on me and told me to get out of the car."

"And you did?"

"Sure I did. What else was I going to do? She looked crazy."

"Go on, please."

"So I get out; I tell her to relax. She tells me to shut up, so I put my hands up and tell her not to do anything crazy. I figure she wants my car, so I tell her she can have it. She tells me to get away from it. I do; then she shoots me anyway. Aims into my gut and pulls the trigger. Didn't say another word. Gets into the car and drives away. Left me there."

"How did you get here?"

"I saw another car. I waved it down. The guy stopped and drove me here."

"Who?"

"Didn't give me his name," Baxter said.

"Where is he now?"

"I don't know," Baxter said. "He told me he didn't want anything to do with the police."

"He left Beau outside the ER and drove off," Salazar supplied.

"Security cameras?"

Salazar shook his head. "I've checked. Didn't get a good shot of the driver's face."

"Can you describe this man, Mr. Baxter?"

"Middle-aged. Black hair. Don't remember much else—I was in the back and trying to concentrate on not bleeding to death. But do I think there was anything about him that you ought to know? Not really. He saved my life, though. I'm sure about that."

Shepherd noted that all down. She turned back to Baxter. "Did you see anything else?"

"No," he said. "I don't think so. Anything in particular?"

"Any other cars?"

Baxter shook his head. "It was quiet." He tried to shift positions and winced with pain.

"You okay?"

"Just sore," he said. "There anything else I can help you with?"

"Can you give me a better idea of where it happened?"

"Outside Goodsprings," Baxter said. "There's an old abandoned gas station out there."

"I know it," she said. "Just after the turning at Jean."

"That's the one. That was where I heard the skipper was hiding out. The woman who shot me was near there."

Shepherd put away her notebook. "Thank you, Mr. Baxter. I'm sorry about what happened. You've been very helpful—I'll go down there to see if there's anything that'll help us find the woman who shot you."

"That's great. If you need me for anything else... well, I'll be here."

Shepherd stood and shook Baxter's hand. "You take it easy," she said.

⁓

SALAZAR AND SHEPHERD reconvened in the corridor outside the room. Salazar finished his coffee and dropped the cup into the trash.

"What do you think?" he asked her as they set off to the reception.

"I think there's a lot we don't know. I mean, for one, the woman—what was she doing down there at that time?"

"I don't know," he said.

"And the man who brought him here—why wouldn't he come inside?"

"He picked up someone who'd just been shot—maybe he didn't want to get involved. Wouldn't be the first time."

"I guess not," Shepherd said. She was silent a moment, mulling something over.

"What are you thinking?"

"I'm thinking there's got to be more to this. A young woman, out in the desert, hijacking a car and shooting the driver? Seems like a stretch."

"So?"

"Maybe it's something to do with Baxter's business, and whoever it was he came down here to find. How'd you know him again?"

"Professionally. There was a guy I wanted in San Diego —he found him."

"And you're sure he's a straight shooter?"

"Don't know him well enough to say."

"We can speak to him again later, but I'm betting he doesn't give us much more. You want to know what I think?" She dropped her cup in the trash. "I think, when all's said and done, this goes in the book as unsolved."

"Camacho's not going to be happy about that."

Shepherd agreed. The lieutenant was already under pressure to increase their clear-up rate, and this wasn't going to help.

They reached the doors to the parking lot.

"We need to go down there and take a look," she said. "You busy now?"

Salazar looked at his watch and exhaled wearily. "I go off shift in a couple of hours."

"Me too. But this can't really wait."

"I know."

"We drive down, check it out, then call it a day. I'll buy you breakfast when we get back."

He brightened. "If you put it like that."

"Come on," she said. "The sooner we get down there, the sooner we can be done."

They opened the doors. Dawn had broken, and the shadows were fading as the sun rose above the horizon. It already promised to be a warm day. They set out across the lot to their cars.

63

The *sicario* awoke at six, as was his habit, and, after preparing a mug of coffee, he sat down in front of his laptop. He opened a Tor browser to mask his location and then navigated to the Gmail account that he used for the receipt of his assignments and clicked over to the draft folder. A new message had been composed. He read it.

He had been given four targets.

Oscar Delgado.

Richard Russo.

Jessica Russo.

John Smith.

There was information on all of them, including pictures and addresses in Las Vegas for Delgado and Russo. There was a brief summation of the events that had been caused by Delgado's ineptitude and Russo's greed. The details were scant and had been included only in the event that it might help him to locate his targets. The *sicario* didn't care. He wasn't interested in why he had been sent, only in how he could complete his assignment.

He deleted the draft email, closed the computer and made his preparations. He dressed in a pair of black jeans and a plain black denim shirt. He hung the Do Not Disturb sign on the door handle and made his way to the restaurant to get breakfast.

64

Shepherd and Salazar drove south in convoy. Shepherd was in front with Salazar following close behind. She would have preferred to have made the drive with uniformed backup, but they had both decided that it would be better to get it out of the way quickly rather than wait around.

She found herself musing over the contents of the conversation with Baxter. The old man had taken the fact that he had been shot and robbed very well, but it was clear to her that this wasn't his first rodeo. A career as a bail bondsman was not one for the faint of heart, and she suspected that he had required medical assistance before; indeed, she suspected that he had sent his fair share of suspects to the emergency room.

She turned off at Jean for the final run to Goodsprings and approached the old gas station that Baxter had said was near to where he had been shot. She saw the vultures circling a quarter of a mile away on the other side of the road. The sun was above the line of the mountains now. She took her sunglasses from the dash, put them on and looked again. There were a dozen of the big birds circling on thermals high above the abandoned buildings.

She felt it in the pit of her stomach: something wasn't right.

Shepherd indicated that she was going to turn off, dabbed the brakes and then pulled over to the side of the road. She opened the door and stepped out. It was still, and, save for the chirping of an insect somewhere close at hand, quiet. The heat was already shimmering up from the ground, lazy waves that spoke of another broiling day.

Salazar's car crunched over the scree and drew up alongside. He got out.

She gestured up to where the vultures were drifting.

"That doesn't look great," Salazar said.

He took off his jacket and tossed it into his car. Shepherd removed her Glock from the shoulder rig and, with the gun held in a loose grip, she led the way toward the buildings. Salazar drew his own service pistol and followed.

She had driven past the gas station before, but had never had reason to come so close. The canopy overhead had been damaged, with a large section missing from the middle. The store was in a similarly bad state of repair, with boards over the windows and paint peeling from the walls. A graffitied face had been sprayed onto one of the walls and, as they approached the open doorway, she saw that the gloomy interior was stuffed with trash.

She felt the sweat bead on her brow as she went around the side of the building to the rear. Salazar followed.

A pair of vultures with bloody beaks flapped up into the air.

Shepherd saw what they had been feeding on: the body of a man, his eyes pecked out, dried blood caked on his skin. She raised the pistol with one hand and adjusted her glasses with the other, the sweat gathering in her eyes and on her top lip. There were three other bodies, surrounded by fragments of glass that glittered in the light, and, at her feet, a Benjamin flapped limply in the insipid breeze.

"Fuck," she said.

She scanned the desert beyond the gas station and saw nothing. They were alone out here with the dead. She narrowed her focus and saw the tyre tracks: one trail led further into the desert, turned around and then headed back. The second terminated nearer to the road, where it appeared the vehicle had been reversed, turned, and driven away.

Two vehicles.

Four bodies.

"Careful," Salazar warned.

She kept her gun out in front of her as she stepped closer to the nearest body. The victim was male, Hispanic, mid-thirties and well built. He had been shot in the head and in the chest. The blood had caked on his shirt, and gory residue had soaked into the sand beneath him. Something larger than the birds had visited him between his death and discovery, for three fingers of his right hand had been chewed off, and the soft flesh of his cheeks had been gnawed away.

Salazar had moved on to the next body, and Shepherd joined him. It was another Hispanic male, same age, the eyes plucked out, dark spaces where they had once been. There was a pistol on the ground next to him, and a scattering of bullet casings. Shepherd knelt down and laid her hand on his bare forearm; the flesh was cold. The third man was near, killed by a round that had gone in just above his nose and out through the top of his head.

She looked back down at the second man. His wallet was

visible in his pocket. Salazar fished it out and flipped it open. A driver's licence was visible through a clear plastic pouch in the wallet.

"Oscar Delgado," Salazar said. "Shit."

Shepherd winced. She looked down at him, ignored the damage from the birds, and realised that she recognised him. It was definitely Delgado.

"Forget about going off shift," she said.

"Yep."

Shepherd could predict the interdepartmental grief that piece of news was going to cause. She had worked a murder last year for which Delgado had been suspected, but they hadn't been able to make the charges stick. He was Mexican and reputed to be connected to one of the groups from down south. Delgado was suspected of being responsible for a good chunk of the product that came into the city, and had recently extended his interest to take in prostitution. There were at least another three unsolved killings that he was pegged for, too.

Shepherd went to the fourth victim. He was on his back, his eyes closed, his body untouched by the birds and the coyotes. She knelt down next to him and reached her hand into his open jacket for anything that she might be able to use to ID him.

The man coughed, loudly and suddenly, and sprayed blood all the way up her arm.

"*Motherfucker!*" She leapt to her feet and took a step back.

Salazar hurried over, his gun aimed down.

"*Agua,*" the man croaked.

Shepherd aimed the Glock down at him, but the man didn't move.

"*Agua, por favor.*"

The man opened his eyes, squinting at the blast of light. He groaned and tried to raise his head.

"Stay down," Salazar warned.

"Agua."

The man lay still, his mouth hanging open. Fresh blood speckled the skin around his lips. His shirt was stiff with dried blood that looked as if it belonged to him.

Shepherd kept her gun trained on the man.

"Call it in," she said to Salazar. "We need an ambulance down here."

65

Milton drove nonstop to San Diego, following the interstate through Barstow, Riverside and Beau Baxter's hometown of Escondido. It was an easy run with no traffic to slow him down, and he arrived in plenty of time.

He left the Porsche in the short-term parking lot and made his way into the terminal. The airport was large, but not so large that it was impossible for him to observe the comings and goings of the passengers. He quickly reconnoitred the building, finally settling for a seat at a table outside a Starbucks where he was able to observe the arriving passengers before they split off to approach their individual check-in counters.

If the Russos were going to catch a flight from here, they would have to pass right by his table. He arranged himself so that the Ruger in the waistband of his jeans didn't press up against his coccyx when he leaned back in the chair. He didn't think that he would need it—or that he would be able to use it in a public place like this—but being unarmed was not an option. Mason Russo had already shown himself to be a ruthless killer, and Milton suspected that his sister would be similarly pitiless in the event that her own back was put to the wall.

And the threat went deeper than the family; Milton knew that *sicarios* who killed in the name of the cartel would wipe them *all* out if the chance presented itself. Jessica had been cunning, but Milton had deduced their escape route. And if he could do it, then the cartel would be able to do it, too. Richard Russo had been questioned by Delgado and had revealed the location of the stolen money along with who knew what else. Was it possible that Delgado had extracted the family's plans from him? Could Delgado have told anyone else before he had been murdered at the exchange?

There was no way of knowing, but the bump of the pistol against Milton's back was a reassurance.

He settled down to wait.

The press started turning up twenty minutes after the additional officers and the ambulances had arrived from the city. Shepherd was leaning against the wall of the building when she saw a van with the KVVU-TV logo park on the other side of the road from the gas station.

Wonderful.

She made her way over to it as Carly Jacobs got out of the van. Her crew climbed out and followed her down to the road. Jacobs worked for the station; Shepherd had been interviewed by her several times. She was tenacious to the point of irritating, and she wouldn't easily be put off. She was thorough, too, and Shepherd knew that as soon as she had confirmation that this was going to be a big story, she would be on the phone to the station so that they could send the news chopper over for overhead coverage. The cordon was only going to be a temporary impediment. They would have to work fast.

"Shep," Jacobs said, "four?"

"I can't comment on that," she said.

"I heard it's four."

"Sorry, Carly. Not yet." Shepherd adjusted her shades.

"What *can* you give me?" Jacobs pressed.

"Multiple homicide. That's all I'm saying right now."

"Shit."

"Feel the same way. It's my day off."

"Not now it isn't."

Shep grimaced. "Stay on this side of the road, please," she said. "Lieutenant Camacho's on his way here. He'll speak to you when he's been briefed."

~

SHE TURNED and crossed the road back to the old gas station, where she signalled to one of the uniforms who had just arrived. He was from Clark County Sheriff's Department, and his cruiser was blocking the track that led around the back of the building, its lights still flashing. The man came over to her, and Shepherd told him to set up a cordon and make sure that no one crossed it without authorisation.

She went around to the rear of the station. Two Crown Vics had delivered three detectives from the Vegas homicide squad: Laura Rooney, Mike DeSouza and Mike Burgener. Salazar was observing the photographer from the forensics team as he took pictures of the dead men. He saw Shepherd and walked over to join her.

"You okay?" he asked.

"TV's here already," she groused. "It's gonna be a circus before too long. You got anything?"

"I do," he said. "Come with me."

He set off into the scrub, picking a careful route through the fist-sized rocks that littered the ground. In the distance, Shepherd saw what looked like a scratch in the landscape.

They closed in on it and she saw what it was: a trench. It was long, perhaps six and a half feet from one end to the other. It was shallow, too, and would have been deep enough to hide a man if he was prone.

Salazar knelt next to it. He pointed to an indentation at the head of the trench. "See this?" he said. "Looks like where a bipod might have been rested. I think someone dug out a place to hide, brought a rifle with them and picked off the guys in one of the cars. I found six casings—.338s, from something big."

She chewed her lip. "What do you think happened?"

"You got an exchange going on out here. Drugs. One party sets up the other one, puts a sniper out here. A couple of the dead guys had pretty big entry wounds. I'm guessing the sniper fires first; then his friends finish off the ones he missed. This was a nicely set trap. Professional."

Shepherd was sweating; she used the sleeve of her shirt to wipe the moisture from her forehead.

"You want some good news?" she said. "I got a call. We got a name for the survivor—Maximilliano Sacca. Mexican. Nasty piece of work. Record for pimping, assault and dealing."

"A gangbanger?"

She nodded. "One of Delgado's crew. He got to the hospital ten minutes ago. He's badly shot up, but they think he's going to be okay."

"What's next?"

"We got two leads. Delgado and Sacca."

Salazar nodded. "You got a preference which one we do first?"

"Sacca's going to be out of commission until they fix him up. Let's go check out Delgado's place."

67

Oscar Delgado's house was ostentatious. The *sicario* was surprised that he would be so crass as to draw attention to himself in this way. According to the file, Delgado explained his wealth by way of the ownership of a legitimate heavy metals business, usefully employing that same business to import the cartel's product. But it would have been prudent to have chosen a slightly less showy property. The *sicario* doubted that La Bruja would have approved, had she known.

The house looked empty. The windows were uncovered and there was no sign of occupation inside, despite the two cars that were parked on the drive leading up to the house. The *sicario* eyed them, then looked up as a man and a woman came out of the house and made their way down to the road. The man was old and doughy and was dressed in a rumpled suit and aviator shades; the woman was wearing dark slacks, a white blouse and shoes with a very shallow heel. She reached into her jacket and retrieved her phone, the action revealing a pistol in a shoulder holster.

The *sicario* had been in this line of business long enough to recognise a cop when he saw one.

He drove on, glancing over to the house as he continued by it. The detectives leaned on the hood of the first car. The woman had her phone pressed to her ear and was deep in conversation with someone on the other end of the line.

The *sicario* turned around and pulled over at the side of the road. He was able to watch the house from here without being seen. He reached into the equipment bag and took out a pair of small binoculars, observing the detectives through them as they went back inside the house again.

He waited there for ten minutes until they came outside once more. The man closed the door. The woman went to the first car and started the engine. The *sicario* watched as the man went to the second car. Both vehicles pulled away.

He thought about waiting and then breaking into the house, but decided against it. His instincts had always been good, and he knew that something was not quite as it should be.

He could always come back to the house later, but, for now, he needed to find out what the police were doing here.

He started the engine and followed them.

68

M ilton stayed at the table for three hours, nursing the same cup of cold coffee for fear that he might miss something if he turned his back. He had been joined by a detective from the San Diego Police Department. Louis Salazar had made a call and requested assistance, and a young officer—looking like he was not long out of his twenties—had been sent. The man's name was Riesenbeck, and he was earnest and serious. Milton had introduced himself to him and had explained what they were looking for, furnishing a description of all three Russos. Riesenbeck had taken up position on the other side of the check-in hall, and the two of them kept in touch by phone.

Milton was still angry, although the red-hot fury that had been generated by Jessica's betrayal, culminating in the shooting of Beau, had subsided a little. But that did not mean that he was prepared to forgive and forget.

Far from it.

He knew that his anger was fuelled partly by his disgust at having allowed himself to be used. He did not consider himself to be a credulous person, but Jessica had made a fool of him. She hadn't been the innocent that he had assumed. The only reason he hadn't eaten his gun when he left the Group was because he had decided that he could use his talents to help those who had no one else to turn to. Jessica had taken advantage of him. More than that, her betrayal had robbed him of the chance to add further balance to his ledger. He knew how irrational that sounded, but it was what it was.

Jessica's family, too, were not innocent. They might not have been as ruthless as Delgado and his cronies, but the Russos were involved in a joint criminal enterprise, and they had used Richard's connection to the cartel to enrich themselves. They must have known the danger in the course that they had elected to take, and the certainty of the fate that would have awaited them had they been discovered. Delgado would have killed them all had it not been for the money that he needed to recover.

They had proceeded with their theft despite the risk and, when it had gone wrong, the children had fomented an ingenious scheme to recover their father that was executed with cold-blooded efficiency. They had enjoyed the element of surprise and had exploited an assumption that Milton could now see was chauvinistic; that a pretty girl like Jessica could not possibly be anything other than what she appeared to be.

Fool me once, shame on you.

There would be no fooling him twice.

Milton checked his watch. It was midday. He looked up at the departures board. The flight from San Diego to Portland was due to take off at half past the hour. The screen announced that the flight would be boarding from Gate 24 and that it was on time. It was a domestic flight, so Milton knew that the gate would close fifteen minutes prior to departure. The Russos were cutting it close. They still had to make it through security. He assumed that they would be careful, would be travelling without hold luggage and would limit their exposure in a public place as much as they could. He tried to put himself in their shoes and imagine what he would have done: stay out of sight until the last possible moment before heading to the gate.

He looked at his watch again. Five past twelve. They would have to show up soon. But even as he concluded that, an insidious thought floated to the surface: what if they had changed their plan?

He called Riesenbeck. "Anything?"

"*Nothing.*"

Shit. Had he underestimated them again?

69

Shepherd and Salazar drove across town to the ER at Southern Hills Hospital and met the doctor responsible for Maximilliano Sacca's care. They followed him up to a room on the third floor.

"Here we are," the doctor said as he brought them to a door that was guarded by a uniformed officer.

"So how is he?"

"Three gunshot wounds and some internal damage, but we were able to patch him up. He'll live. He's dosed up pretty good, but he's fit to be questioned if you go easy."

"Thanks," she said.

Shepherd led the way inside. Sacca was sitting up in bed, propped up by pillows that had been arranged behind his back. A cannula had been fitted to the back of his hand and that, in turn, had been fitted to a drip. His vitals were being monitored, with his heart rate and blood pressure displayed on one of the screens that was fitted to a moveable stand behind the bed. He was a large man, with a shaved head and tattoos on his exposed skin. He had inked lipstick kisses on either side of his face, a design around the crown of his head, and some sort of gang design—Shepherd didn't recognise it—was visible above the bandages that had been wrapped around his stomach.

Shepherd took a chair and placed it next to the bed. Salazar went around to the other side of the bed and stood over Sacca there.

Shepherd took out her notebook. "Hello, Señor Sacca," she said. "I'm Detective Shepherd. That's Detective Salazar. We're with the Las Vegas Police Department. We need to ask you some questions about what happened out in the desert last night."

The Mexican glared at her, but said nothing.

"Look," Salazar said. "I'm going to be straight with you. You're in a lot of trouble. I mean a shit-ton of it. We've got you at the site of a multiple homicide. I'm guessing we're gonna find your prints on one of the weapons we found there. We know that you run with Oscar Delgado's crew. And we know that Delgado is one of the dead men. All we need is for you to tell us what happened down there. That's it."

Sacca glared at Salazar and then turned back to Shepherd.

"You're going to have to talk," Shepherd said. "It'll be much better for you if it's now."

"*Inmunidad*," he said, his voice weak and breathy.

"Immunity?" Shepherd said. "Sure. We can talk about that."

"*Inmunidad*," he said again, with more strength.

"If you cooperate, tell us what happened and help us catch whoever it was who killed your amigos, then I'll make a case that you should receive favourable treatment."

"*Immun*—"

"But that's a one-time deal," Shepherd said, cutting him

off. "You got my word that we'll make it easy for you, but that's only if you answer my questions right now. You don't answer them, or you mess around with us, then what can I say?" She shrugged. "We throw the book at you. *Comprende?*"

He scowled.

"I'm serious," she said. "We can leave, but if we do, you won't get the same offer again. Your call."

He leaned back a little, wincing from the pain. His expression changed from resentment to acceptance. "What you want to know?"

"What happened out there?"

His voice was strained and his English halting, but Shepherd could make him out. "There was to be an exchange."

"Drugs?"

He shook his head. "No. There was a gringo. He stole from us."

"Name?"

"Russo."

Shepherd noted it down. "First name?"

"Richard."

"Go on," Shepherd said.

"This man? He was *estúpido*. Oscar said he took five million dollars. Five million, from the cartel! He must have thought that Oscar was *estúpido*, like him, but he wasn't. Oscar was smart. He knew. We went to his house and we took him."

"Took him where?"

"The warehouse."

"Where's that?"

"Sunrise Manor. East Cartier Avenue. It's quiet, no one nearby. We took Russo there. He was a pussy. Folded after the first question. We beat him some anyway, but it was easy."

"What did he say?"

"That he had taken the money. Admitted it, straight up. Said he had it in a storage place up in Silver Spur."

"Five million dollars in storage?"

"Hundred and fifty in cash, the rest in Bitcoin. Oscar sent two guys to go and collect it, except they got lost on the way and, when they got there, they were too late. It was gone. Russo's daughter and this other gringo had got there first."

"The other guy?"

"John Smith. Him and a second gringo were working with the Russos. The old man was on his own when we took him, but, as we were driving away, we saw a car with the daughter inside heading back to the house. Oscar wanted her, too, so we turned around. We get back there, the daughter and the guy she was with are inside the house. We go in, too, all of us, all packing. The guy takes out Pérez, Lòpez and Morazán—"

"Takes out?"

Sacca put his fingers together in the shape of a gun.

"He shot them?"

Sacca nodded. "Puts the girl in the back of her *papi's* car and runs. We chased him, but this guy is fast, like NASCAR, and we lost them."

Shepherd listened intently. Clearly, what had happened in the desert was a lot more complicated than it had initially appeared.

"And then?" Salazar probed.

Sacca reached out for his water and took a sip. "Oscar gets a call. It's the guy. Smith. He says he's got the money and he'll exchange it for the old man. Oscar says yes. Smith says we meet him at Jean and he'll take us to where it's gonna go down."

"What happened next? Take your time."

"There were the two gringos and Russo's daughter. One of them was Smith. English. He had the accent."

"Describe him?"

"Forties. Same height as me, not as big. Dark hair, scar across his face, blue eyes."

"The other guy?"

"Older."

"How old?"

"Late sixties. Dressed like a cowboy."

"How do you mean?"

"Big belt buckle. And he had these snakeskin boots. White and black."

Shepherd remembered the boots that she had seen in Beau Baxter's room. He was late sixties, too.

Surely not.

She paused, distracted, as Salazar pressed Sacca to continue.

"So Smith gives Oscar the briefcase," he said. "Oscar looks—there's money there, but not all of it. And then it all goes crazy. They got another guy out in the desert. He shoots Oscar; then the gringos take the rest of us out."

"And then?"

"Don't know what happened after that," he said. "I was out of it. Next thing I know, I wake up covered in blood and you're there." He shrugged, his hands spread.

The Mexican looked tired. The doctor, who had been standing just outside the door, put his head through. "Time to stop," he said.

Shepherd acknowledged him and stood. "We'll be back tomorrow when you're stronger."

"You leave someone here?" he said.

"You feel like we need to?"

He looked at her as if she were mad. "Those dudes were *despiadado*—you know?"

Salazar translated. "Ruthless."

Sacca nodded. "*Muy despiadado*."

"We'll leave an officer outside," she said.

70

Salazar led the way out of the hospital room. He had seen the way Shepherd had reacted when Sacca had said that the older of the two shooters had been wearing white and black snakeskin boots. He knew what she was thinking: Beau Baxter had a pair of white and black boots in his room, and, by his own testimony, he had been shot near to where the massacre had taken place. The plan that Baxter and Smith had put together was looking like it was about to fray.

"Shit," Shepherd said to him.

"No kidding. What do you make of it?"

"We got to speak to the precinct. We need to see if they've got anything on this Russo."

"You want me to do it?"

She shook her head. "I got it. Get me a coffee?"

"Sure. See you downstairs."

Salazar took the elevator down to the first floor and went to the waiting area. He bought two coffees and sat down. He took out his phone and looked to see if there were any messages from Smith. There were none. He thought about how things might go south. Would Sacca be able to identify Baxter and Smith? It seemed possible. If he was able to do that, the lies that they had told would quickly be debunked. Salazar started to think about his own self-preservation.

Shepherd joined him after ten minutes. Her eyes glittered with excitement as she sat down.

"What is it?"

"So," she began, "I just spoke to Dutch. He ran Russo through the system. Turns out that financial crimes have been looking into him for the last six months. Dutch says that Russo's behind a big scam on the Strip—setting up credit lines using stolen IDs, getting third parties to use the credit to post big bets and then, when they win, taking off with the proceeds."

"Working with Delgado?"

"Dutch said that a couple of the gamblers they picked up had connections. Doesn't seem like a stretch, given the circumstances."

"So what are we saying? Russo and Delgado were working together, Russo rips Delgado off, Delgado abducts him?"

She nodded. "And his daughter and these two mystery men set them up at the exchange to get him back. I don't think that sounds too wide of the mark." She sipped the coffee.

"Anything else?"

"I'm just getting started. Financial crimes subpoenaed Russo's bank records six months ago. They've seen money going in, tens of thousands every month, and then, last month, a big sum was transferred into the client account of a real estate agent in Florence. Turns out that Russo bought a farmhouse near Siena. Put down six hundred grand and funded the rest with a mortgage. Look—Dutch even has a picture."

She took out her phone and handed it to Salazar. There was a PDF brochure from a property agent. The property advertised was called Casa Tulipano and, from the pictures at least, it looked stunning.

Salazar thought of John Smith waiting at the airport and wondered if he had been able to pick them up. Was that where the Russos were going to run to?

"We got an address in Vegas for him?"

"Summerlin. Dutch is already on it."

"What about the two guys?"

"Nothing obvious," Shepherd said.

Salazar watched her as she answered, looking for any indication that she had made the connection with Baxter. Her face gave nothing away. Maybe she hadn't seen the boots.

"What now?" he said.

"I don't know about you, but I'm cooked. I should've been off shift hours ago. We can speak to Sacca again when he's recovered, and I'm thinking we can leave Russo to Dutch. Maybe we pick this up again when we get back on shift. What do you say?"

"Works for me."

Salazar finished his coffee and dropped the cup in the trash. "You still owe me breakfast."

"I'll buy you a burger tonight."

71

Shepherd and Salazar went out to their cars. Salazar drove away, waving as he went by. Shepherd opened her phone and navigated to Google. She searched on Beau Baxter's name and scrolled through the results until she found the one that she wanted.

Baxter's Bail Bonds.

She tapped the result and waited for the next page to load. It was bright red, with the name of the business running across the top of the screen in large white letters. There was a picture beneath it: Beau Baxter in a Stetson standing next to a steer, his hand resting between the beast's horns.

Shepherd got out of the Crown Vic and went back up to the room where Sacca was being treated.

The doctor was looking at the man's charts on the clipboard that was attached to the foot of the bed. He saw Shepherd and indicated that he would speak to her outside the room.

"What is it?"

"One more thing."

"I've just sedated him. He needs to rest."

"Won't take long. I just need him to look at a photograph."

The doctor looked as if he was going to protest, but Shepherd held his eye and he relented.

"Fine. But be quick."

"Thank you."

Shepherd went back into the room. Sacca looked up at her through glassy eyes. He looked close to sleep.

"It's Detective Shepherd. I need you to look at a picture for me. Can you do that?"

He gave the slightest incline of his head. Shepherd took her phone from her pocket and held it out so that Sacca could look at the picture of Beau Baxter. He blinked, once and then twice and then a third time, as if willing his eyes to focus. Shepherd watched his face for a reaction and was rewarded: his nostrils flared and he scowled.

"Is that him?" she asked. "Is that one of the men from the exchange?"

"*Sí*," he said.

"Are you sure?"

He nodded.

"Thank you," she said.

Shepherd left Sacca and went back outside.

She knew that Salazar was prone to sailing a little close to the wind from time to time, but she hadn't sensed anything that might have suggested that he was involved with Baxter in whatever it was that had gone down in the desert last night. Baxter, though, was a different matter. She wondered whether it might be prudent to arrest him now and then formally question him. She would speak to the lieutenant. One thing was for sure: Salazar couldn't be involved in that, at least not until she was absolutely sure that his hands were clean.

What a mess.

She sat down and stretched out her legs, the fatigue that she had been ignoring suddenly overwhelming her. She needed to sleep, but it was going to have to wait a little longer. She wanted to check with the doctor that security had been arranged, but the doctor wasn't there.

A man came out of the restroom opposite. He was dressed simply, in a black denim shirt and black denim jeans. His face had a monumental quality about it: his nose was a little bulbous, his cheekbones were prominent, his brow was a slab that ended with thick eyebrows that, in turn, surmounted dark and soulless eyes.

He had a pistol in his hand and it was pointed straight at her.

"Inside, please, Detective."

72

M ilton looked at his watch again. It was one
o'clock now, and the flight had taken off on
time half an hour ago. Milton and Riesenbeck
had kept watch in the arrivals hall, with Milton staying in
the café and Riesenbeck heading over to a line of stores
where travellers could buy books, magazines, toiletries and
other ephemera.

There had been no sign of the Russos.

Milton leaned back in the chair and exhaled
impatiently.

Riesenbeck was crossing the hall toward him. "They're
not coming, are they?"

Milton got up and stretched the kinks from his shoulders. "It doesn't look like it."

Milton thought back to the items that he had found in
Jessica's Tesla: the itinerary, the guidebook. She had clearly
been intending to take that flight, and Italy was to be their
final destination.

What had changed?

"You need me anymore?" Riesenbeck asked him.

"No," Milton said. "Sorry for wasting your time."

The detective shook his hand and made his way to the exit. Milton stayed where he was, thinking. What had happened? Jessica was smart: might she have anticipated that he would have gone back to search the car? That seemed like a stretch, especially given that she must have assumed his attention would have been taken up with tending to Beau.

Milton took out his phone and called Salazar.

"How's it going?"

"Not good," Milton said. "They didn't show."

"Might only be a temporary disappointment. I got something for you—turns out that Richard Russo is a person of interest for the department. He's been under investigation by the fraud team for months."

"For what?"

"Hacking guest information at the casino and using it to set up fake lines of credit. We're talking serious money. They were close to making an arrest. I just found out. Gets better, too. They've been in Russo's bank accounts for months. Your hunch about Italy looks like it might be right. He bought a farmhouse near Siena. You got a pen and paper?"

There was a store selling newspapers and stationery next to the café. Milton took a pen from the shelf, wedged the phone between his shoulder and chin, and held out his left hand. "Go on."

"Place is called Casa Tulipano. Near San Quirico d'Orcia."

Milton wrote the address on his hand. "Got it."

"You think they'll still go out there?"

Milton put the pen back. "Where else are they going to go? Have you had to deal with anyone leaving the country before?"

"*I work Nevada, buddy. Most of the low-lifes I deal with have never even left the state boundary, let alone the country.*"

"How many other big airports are close to Vegas?"

"You think they booked another flight?"

"It's possible."

"*You got LAX and San Francisco if they went west.*"

"What about south or east? Phoenix?"

"*Sure. Albuquerque, Tucson, El Paso. Denver's eleven hours away. They could transit to one of the hubs and head to Europe from there.*"

"What about Vegas?" Milton said.

"*You think?*"

"It's worth considering. They've created a big diversion. Maybe they go straight to the airport and take the first flight out. Can you check?"

"*Yeah,*" he said. "*I can get someone back at the precinct to pull the manifests.*"

The more Milton thought about it, the more likely that seemed to be. Jessica was shrewd; the notion that she had outsmarted him again was not so hard to credit, given what she had already achieved.

"What about the investigation?" he asked.

"*We caught a break—one of Delgado's guys survived. He laid it all out—the exchange for Russo, what went down, the whole bit.*"

"Can he identify me or Beau?"

"*I don't know.*"

Milton swore under his breath.

"*What are you doing now?*"

"I'll stick around here for a while longer, just in case. Maybe they got a later flight. Will you let me know if you get anything?"

"*Sure.*"

Milton thanked him and hung up. He looked at the address that he had written on the back of his hand and wondered what to do next.

Beau had been spinning his wheels all afternoon. He was still sore from his injury, but when he looked down at the wound when the nurse changed his dressing, he could see that it had not become infected. They had done a good job of removing any foreign material, and that, together with the antibiotics that had been delivered intravenously since he had been admitted, had seemingly ensured that he would recover well enough. He knew he had been fortunate. He could easily have died in the desert, or in the back of the car as Smith had delivered him here, or from complications afterwards. He had lost a lot of blood, too, and the doctor had told him that they had transfused several pints as they'd sought to stabilise him. He was bound to feel weak.

He was grateful, but now he was ready to leave. He had asked the doctor when he thought he would be able to discharge him and had received the reply—not that he was surprised by it—that they would like to keep him in for another couple of days, three at the outside. He had been very badly hurt, the doctor said, and he wanted to make sure that everything had been properly patched up before he was prepared to let him out. Beau hadn't argued; he knew that there was no point, and presenting himself as anything other than a compliant patient would make it more difficult for him when he was ready to leave.

There was also the small matter of the police. He was confident that the story that he and Smith had concocted was sound, and that his delivery of it had been persuasive, but there were things about the police investigation that they did not know, and that meant that it was possible that they might come across evidence that would undermine his telling of the tale. He was limited in what he could learn while he was stuck in the hospital; Salazar might be able to give him an update, but that was it.

There were windows in the wall that separated Beau's room from the corridor, but the glass was frosted, and all he could see of the people outside were their shapes as they passed. There had been a silhouette there most of the afternoon; Beau had hobbled outside earlier to see about getting a coffee and had seen that the silhouette belonged to the police officer who was guarding the room. Beau had thanked him, and the man had acknowledged his gratitude with a nod of the head.

Beau was wondering about the best time to discharge himself when he saw another silhouette draw up to the guard. He heard the sound of voices—too low and muffled for him to decipher them from behind the door—and then watched as both shadows disappeared to the right.

He turned away, his thoughts running back to how the next day or two might develop. He needed to get out so that he was in a position to stay ahead of events. He felt as if he was just waiting for things to happen while he was sitting here on his ass. At a minimum, he was going to have to get

Chase to fly over so that he could collect the skipper and take him back to San Francisco. He didn't like to lie to family, and he was going to have to think about exactly what he could tell his son to explain what had happened. Chase had been nagging him for months that maybe it was time to hang it up, and seeing him laid up in a hospital bed was going to be more grist for that particular mill.

He heard the sound of footsteps and saw a dim shape passing across the window from right to left. The shape reached the door and he saw the handle being pushed down. The doctor? Beau shuffled back a little in the bed, wincing from the ache as he straightened his back against the headboard.

The door opened.

It wasn't the doctor.

It was a man Beau had not seen before. He was dressed all in black—black denim shirt and jeans—with black hair that framed an unhealthily white face. The man stepped inside and closed the door.

"Hello, Señor Baxter," he said.

"Who are you?"

The man ignored the question. Instead, he brought his arm up to show his hand; he was holding a pistol with a long suppressor screwed onto the barrel.

"Please, señor, keep your voice down. I would like to ask you a few questions. I would much prefer it if our conversation was civil. Do you think that might be possible?"

Beau was too long in the tooth to be panicked by the sight of a gun, but he was also more than experienced enough to know that he was in something of a situation. The reason guns did not normally concern him was that he always had one himself, and made it his practice to have it drawn and ready before the bad guy drew his. It was easier to be relaxed about the prospect of an armed man when you had your finger on the trigger before he did. That wasn't the case now. Beau was unarmed, and, as he carefully glanced left and right, he could see nothing with which to improvise.

"Where's the guard?"

"In the restroom," the man said, as calmly as if he had just described the weather.

He didn't elaborate; he didn't need to.

Beau decided to play it dumb. "What do you want?"

"You were working with Señor Russo."

"Say what?"

"Señor Russo and his children—Jessica and Mason. What was your relationship with them?"

"Don't know those names."

"I think you do. Detective Shepherd told me that you and another man—a man who spoke with an English accent —were involved with the Russos, and that the two of you shot Oscar Delgado and his men during an exchange in the desert."

"Delgado? Don't know that name, neither."

"You would say that, Señor Baxter. But one of Señor Delgado's men survived—a man called Sacca. I spoke with both him and Detective Shepherd before I came here. The detective told me that she showed Sacca your picture, and he identified you. So, please, it would be much better if you did not waste my time. Let me ask you again—how did you come to work for the Russos?"

Beau thought of the button that he used to call the nurses. It was tethered to the rail of the bed.

"No," the man said, noticing the dart of Beau's eyes. "That would not be a good idea."

Beau put the thought of using the button to one side. He wouldn't be able to reach it before the man could fire; even if he had been able to reach it, he knew it wouldn't do him much good.

"Señor Baxter—please. Answer my question."

"Buddy, I don't know what you want me to say. I don't know anything about the girl, and I certainly don't know anything about some shooting in the desert. I ain't got nothing for you."

"What about the Englishman?"

"I don't know no Englishman. I don't know no one from England. I was down here looking for a bail skipper, and then this whole mess happened around me. I work alone. I was alone in the car when it happened. That's it."

"Where do you think the Russos have gone?"

"I just told you—I don't know no one called Russo."

"Your last chance, señor."

"I ain't got nothing for you."

Was there a flicker of something across the man's face? Satisfaction, perhaps. He took a step back and—before Beau could protest or react or do anything that might have helped his situation—pulled the trigger. The first shot hit Beau in the chest, punching into his heart, blowing out of his back and into the mattress.

The second shot, aimed with languid ease, was into his head.

74

Milton stayed at the airport all afternoon. There were no direct flights to Florence, but the Russos could have chosen to fly out from any of the main hubs. His phone ran out of charge just after two, and he changed his observation point to a bench near security where he could plug the phone in for more juice.

He allowed his thoughts to wander a little. If the Russos had already left the country, then at least he had a very good idea where they would go. The Nevada police would be able to request assistance from their foreign colleagues; if they could find them, perhaps it would be possible to begin the process to extradite them back to the States.

He pressed the button to turn on the phone. It immediately buzzed with inbound notifications.

He picked it up and saw that he had missed calls from Louis Salazar.

Ten of them.

His stomach dropped. He dialled Salazar's number.

"At last," Salazar said as soon as the call connected. *"Where've you been?"*

"My phone died."

"Beau's dead."

Milton felt sick. "What?"

"He's been shot. The guard we had on the door—shot, too."

"Oh no."

"It's worse than that," Salazar said. *"My partner was found dead in Maximilliano Sacca's room. Sacca was shot, too, and the doctor who was looking after him. Looks like the same gun was used to kill all five of them—we'll know for sure when the ballistics are checked. It looks like the killer took out Sacca and Shepherd first, then crossed town for Beau."*

Milton's head was spinning. "It can't be the Russos."

"It isn't. A Denali Yukon matching the one you said you were driving was found in a parking lot at a mall in Crystal Springs. We've got security camera footage from the mall showing the three of them leaving the car on foot two hours ago. So it couldn't have been them."

"You have CCTV from the hospitals?"

"We're looking."

Milton gripped the phone tightly.

"You still there?" Salazar said.

"I'm here."

"It's a shitstorm. The press are on to it. You got a murdered detective, a murdered gangster, a murdered doctor and two murdered civilians. Five homicides, plus the three from last night."

"It's the cartel," Milton said. "They've sent someone to find the money."

"But the money's not here."

"And whoever it is that they've sent, he'll know that by now."

Milton closed his eyes and thought. He needed to piece this together.

"Did your partner know about Beau?"

"I think so. I'd just been with her when she spoke to him. She waited until I was gone and went back. Maybe she suspected something and didn't want me around when she asked because she knows I knew Beau."

"She *must* have known," Milton said. "The killer couldn't have known about Beau unless she told him."

"Or Sacca."

"Either one could have told him," Milton conceded. He squeezed his eyes closed tighter. "He finds out about Beau, kills them and then goes across town. He questions Beau. So he knows about me now."

"Beau was tough."

"It doesn't matter. Everyone talks. It's biology."

"Okay. He knows."

"He's trying to work out what happened in the desert. He'll know about the Russos by now—someone would've told him. He'll be after them." Milton paused. "Did your partner know about Russo's place in Italy?"

"Yes. She told me."

"So the killer knows about that, too."

"What next? We can't let that motherfucker get away with what he's done."

Milton stood up. "We're not going to."

"So?"

"He'll go to Italy. He'll find the property and wait for the Russos to show."

Milton started towards the airline ticket desks.

"What are you going to do?"

"I'm going there, too," Milton said.

75

J essica got out of the car and stretched, trying to work out the kinks that had accumulated over the course of the long journey north. They were all exhausted. They had covered the twelve hundred miles between Las Vegas and Vancouver in twenty-one hours. They had stopped in Crystal Springs to change cars, but, since then, they had paused only to use the restroom, refuel and change drivers. Mason had driven the first leg before Jessica had taken over just outside Twin Falls. She had taken them up to Baker City, and then, after sleeping for much of the journey, their father had insisted that he was fit enough to take his turn. He had delivered them to Blaine, and Mason had taken over again for the trip across the border to White Rock and then the final run to Vancouver International Airport.

The first few hours, while they were still within easy distance of Las Vegas, had been the worst. Jessica had looked back often, half expecting to see the strobe of police lights prickling the darkness behind them. Her fearful thoughts had then turned to Smith when the police lights did not appear: would he come after them? It was panicked thinking, she told herself. Smith and Baxter had been left in the middle of the desert, and Smith's focus would have been on getting Baxter to the hospital before he bled out. Even assuming that he was prepared to involve the police—and she doubted that, given his involvement in what had happened behind the gas station—she and her father and brother still had a significant head start on any pursuers.

Of course, anyone who wanted to give chase would have had to know where they were and where they were going. Their father assured them that he had not mentioned their destination to Delgado, and, even if he had, it wouldn't have mattered: Delgado was dead. They had decided that they could still travel to Italy, but, just to be safe, they would change their route. They would eschew the tickets out of San Diego that Jessica had bought and, instead, would take the longer—but safer—trip north.

Crossing the border had been big. It had been a relief to get out of the country, and it would be an even bigger relief to leave the continent. The next leg of their journey was the 00.05 Air Canada flight to Montreal, where they would lay over for nine hours before connecting onto the 16.50 flight to Zurich. They would have a further short layover in Switzerland before the final Swissair flight to Florence. They would be travelling for another seventeen hours before they reached the safety of their final destination.

Mason helped their father out of the car.

"Halfway there," he said.

He looked tired and fragile. She didn't know how much of that was the cancer and how much was just his age, but she was pleased to have him back again. Delgado had treated him roughly, but, even so, it could have been worse. They didn't know how long he had left, but he had always wanted to live in the Tuscan hills. Now, at least for a few months, that was what he would do.

They were travelling light; her luggage was in her Tesla, and Mason's and her father's were still in the house back in Vegas. It didn't matter. It wasn't as if they were short of cash. Mason took out their passports and handed them around.

Their father straightened up and put out his chest. "Ready?"

Jessica and Mason said that they were.

"Let's get out of here."

They made their way into the terminal. She felt a twist of nervousness in her stomach, and although she tried to keep it off her face, her father noticed.

"There's no reason why they would be looking for us here."

"I know," she said.

They made their way into the departures hall and followed the signs to the desk for Air Canada. Jessica had purchased three one-way business-class tickets on her phone and there was no line at the check-in. The attendant welcomed them with a smile that was surely reserved for the airline's more affluent customers, and quickly ran through the procedure. They said that they had no luggage to check and, once their passports had been checked and their seats had been assigned, they made their way to security.

Jessica couldn't help but look around as they waited to go through the scanner. The other passengers were nondescript, and she saw nothing that would lead her to think that anyone was observing them. She found, to her surprise, that it was Smith to whom her thoughts returned. He had been good to her and she had betrayed him. She could live with that; his assistance had been helpful in collecting the money and rescuing her father. He had served his purpose. But she found it difficult to forget the way in which he had conducted himself. It was more than just his obvious competence; he knew his business and perhaps he would know how to find them.

"Madam?"

She looked up. Mason and her father were waiting for her on the other side of the arch, and the guard was beckoning her forward. She stepped through and was pleased not to set off the device. On the other side, she pocketed the coins that she had deposited in the tray and went to her father's side. He offered her his arm and she took it.

"Shall we?" he said.

She smiled at him. "Let's."

PART IV

76

Milton had been lucky. He had managed to book a Lufthansa flight from San Diego to Frankfurt that departed within two hours of his enquiry at the desk. He had an hour's layover in Germany before the connecting flight to Florence, and he had spent that time making a telephone call to a contact to ask for his help. He had a plan to deal with the Russos, but there were certain technical elements that were beyond him, and Ziggy Penn— a man who had worked as an analyst for the Group at the same time that Milton had been deployed—had been able to assist, especially when Milton promised to pay him for his time.

The Air Dolomiti Embraer ERJ-195 started its descent into Florence and Milton allowed himself to think—again— about the events that he had left behind him. A riot of thoughts ran through his head. There was no shock at the thought of death, since death had been a constant presence in his life for two decades, and familiarity had inured him to its sting. Instead, there was confusion and dismay and anger.

There was self-recrimination there, too, the first stirrings of blame: Beau had no business in Milton's affairs and had only involved himself in the Russo business at Milton's request. Beau had done him a favour—another one, *again*—and now, because of that, he was dead. Milton knew himself well enough to know where he would point the finger of blame, and that he needed to get to a meeting quickly if he wanted to resist the demon that was already beginning to stir. Vegas had been a challenge to his sobriety before this, but if his self-loathing was allowed to stir and flourish... he knew where that would end up.

"Could you open your blind, please, sir?" the attendant asked. "We'll be landing shortly."

"Sorry," Milton said. "Of course."

She smiled an automatic smile and continued back along the aisle. Milton pushed the blind up and looked down at the verdant green hills that swaddled the city ahead of them. Florence. He had been here before, years earlier, and for once it had been for pleasure and not for business. He had brought a girlfriend here to see the Ponte Vecchio and the Uffizi Gallery and to eat the ribollita and penne strascicate and the gelato. It had been a magical visit, and he had retained fond memories of it ever since.

This, though, was not pleasure.

This was business.

～

MILTON DESCENDED the steps to the asphalt and made his way around the wing to a waiting bus. He pushed inside, fighting for space with the other several dozen passengers who had no patience to wait for the next one to arrive. The driver put the bus into gear and moved forward perhaps a hundred metres, then hit the brakes and opened the doors. Everyone disembarked, a few sharing a joke about how idiotic the need for the bus was given the distance between the jet and the terminal. Milton followed the crowd into the baggage reclaim. He had no luggage save a small pack that he had purchased in San Diego, so he bypassed the renewed scrum at the mini-carousels and made his way through immigration and into the arrivals hall.

He changed six hundred dollars into euros, put the notes into his pack and went to the Autoeurope desk. He rented a car and headed south. The airport was on the autostrada and the traffic was light. His satnav indicated that there were seventy-six kilometres between here and Siena, and that he would arrive in an hour and twenty minutes.

He decided that he had time to make a short stop. He pulled off the road and stocked up on food from the first Autogrill he passed: he bought several pastries and sandwiches together with a *spremuta*, the juice of four blood oranges that was squeezed into a tall glass.

~

HE REACHED Siena in good time and left the car in a lot on the edge of town. He took out his phone and searched for the nearest store that sold camping equipment and outdoor gear. It was on Casato di Sotto. He found his way there and went inside. The store was small, but had a good range of equipment. Milton walked the aisles, selecting the things he thought he might need if he was forced to stay outdoors for a reasonable length of time. He selected a small one-man tent, together with the associated accessories. He added a sleeping bag, a flashlight, a hunting knife with a sheath that could be fixed to his belt, a water container and a selection of ready-to-eat meals. Finally, he took waterproof matches, a bag of cable ties, a candle, a flint, a compass, a pair of binoculars and a simple medical kit including an analgesic, Imodium, an antibiotic, antihistamine, water purification tablets, a can of bug repellent and potassium permanganate. He chose a rucksack that was large enough to carry everything and went to the counter. He paid cash and took the equipment outside.

He would have liked to have spent an hour or two wandering the cobbled streets, but he didn't have the time to spare. He slung the rucksack onto his back and hauled it back to the car.

~

HE CONTINUED SOUTH. He felt underprepared, with no weapon and no real prospect of finding one. But he had formulated a plan during the flight and was anxious to put it into action. He had very little to go on, and didn't even know whether the Russos would come here. He was as confident as he could be that they would—and had no idea where else they would go if it *wasn't* here—but had no clue as to whether they might have already arrived or whether he might have beaten them.

He also did not know whether they would be alone.

He needed to check the house out as quickly as he could.

77

Milton drove into San Quirico d'Orcia. It was a small town in the Val d'Orcia. It was arranged around its church, the Collegiata, which was decorated with sculptures and with weather-beaten lions guarding the entrance. Milton found a place to leave the car and took out the map he had purchased of the area. He found and marked the Russo property on the map and then took his bearings. The farmhouse was a five-mile hike to the south.

Milton went around to the back of the car and took out his rucksack. He hoisted it onto his shoulders, tightened the straps until they were comfortable, locked the car and started to walk.

~

It took him over an hour to find the property. It was located to the southwest of the town, beyond the signs that directed visitors to the Poggio Grande vineyard. The house was accessed by a dirt track that branched off the picturesque

Strada di Ripa D'Orcia, a hand-painted sign identifying it as
Casa Tulipano. The flowers that gave the property its name
were much in evidence, with the bank to the right of the
track showing a multicoloured display and infusing the hot
air with their heady scent.

There was a mailbox next to the sign. Milton opened it,
hoping to find something that might suggest that the Russos
were in or about to be in residence, but it was empty.

The terrain here was steep, with a series of small hills
rolling into more impressive climbs. Two stands of majestic
cypresses had been planted on either side of the track, and a
copse of fir and ash could be seen on the slopes of the hills
to the north and south. The track wound between these
hills, headed due west.

Milton's map suggested that the farmhouse was another
two miles in that direction. He turned off the road and
climbed up the bank, continuing to the north and then
following the route of the track from inside the tree line. He
traversed carefully, on high alert, stopping regularly to scan
the terrain ahead and behind. A tractor chugged through
the fields of the vineyard to the south but, save that, there
was no sign of anyone in the vicinity.

Milton proceeded with care.

～

MILTON CRESTED A SLOPING HILL, and the farmhouse
presented itself. It sat atop a shallow plateau at the bottom
of a depression, the terrain sloping up around it on all sides.
It was a large building, the end facing him clad entirely in a
cloak of thick ivy that was punctuated only by windows. The
track switched back on itself as it climbed to the plateau,
terminating in a wide parking area. He saw the crystal blue

of a swimming pool from within a screen of trees, a summerhouse and a collection of outbuildings that must have served the vineyard. Those cultivated fields stretched around the property, with the largest acreage laid out between a large barn and the start of the foothills perhaps a mile to the west. It was an impressive estate. Milton was not an expert on Italian real estate, but the similar properties that he had researched online had price tags of anywhere up to three million euros.

Milton put the binoculars to his eyes and scanned the estate. He started with the distant fields and then continued until he was looking at the property itself. There was no sign that anyone was in attendance. The fields were in good order, with the vines laid out in neat rows, clearly given the attention necessary for them to continue to be farmed. The lawns around the property looked to have been cut within the last few days. They sported back-and-forth stripes and were a verdant green—noticeable given the parched yellows and browns of the scrub—signalling the ministrations of a diligent gardener. There were no cars beneath the porte cochère, nor on the gravel turning circle that had been laid out in front of the house.

Milton scrutinised the area closer to his present position. There was a copse behind him, slightly up the slope, and Milton climbed up to it. He pushed his way through the bracken that had gathered between the trunks of the hornbeams and linden and then turned back to consider the scope of the view. It was promising. There was a narrow clearing inside the tree line where he would be able to erect his tent so that it wasn't visible from the house, and, with a little judicious clearing of the underbrush, he would have reasonable sightlines into the valley. He would be able to see the track until it disappeared over the ridge, two aspects of the house, the turning area and the pool, and much of the vineyard. He was satisfied.

He took off his pack and dumped it against the nearest trunk. He would put the tent up later; for now, he wanted to take the opportunity to scout the property while it was unattended.

He picked a route that would offer frequent cover and started down the slope.

78

Milton proceeded carefully, staying low and hurrying through the stretches where he could not quickly retreat to cover. He was aware that it might not just be the Russos who were on their way to the house, although they had shown themselves to be more than dangerous enough to earn his caution; there was also the chance—the *hope*—that whoever had murdered Beau was also on their way.

He passed through a grove of olive trees that showed signs of cultivation, and then through the formal gardens that were marked by a row of tall Tuscan cypresses, matched to the double line that followed the track leading back to the road. Milton reached the first of a series of outbuildings and pressed himself against the wall, grateful for the shade. He peered around the corner and still could not see any sign of activity from within the property or in the grounds that surrounded it. He was as satisfied as he could be that he was safe to continue.

He turned around the corner and moved ahead, hurrying by an ornamental garden until the hard earth was replaced by the gravel of the drive. He went around the house, moving to the rear so that his presence would be masked should anyone approach.

The windows at the back of the house were covered by shutters that had been closed and secured from the inside. Milton was unable to see through them to the interior, so he continued along the wall until he got to a wide pair of French doors. He tried the handles, but the doors were locked. They weren't shuttered, though, and by cupping his hand to the glass, he was able to cut out the glare from the sun and look inside. It was some sort of anteroom, with a tiled floor and an ornate archway that opened onto a corridor that went deeper into the house.

He heard the sound of an engine.

He froze, closed his eyes and listened: it was approaching from the other side of the house, most likely from the track. He heard the squeak of the vehicle's suspension and then the crunch as it passed from the rough surface to the gravel. He opened his eyes and assessed his options. He wouldn't be able to get back to the copse where he had left his tent without being seen from the front of the house. The vineyard was close at hand, but he dared not go there in the event that whoever had just arrived was responsible for tending to the grapes. The same went for the brick shed that faced it; he guessed that the equipment was stored there.

He moved around the house, turning the corner and looking down on the glittering azure rectangle of the pool. There was a pool house next to it. It would have to do. He crossed the lawn until he reached the building and slipped into the shade behind it.

He stopped, closed his eyes again, and listened.

The engine switched off and he heard the sound of

voices drifting down to him on the breeze. They were too far away for him to be able to pick out the words, but he could tell that there was more than one speaker. He thought he could distinguish three speakers: two male and one female. He heard laughter.

It had to be the Russos.

He shuffled around to the door that led into the pool house and tried the handle. It was unlocked. He opened it and slipped inside. The interior was messy: to Milton's left were an oil-fired boiler and the hydraulics for the pool cover; the wall to his right had been fitted with shelves that held the chemicals and cleaning equipment used to maintain the water quality. There was a window on the other side of the boiler that faced the house, and Milton picked his way cautiously across the floor until he was alongside it. He peered out: the window faced one of the large shuttered windows on the ground floor of the farmhouse and, as Milton watched, the shutters were opened and the interior revealed.

It was the kitchen. Jessica Russo was looking out of the window, her head angled so that she could look down the slope to the pool. She was speaking to someone else and, as Milton waited, holding his breath, he saw Mason Russo and then Richard Russo.

Milton retreated from the window and crossed back to the door. He knew that now would be a good time to take action against them. They had no idea that he was here, and subduing them—even without a weapon—would be a simple enough thing to do. He would take them out in the order of the threat that they presented: Mason, Jessica, their father. He would secure them and then call Salazar. The family must have been charged with an extraditable offence after what had happened in Nevada—murder and theft, for a start—and the Carabinieri would be obliged to hold them in custody until the application to repatriate them had been heard. Milton had given that course of action serious thought on the flight from San Diego. There would be no consequences for him: the Russos could allege that he was involved, of course, but in the deaths of Beau and Sacca, there was no independent third party to support the claim. Of course, that was all moot given that Milton could just as easily disappear once he had left them for the Italians to find. It would be an easy thing to accomplish, and it would be the safest course of action, at least when it came to the family's continued well-being.

But Milton had dismissed the idea then, and he did so again now.

He wanted them to face justice, and they would.

But, more than that, he wanted justice for Beau, and that meant he needed to wait to see whether the *sicario* who had killed for the cartel smelled the bait and took it.

Milton opened the door, stepped out into the heat of the afternoon, and closed it behind him. He couldn't retrace his steps without risking discovery, so, relying on his reconnaissance from earlier, he descended the slope into the vineyard and started on a longer, more circuitous route that would bring him back to his observation point while minimising the risk that he might be seen.

He settled into a steady jog, the sweat gathering on his forehead and running down onto his brow. He wanted to take up position. He felt it in his gut: the *sicario* was coming, and, when he did, Milton was going to show him the error of his ways.

79

Milton returned to the copse and took up position beneath the branches of the carrubo and myrtle that thronged the spaces between the trunks of the trees. He decided that there was no need to put up his tent. He was sheltered beneath the thick canopy overhead, and, in any event, the forecast for the next three days was for warm and dry weather. He laid out his sleeping bag, using that to soften the ground. He suspected that he was going to be prone for several hours, and the last thing he needed was to punish his body while he waited.

He took out the binoculars and peered through them at the activity at the farmhouse below. The shutters on the ground floor had all been opened, and, as he settled down, the windows on the first and second floors were opened, too. He saw flickers of movement in the windows that faced his position, and, for a moment, he caught a glimpse of Jessica as she pulled back a set of shutters and then stood there, gazing out over the estate. Milton was adjusting the focus when she turned and disappeared again.

He scoped the rest of the estate instead. The Russos had travelled to the house in a rental car, a dusty Audi A5 that was now parked beneath the porte cochère. He scanned farther out, looking for any sign that they might have been followed, or that anyone else was watching the house, but he saw nothing.

He had time to prepare, so he took out the packet of zip ties that he had purchased from the camping equipment store. He removed two of them, made one into a loop that was big enough to slide around a large hand, and then threaded the second through the first before looping that one, too. It was a decent homemade restraint, and the best he would be able to do on short notice. He made more of them and put them into his pocket.

∾

MILTON HAD BEEN WATCHING for fifteen minutes when Richard Russo stepped out of the open front door and, seemingly without a care in the world, crossed the turning circle to one of the barns. He unlocked a padlock and went inside. Milton was a decent distance away, but, even so, he heard the throaty rumble of a powerful engine and watched as a red Ferrari 348 Spider was driven out.

Mason Russo came out of the door and watched his father as he parked the car, opened the door and got out, grinning broadly. Father and son enjoyed a conversation that was evidently amusing, given the faint laughter that floated up to where Milton was hunkered down. Milton focused on the younger of the two men and gritted his teeth; Richard was smart and Jessica was cunning, but it was the hollowness that he had observed in Mason that Milton found the most perturbing. He had taken out Delgado and his men without pity or feeling, and had only been persuaded against killing Milton and Beau by his sister's entreaties. And, despite them, he had coldly put a bullet into an old man's gut. There was a nihilism about him that he recognised in himself.

He took out his phone and dialled the number for Louis Salazar.

"Hello?"

"Salazar—it's me."

"Where are you?"

"Italy. They're here."

"Shit. They're gonna wish they went somewhere else. I've made some progress."

Milton shifted position. "Go on."

"Richard Russo has been charged with fraud. That was a slam dunk—they've been sitting on that for a month. The kids are a little more difficult. The witnesses to what happened in the desert are dead."

"All except one," Milton said.

"Uh-huh. It'd be easier if you were prepared to give evidence."

"I'd much rather not."

"I thought you'd say that. It might not be necessary. We've checked Beau's rental. We've got prints that we've matched to Mason Russo on the wheel. We don't have prints for Jessica or their dad, but I'm betting we'll be able to match them once we've got them back here."

"My prints will be in there, too."

"Are they on file anywhere?"

"A couple of places," Milton said. "I was arrested in Texas a couple of years ago. And Michigan after that."

"I'll see what I can do."

"I'd appreciate that."

"We know that Beau rented that car, and we've got Jessica

inside it—that backs up the story you two cooked up about Beau being jacked. We got the three of them on the passenger manifest of an Air Canada flight out of Vancouver to Montreal. We worked back from that and got video of them going across the border at Blaine. We got enough to charge them with attempted murder to go with the fraud. It'll be enough to apply to have them extradited."

"Have you started that?"

"I was told we spoke to the DOJ last night. They'll speak to Interpol and put out a Red Notice. The locals will go and grab the suspects. What are you thinking?"

Milton saw motion down below. Jessica had come out of the front door. She went to her father, and the two of them had a conversation.

"The department will tell the Italians about Russo's house, right?"

"It's an obvious line of enquiry. Why?"

"I want to dangle them as bait for as long as I can," Milton said. "Whoever killed Beau knows about the house, too."

"That's an assumption."

"I don't think so," Milton retorted. "He's coming."

"And what then?"

"I'll call you. You can send the Italians to get the Russos. You can leave the rest to me."

Jessica took something from her father and made her way to the Ferrari. Salazar was saying something, but Milton told him he would be in touch and killed the call. He brought the binoculars up to his eyes and watched as Jessica opened the door and lowered herself into the front seat of the Spider. He heard the rumble of the engine and then a roar as Jessica revved it, once and then twice. Another broad smile broke out on her father's face as he watched. The

Ferrari pulled out, crunching over the gravel and then proceeding carefully onto the rough track that led to the road.

Milton watched the car climb up to the ridge and then disappear down the other side.

80

Milton stayed at his observation point all afternoon and into the gloom of dusk. Mason Russo went down to the pool and swam laps for half an hour while his father took a book out to a summerhouse near the vineyard and read. Milton could see both of them. He swept the rest of the terrain without seeing anyone else, save for a farmer who passed along a nearby field on a tractor. Both Richard and his son eventually went inside, reappearing out of the kitchen doors a short while later with drinks and lit cigars. Milton could see the glowing tips as the daylight slowly faded into the gloom of night.

It was nine when Milton saw the rake of a car's headlights arrowing into the sky above the ridge as the approaching vehicle neared the crest. Milton listened, heard the sound of a powerful engine and then saw the Ferrari as it reached the top and then continued down the track to the house. He watched, waiting to see whether Jessica had returned alone. It appeared that she had; there was no sign of anyone else.

She reached the turning circle and parked near the

house. Mason came out of the front door and intercepted her as she got out. He had changed his clothes since Milton had seen him with the cigar, and now, instead of his swimming shorts, he was wearing a leather jacket and jeans. He spoke with Jessica, pointed at the Ferrari, and took the keys. They were too far away for Milton to be able to hear their conversation, but the sentiments were clear: Mason was going out, he wanted to take the Spider and, Milton guessed, he was irritated that Jessica had taken so long to bring it back.

The conversation ended and Jessica went inside. Mason opened the door to the car, started the engine and pulled out, giving the car a little more juice than Jessica had done, and sending it racing over the gravel and onto the track. Milton followed the car with the binoculars. He assumed that Mason was going somewhere he might get a drink and enjoy some company, perhaps to San Quirico d'Orcia.

The car raced around the corner and started up the slope toward the ridge. Milton was about to turn the binoculars back to the house again when the brake lights glowed a sudden, urgent red and the car swerved over to the side of the road and crashed into one of the cypress trees. Milton froze, focused the binoculars and watched. The car was out of sight of the main house now, screened off by the trees but visible to Milton from his elevated position.

Milton held his breath, adjusted the focus and watched as a man emerged from between the trees. He walked to the car and raised his arm so that his hand was pointed at the driver's side window. Milton thought he heard the muffled puffs of suppressed gunshots.

Milton judged the distance between the crashed car and the farmhouse. It was half a mile at most, perhaps a little less. It would take the man six or seven minutes to reach the main building on foot. Milton was a quarter of a mile from the house, but he had the disadvantage of more difficult terrain and the need to remain out of sight, both to the occupants of the house and the shooter.

Milton focused on the car again and watched as the shooter turned and left the road, disappearing between the trees again.

Milton couldn't wait. He left the binoculars, checked his pocket for the zip ties, clipped the sheathed hunting knife to his belt, and started the descent to the farmhouse in the valley.

81

Jessica went outside to the lime tree that was growing between the house and the pool. She reached up and twisted off one of the fruits; it was plump and glossy, and the skin was almost moist from the juice within.

Her father was lying on a lounger, his legs outstretched and his book resting face down on his chest. He had his fingers laced behind his head and he looked peaceful and at ease. His face still showed the bruises that Delgado had inflicted during the night that he had been in the Mexican's custody, but they would fade over time. He was as relaxed as she could remember seeing him, certainly since her mother's death. She knew that he had been weighed down by the audacity and risk of the plot that he had mounted against the cartel—or, more particularly, by the consequences that would have been meted out to him in the event that Delgado had realised what he was doing. But Delgado was foolish and her father was smart, and, at least up until the end, the plan had been a remarkable success. The last few days had been as stressful as any she could remember, but they were through to the other side now. They had this house and five million dollars' worth of Bitcoin, and no one knew where they were. She could allow herself to relax.

It was late now, but still warm.

"What are you doing?" her father said as she plucked a second lime.

"Cocktail hour," she said. "You want one?"

"I'm good with my wine," he said.

He reached down for the bottle of red that he had stood next to his lounger, hooked it by the neck, sat up, and poured another glass. The vineyard was tended to by a local man called Carlo, who had been working on the estate for forty years. He came in every morning to check on the grapes, often working all day in the broiling heat. Last year's crop had produced an excellent vintage. He had big vats of it at his house and had provided several bottles when the Russos had stopped on their way to the property earlier that afternoon.

Jessica went back into the kitchen. She opened the cupboard where she had put the bottle of gin, took a bottle of tonic from the fridge and lifted a bag of ice from the freezer. She put one of the limes on a chopping board, then halved and quartered it. She filled the bowl of the glass with ice, poured in a double measure of the gin, added tonic, then squeezed a piece of the lime and rubbed the pulp around the rim of the glass, finally dropping it into her drink.

Mason had gone to see the girl he had met when he had been out here with his father to buy the house. Jessica had not had the pleasure of an introduction but had been informed—by Mason, so she took everything with a pinch of salt—that she was beautiful and into him. Jessica's initial reaction to his suggestion that he go and see her tonight was to tell him not to be so stupid, that they had only just arrived and that he should lie low for a day or two. He had reminded her—correctly, she conceded—that there was no need to lie low any longer.

They were safe.

They had done it.

She went outside again and stood next to her father.

"Cheers," she said, holding her gin out.

He touched his wine glass to hers. "*Saluti,*" he corrected her.

"*Sì,*" she said, and grinned. "*Saluti.*"

Jessica sat down on the lounger next to her father's and gazed out onto the pool and the vineyard beyond it. She hadn't come with her father and Mason when they had purchased the property, and the pictures that she had been shown didn't do it justice. The Tuscan countryside, the climate—hot, but without the brutal heat of Vegas—the food, the wine; it was heavenly. She had no ties to the States, and she doubted that she would miss it. Her father had said that it would be best if they stayed away for a few years, but she wondered whether she would ever go back. His cancer was going to get worse, and she wanted to be here to care for him. The house would pass to her and her brother once he was gone, and she could imagine herself staying.

A bird hooted from somewhere nearby.

"It's a tawny owl," her father said. "I've seen her hunting in the vineyard. She's a beauty."

She was thinking about her father's love of nature and the satisfaction he was going to derive from it here, when she heard something from the house. The kitchen door squeaked a little when it was opened, and she wondered if it had been that.

"Mason?"

There was no response. She swung her legs off the lounger and stood up, turning towards the house.

There was a man standing on the patio. She had never seen him before. He had dark hair badly cut into a bowl, white skin, and a heaviness to his features. His nose was thick, his brows solid. His eyes were cold. He was dressed in black: black denim jeans and a black denim shirt.

Her eyes were drawn down to the pistol that he was pointing at her.

"Dad," she said.

Her father grunted as he sat up. "What is it?"

He turned to look back and saw him, too.

"Señor Russo," the man said. He turned his head to Jessica. "Señorita Russo."

Jessica swallowed; despite the gin, her throat was dry. "Who are you?"

"I represent the cartel. They have asked me to find the money that you have stolen."

Jessica's father stood. "Please," he said. He raised his hands, palms facing out, and made a calming motion. "Please. There's no need for unpleasantness."

"They would disagree. You should not have stolen from them if you were not prepared to face the consequences."

Jessica thought of Mason. "Where is my brother?"

"I found him," the man responded, cool and emotionless.

Her father's face blanched.

The man did not elaborate, but he didn't need to. Her father took a step toward him, his fist raised, but the man switched his aim and just shook his head. "Señor—you really have no reason to complain. You brought this all upon yourself. Now—*por favor*—sit back down, both of you. We need to talk about the money that you stole."

Jessica looked at her father; he was shaking, his hands trembling uncontrollably. "Sit down, Dad," she said, worried that he was about to collapse. "We can talk this out."

The man smiled; there was no humour there, no warmth, simply a look of amusement that she still dared to hope.

82

Jessica sat down on the lounger. Her father sat down again, too. The man with the gun took one of the seats from the patio table and set it down so that he could address them both, but not so close that he wouldn't be able to aim and fire if either of them was foolish enough to try to impede him. Jessica could tell that the man was capable. There was an easy confidence about him: the way he held the gun, relaxed but not too loose; the nonchalant demeanour; the polite way of speaking that might even have been considered pleasant were it not for the pistol.

"Where is the money?"

"You're looking at it," her father said.

"No," the man replied. "You bought this property some time ago, I believe. We can get to that later, of course. But, for now, I am interested in the money that you stole before you left. Five million dollars. I understand that it was converted to Bitcoin. You are going to transfer those Bitcoin to an account that has been set up for that purpose."

Jessica felt as if she was about to be sick. Her satisfaction with what they had achieved—so pleasing just five minutes ago—had turned to ashes in her mouth. She thought of Mason and the unavoidable implication in the man's words. She knew enough about the cartel that any emissary that was dispatched to do its business would be ruthless, and that this man would have been given instructions to punish them—or worse—once the money had been recovered. She and her father would have to delay him long enough that an opportunity to save themselves might present itself; the trouble was, they were in the middle of the countryside, with no one nearby and no way of calling for help. She was unarmed, and her father was frail from his cancer and the beating that he had taken. They were helpless against their fate.

"Señor Russo," the man said, "where is the money?"

Jessica looked at her father. The contentment was gone; it was as if he had been hollowed out, an empty vessel that had now been filled with weakness and fright.

The man aimed the pistol at Jessica while continuing to look at her father.

"This is the last time I will ask in a pleasant way," he said. "I do not bluff, señor."

"Dad," Jessica said, "tell him."

She saw the flicker in her father's face, a reaction that he was not entirely successful in suppressing. The man saw it, too, and turned back to the house just as Jessica looked in the same direction. Her first thought, even as she blinked to focus on the shadow that was approaching them through the gloaming, was that Mason was still alive. The shadow took another step, passing through the oblong of light cast through the kitchen window, and she saw that she was wrong. The man wasn't quite as big, his hair was dark rather than light, and he moved with an animal stealth that her brother would not have been able to match.

The man was clutching something in both hands, his left shoulder slightly further forward as he set his stance and swung as if addressing a fastball over the plate. The swing brought the object—long and thin and sparkling in the light—through a full arc that terminated in the man's head. He had half-risen from the chair—too late—and now he fell to the side. He landed on his left shoulder, twitched once, and then lay still.

The gun fell free. Jessica scrambled for it, but was too slow. The newcomer picked it up and aimed it back at her.

He shook his head. The man was in the light now, and the glow illuminated his face: the scar across his cheek, the cold blue eyes.

"Sit down, Jessica," John Smith said.

83

B lood dripped from the tip of the wrench that Milton had used against the *sicario*. He had found it in the outbuilding that he had passed on his way down to the house, and it had served its purpose well. He had given the *sicario* a heavy blow, but not—he hoped—a terminal one. They had things to discuss.

Milton held the *sicario's* pistol in his hand as he waited for Jessica to sit down. It was a Czech weapon, the CZ 75B Shadow. A smooth-shooting pistol with minimal recoil. Milton had used it before.

"What happened to Mason?"

"He's dead," Milton said.

"How?"

"I was watching up on the hill." Milton nodded down to the unconscious man at his feet. "He was waiting along the track. He stopped the car and shot him."

Richard Russo's face crumpled, and Jessica blinked back sudden tears. Milton didn't care. He wasn't sorry about what had happened, and he wasn't about to pretend that he was.

Mason had brought it upon himself. They all had. The
family had invited calamity, and now that it had visited
them, they could hardly complain about the consequences.
Jessica and her father were fortunate that he had been here
to intercept the *sicario*, because their evening would have
become even more unpleasant than it had already been.

Milton took the homemade cuffs from his pocket and
tossed them to Jessica.

"What am I supposed to do with these?"

Milton nodded to Richard Russo. "Get up, please. Turn
around and put your hands together behind your back.
Jessica—you're going to secure his wrists."

"There's no need to—"

"Now," Milton said.

She looked at him, and he noted that her stubbornness
wilted in his withering stare. Her father got to his feet and,
at a nod from Jessica, turned around and put both hands
behind his back. She looped the first cuff around his right
wrist, the second around his left, and, at a curt nod from
Milton, she closed them tightly.

"Now you," Milton said, indicating that she should turn
around.

Milton secured her wrists and sent her and her father to
stand on the other side of the patio. With one eye on them,
he kept the gun trained on the *sicario* and used his left hand
to secure the man's wrists. Satisfied that all three people
were now properly restrained, Milton pushed the pistol into
the waistband of his jeans and stood.

"Come with me, please," he said to the Russos.

He dragged the man down the slope to the pool house
that he had visited earlier. He opened the door and
deposited the man inside. He secured his feet with another

restraint, then closed the door and turned the key in the lock to secure it.

He nodded back up to the house. "Move," he said to Jessica and her father. "We have some things to talk about."

84

Richard Russo went first, followed by Jessica and then Milton. The door led into the kitchen. Milton glanced around the room, taking in the details: there was a large stove, cupboards and a dresser that bore a host of colourfully decorated plates. There was a generous-sized oak kitchen table with chairs arranged around it. An open laptop sat on the table, insects buzzing around it, drawn by the light from the screen.

"Sit down," Milton said.

He waited as they used their feet to drag the chairs out from beneath the table and then sat down awkwardly.

Jessica looked up at him. "Why are you here?"

"Because of what you did," he said.

"Your friend?"

"He's dead," Milton said.

"No, he isn't," she shot back defensively. "I read about it online—the police said that he was shot, but that he was going to be okay."

"He would have been," Milton said. "But the man who shot your brother killed him. He killed a lot of people,

Jessica—a detective, a doctor, a security guard, one of Delgado's men, and my friend. None of that would've happened if you hadn't done something so monumentally *stupid* as thinking that you could steal from a Mexican cartel and that nothing would happen."

She looked as if she was about to reply, but her mouth opened and closed uselessly as she struggled to find the words.

"I'm not here because of you," Milton went on. "That's not the main reason, at least, although I am going to see that you pay for what you've done."

"So why are you here?"

Milton nodded his head in the direction of the *sicario* in the pool house. "I'm here for him. I'm going to find out who sent him, and then I'm going to find them."

Milton had no interest in a discussion with the Russos, and he wanted to be away from the property as quickly as he could. Salazar had made it clear that the lead to Russo's Tuscan farmhouse was one that the fraud team in Las Vegas would follow, especially now that they knew that the family had flown to Florence. He didn't know how long it would take for an arrangement to be made with the Carabinieri, but he doubted that it would be very long. He was counting on that, in many ways, but he would have preferred a delay while he did what he had to do.

"How much?" Russo said.

Milton frowned. "What did you say?"

"How much will it take? How much do I have to pay you?"

"All of it," Milton said.

"And then you'll leave us in peace?"

Milton shook his head. "You don't get it. You can't buy me. I don't care about money."

"But you said—"

"I have a purpose for the money, but it's not going to help you."

Russo started to protest, but Jessica stopped him with a glance. "Fine," she said. "You can have it."

Milton glanced at the laptop. "Where is the Bitcoin?"

"On the thumb drive," she said.

"And where is that?"

"In my bag. On the counter—over there."

There was a leather shoulder bag on the counter. Milton went over to it, opened it, and tipped the contents out. The drives that he had seen in the briefcase were both there. He took them back to the table and put them down in front of Russo.

"Transfer all of it into a wallet that I'm going to give you. Do you understand?"

Russo looked reluctant but, as Milton held him in his stare, he nodded.

Milton took his knife and sliced through Russo's cuffs. He watched as the man plugged one of the drives into the USB port on the laptop, navigated to an online cryptocurrency exchange and hit the button to send Bitcoin. Ziggy Penn had explained the basics of cryptocurrency when Milton had called him during his layover in Germany. He didn't pretend to understand it—his obtuseness had been a source of great amusement for Ziggy—but he had paid attention and knew what to look for to ensure that Russo didn't try to trick him.

"Where am I sending it?"

Milton took out the details of the destination wallet that Ziggy had provided and put them on the table. Russo typed, slowly and deliberately, as if taking his time about it might cause Milton to change his mind.

It did not.

Russo sighed wearily, tapped return and sat back in the chair, all the strength drained out of him.

Milton felt the buzz of the phone in his pocket. He took it out and saw the message that had just arrived from Ziggy. The money had arrived.

"Thank you," Milton said.

He took out the last of the restraints that he had made, told Russo to stand, moved his arms behind his back and cuffed him again.

"Up," he said to Jessica.

"Where are we going?"

"Back to the pool house."

He followed behind as they walked, and pulled the pistol from his waistband as they approached the pool house. There was no sound of movement from inside, but Milton carefully turned the key in the lock and stepped back, allowing the door to fall open. The *sicario* was still unconscious on the floor.

"Inside, please."

Russo and Jessica did as they were told. Milton followed, then grabbed the unconscious man by the shoulders and dragged him outside once again. He coughed and then groaned. That was good; he was still alive.

For now.

Jessica drifted back to the door. "Please, John," she said. "I didn't mean for any of this to happen the way it did."

Milton put the gun back into his jeans, ignoring her.

"My father's dying. He doesn't deserve to spend the time he's got left in an Italian jail."

"It'll be an American jail, I expect. You'll both be extradited."

"Please, John. *Please.*"

Milton turned and stared into her eyes. "I don't have many friends. One of them was murdered because of what you and your family did. You're lucky I live my life by a different set of rules now than I did before. Ten years ago, I would have killed him"—he gestured to the man on the ground—"and then I would have killed you. All of you." He felt the flash of anger and paused to let it pass. "You and your father are going to wait in here. If you're lucky, you'll never see me again."

"You're going to leave us here?"

"I'll send the police to get you when I'm out of the way. Now—step back."

She did, fading into the gloom. Milton closed the door, twisted the key to secure it, and turned back to the man. He was awake now, his eyes open and staring balefully up at Milton. The hair on the back of his head was matted with damp blood, and a bruise had discoloured his ear.

"Who are you?" he said.

"You killed my friend."

"The gringo?"

"The gringo."

"What do you want?"

"We're going to have a little chat," he said.

PART V

85

A storm rolled in off the Pacific on the day of Beau Baxter's funeral. The skies were leaden, and lightning had crackled through the clouds like veins, thunder booming over the ocean. Milton arrived at Mount Hope Cemetery just as the rain began. He didn't have an umbrella, and as he left the car and made his way into the beautifully tended grounds, he was quickly wet through.

He made his way into the cemetery until he could see the proceedings. The funeral was well attended; Milton estimated that there were a hundred mourners gathered around the grave. Salazar was there, standing at the back beneath a dark umbrella. Chase Baxter was standing next to a woman, and from the way he had his arm around her shoulders, Milton guessed that it was his mother. He remembered what Beau had said to him as he lay bleeding in the back of the car as they made their way to the ER after the shooting. Milton had promised to deliver a message for him, and he intended to honour it.

Milton made his way a little closer, sheltering beneath the spreading boughs of a eucalyptus tree. The priest said a few words, and then Beau's casket was lowered into the ground. Beau's wife cast a handful of dirt down onto the lid, and then Chase did the same; some of the mourners waited to take their turn, and others started to drift away.

Milton caught Salazar's eye and waited beneath the tree until the detective reached him.

"I didn't think you were coming," Salazar said.

"I wasn't going to. But I want to pay my respects."

"You okay?"

"I'm fine."

"You going to the reception?"

"No," Milton said. "I have a flight to catch."

"Where to?"

"That doesn't matter."

"But it's to do with what happened?"

"It is."

"You gonna tell me anything?"

"No," Milton said.

"I didn't think so." Salazar nodded over to the parking lot. "Walk with me?"

They set off together. Thunder boomed overhead as Milton wiped the rain from his face.

"I got some good news for you," Salazar said. "The security cameras at the ER didn't catch anything, and the prints we found in the back of Beau's rental won't be matched to you. I made them disappear."

"Thank you."

"The only people who can tie you to what went down in the desert are Richard and Jessica Russo. Now, no one's gonna give too much credence to anything they say, but it did cross my mind that she might say that she was on the security cameras with you and Beau at the El Cortez. I went over there yesterday before I got the plane here. You'll never guess what they said."

Milton shrugged.

"Said they had a break-in last week. Someone picked the lock into the back office and took the hard drives with the camera footage on them."

"That's a stroke of luck," Milton said.

"Isn't it."

They reached the lot.

"What about the Russos?" Milton said.

"That's underway. They're being held in Florence until the extradition proceedings are finished. The DOJ told us the hearings are a slam dunk—they'll be back in Nevada by the end of the month. We got a couple of nice cells waiting for them in Ely State."

"And then?"

"They've been charged with fraud, and murder will be added soon. The email you sent with Russo's statements has been helpful. On top of all that, we've got evidence of Mason Russo buying a Sako TRG M10 from Northwest Arms the day before the shootings, and we got forensics from all of them in the back of Beau's rental, plus the fact that they bugged out to Italy. The story you and Beau came up with looks like it'll hold up. We'll say that Jessica Russo hijacked him and stole his car. The rest writes itself—she picked up the rest of the family and ran."

Milton nodded in satisfaction. He didn't care about the Russos now; Mason had been punished for what he had done to Beau, and Milton was happy to let the justice system deal with his father and sister. The family had made a series of catastrophic errors, and now they were going to have to pay the price.

"The Italians are still investigating what happened to Mason," Salazar went on.

"It was the guy they sent," Milton offered.

"The Mexican?"

Milton nodded.

"The Italians didn't find anyone else there. What happened to him?"

Milton flashed back to that night in the hills outside Siena. He had taken the *sicario* into the woods and got all of the answers that he needed.

"He won't be found," Milton said.

The other mourners started to amble into the lot, the rain pattering onto their umbrellas. Milton saw Beau's widow making her way to a waiting car.

"I have to go," he said to the detective. "Thank you for your help. For everything."

"What are you going to do now?"

"The man who killed Beau was following orders," Milton said. "He's responsible, but he's not the only one. I'm going to make the others pay."

∾

MILTON MET Debbie and Chase Baxter as they reached the limousine that was going to drive them to the family reception. Beau's widow was in her fifties, with long, dark hair. Her eyes were ringed with red. Chase was holding an umbrella over his mother and eschewing it for himself; as a result, his suit was sodden and his hair was plastered against his scalp. He saw Milton and evidently recognised him; his jaw bulged as he clenched his teeth, and there was heat in his stare. Milton wondered about the good sense of speaking to the two of them, but knew that he had to; he had given his word to Beau, and there was no guarantee—given what he had decided to do—that he would ever get this chance again.

"Mrs. Baxter."

"Yes?"

"My name's John. I was a friend of your husband. I just wanted to say how sorry I am for your loss."

"Thank you," she said. "That's very kind of you."

"I saw him in the hospital."

"My husband?"

"Yes. And he told me that if he didn't recover, I was to make sure that you knew how much he loved you."

"Thank you," she said again, her voice trembling. She bit her lip and blinked back fresh tears.

"Here," Chase said, reaching over to open the door of the car. "Get in, Mom."

Milton nodded to the younger man, turned and started to walk away.

"Hey!"

He turned back towards the car to see Chase Baxter coming towards him. His face was twisted with anger and his fists were clenched. It wasn't difficult to anticipate what might be coming and, to try to minimise the potential for the mourners to witness an embarrassing scene, Milton stepped around the side of a large SUV.

Chase followed him. "You got a fucking nerve," he said. "Coming here after what you did."

Milton faced Chase head-on. "I didn't do anything, Chase."

"I don't believe you."

"I'm sorry about what happened."

"Yeah? Really?"

"I am."

"Why don't you prove it? Start by telling me what really happened to my dad."

"He was hijacked—"

Chase shoved him, hard, sending him back into the side of the car. *"Bullshit!"*

The younger man clenched his right fist and raised it. Milton could have taken him down with ease—his balance was all wrong, his weight on his front foot rather than spaced evenly between front and back, and his hips were turned a little too far—but he decided that he wouldn't do that. If Chase wanted to strike him, Milton would allow it.

He didn't.

"Tell me," he said instead.

Milton knew he had a choice: stick to the story or give him the truth. The line that they had fed to the authorities was sturdy and would be difficult to disprove, and telling Chase would open up potential consequences that Milton would not be able to control. Chase might go to the police and tell them whatever Milton told him now. But how risky was that? Milton would be gone, and there would be no evidence that would prove one version of events over another. Milton knew that reassurance was there, but he set it aside. It was irrelevant. Chase Baxter's father had been murdered; he deserved to know what had happened. It was his right to know, and he would be much better placed than Milton when it came to what Chase decided to tell his mother.

"I want to know what happened," he insisted.

Milton nodded. "Okay. But not here."

"Then where? When?"

"I'm booked on a flight tonight. Meet me at the airport. Eight o'clock."

PART VI

86

The meeting was held in a social club in a leafy, upscale part of the city. It was a Twelve Steps Study Group and was advertised online as suitable for English speakers. Milton had attended many similar meetings around the world since he had stopped drinking. He looked around the room and saw that the others fit the usual archetypes: embassy officials, businessmen, tourists. Milton had waited at the entrance, weighing up whether to go inside or not. He had watched the others arrive. They had been shifty and nervous as they had turned off the street, but now that they were in the company of those who understood them, they had relaxed.

The meeting was ordinary and could have taken place anywhere: in London or Los Angeles or Paris. The secretary opened proceedings, a volunteer shared their experience, and then the men and women in the audience shared back, encouraged, as ever, to find the similarities and not the differences. Milton listened dutifully, but did not enjoy the peace that he had persuaded himself that he had come here to find.

He didn't want peace, not now.

He wanted affirmation. He wanted to admit to himself what he was proposing to do.

"Does anyone else have anything they'd like to share before we close?"

Milton raised his hand.

The secretary pointed to him and smiled.

"My name is John and I'm an alcoholic."

"Hello, John," the room responded as one.

It always felt unnatural and awkward; Milton was not one of the drunks who found it easy to speak about how they were feeling. He almost flinched at the sound of his own voice. He knew plenty who craved the attention that came with a share. He did not. He hated it, but he found now that he had a compulsion to speak.

He cleared his throat. "I don't come to meetings enough," he began. "I know I should try harder... It's not as if I don't know what happens when I stop. I haven't been attending enough, not recently, and what's happened is the same thing that always happens. Things have gone to shit, and I feel like I'm in a dark place."

He looked up and saw that the secretary was smiling at him, encouraging him to carry on.

"I've been sober long enough to know why I drink. It's like I have something on my shoulder. My worst self. The part of me that I tried to keep down with booze. I drank and drank so I could drown it out—the things it whispered to me, wanted me to do." He paused, but he found that he wasn't ready to stop. "It's different this time. I don't *want* to ignore it. I want to bring it back. I *need* it. Something bad happened to a friend of mine. It happened because of what I asked him to do, and now, because he was a good man and he wanted to help me, he's..."

Milton didn't finish the sentence; instead, he paused. There was an uneasy silence in the room. They had all seen these kinds of shares before: drunks, white-knuckling it, hanging on to sobriety, ready to let go. Some of them would have been lost forever, back to the drink, and then, weeks or months later, found dead in a fetid apartment that stank of alcohol, excrement, desperation and fear. Milton had seen plenty of men and women who had fallen off the wagon.

And yet...

The secretary looked over with fatherly concern. "But that's not your fault, John."

"No," he said. "It *is*. It's all my fault."

"You can't blame yourself. Drinking won't solve your problems."

Milton looked at him as if unsure of what he had just suggested. "It's not that," he said. "I'm not going to drink. I used to get drunk because I wanted to ignore what I am. There's no point in ignoring it anymore. I know what I am."

~

MILTON HAD no intention of sticking around after the meeting. He had said what he had wanted to say, and he knew that the others would want to talk to him. Milton had no interest in their concern. He hadn't come to the meeting to be persuaded that his course of action was the wrong one. He knew, with iron certainty, that it was *exactly* what the situation demanded. He had come to admit to himself that he had made the decision to embrace the demon that he had been stifling for so long. The decision bore risks. He knew that he might not be able to go back to the uneasy truce that he had established with his dark side since he had stopped working for the Group. That, in turn, might lead to more nightmares and then back to the bottle.

He would deal with the consequences of unshackling the demon if he had to. For now, he needed what it offered: the amorality, the capacity for violence, the disdain for his own safety.

There were people who needed to pay for what they had done.

They would have to account for the deaths that had been authored in their names.

A doctor.

A cop.

A security guard.

And Beau.

Those people were dangerous. Milton needed his worst self or else he would stand no chance.

He stepped outside. It was midday in Amsterdam, and the sun was shining down from a clear blue sky. Milton took out the Ray-Bans that he had purchased at the airport and slid them onto his head.

∾

MILTON TOOK AN UBER TO P.C. Hooftstraat and made his way to the Prada store. He had purchased a new suit the previous week and it was ready for collection. He took it into the changing room and put it on. He hadn't worn decent clothes for months, but it felt good on him. His outfit—the suit, a crisp white shirt with double cuffs fastened by solid gold studs, and a pair of Gucci loafers—had cost the better part of eight thousand dollars. The platinum Rolex Daytona on his wrist had cost another eighty thousand. Milton was not used to such ostentation, but he had an image to establish. His new legend was rich, flush with the proceeds of a successful and illicit business, and not ashamed of flaunting his wealth.

The clerk put Milton's previous outfit into a bag and wished him a good day. Milton put the shades on and stepped outside. He looked left and right, searching for any sign that he was being watched, and found none. He didn't expect to be tailed, not yet, but he intended for that to change. Drawing attention to himself was anathema, but, this time, it was going to be necessary.

He took out his phone and called another Uber.

~

MILTON HAD RENTED a penthouse apartment in the Pontsteiger building. It was a spectacular new block in the Houthaven district, an up-and-coming area that had once been a port where lumber was unloaded. There were new houses and houseboats, surrounded by green spaces and water. Many properties—including the one that Milton had rented—were exorbitantly expensive.

He got out of the Mercedes and looked up at the vast building. There were two towers, each ninety metres tall, with a 'bridge' hung between them. It was a striking design, the sort of place that could only attract the richest clientele. Milton would be followed as soon as he made contact with the go-between and his circumstances reported upon. Living in a place like this was exactly the kind of statement that he wanted to make.

He made his way into the building and rode the elevator to the top floor. He took a key from his pocket and opened the door. The penthouse had been on the market for six million dollars, but Milton had secured it on a six-month lease for thirty grand a month. It was set on two storeys and had been constructed in the loft style that would not have looked out of place in New York. It had a three-hundred-and-sixty-degree view of the city, all of the neighbourhoods and the suburbs and then the flat country beyond.

There were three men waiting for him.

Ziggy Penn was sitting at the large eight-seat kitchen table with three laptops arranged around him. He was wearing a pair of headphones, and his attention was caught somewhere between the three screens.

Alex Hicks was on the sofa, his feet up on the coffee table while he watched the Premier League on an illegal stream that Ziggy had somehow conjured up. The weapons were on the table: two Glocks, a Heckler & Koch MP5 and all the ammunition that they would need.

Chase Baxter was on the terrace, smoking a cigarette.

Milton took off the dark glasses and put them on the kitchen counter. He removed the suit jacket and hooked that on the back of one of the chairs.

Hicks was ex-SAS and had worked with Milton before. He looked away from the television. "Everything okay?"

"All good," Milton said.

Chase heard him and came inside.

Ziggy was still absorbed by whatever it was he was doing.

"Ziggy," Milton said.

He didn't hear.

Milton reached over and swiped the headphones off his head.

"What?"

"I want to talk to you all."

Milton had arrived in the city first to reconnoitre the lay of the land, and then he had sent for Hicks and Ziggy to ask whether they would be interested in working a job with him. Both, more to the point, had long relationships with Milton. He had made it very plain that he was not calling in favours owed, because the assistance that he was requesting would be much more perilous than anything that he had done for either of them. Instead, he had offered them a quarter of a million dollars each. Ziggy was venal, and his acceptance was no surprise. The cancer that Hicks's wife had been fighting for several years had returned, and her treatment was expensive; he had gladly accepted. Milton had given further thought to Chase's demand that he be involved, and had ultimately decided that he was not in a position to deny him the chance to avenge his father's death. He looked capable, too, and Milton knew that doing what needed to be done was not something that he would be able to do alone. There had been no mention of payment for his assistance, but Milton would transfer the same quarter million to him, too, in due course.

Hicks switched off the TV.

"This is it," Milton said to them. "Last chance. If you go any further, there might not be a way back."

"You're giving us a chance to walk away?" Hicks asked.

"I am."

"I didn't come all the way here to go back home. I'm in."

Milton looked at Ziggy. "What about you? Are you sure?"

"No," he replied. "I'm not sure. But you've made a persuasive case."

"You mean he offered you a lot of money," Hicks suggested.

Ziggy grinned. "Also true. I'm in."

Milton turned to Baxter. The younger man didn't give him the opportunity to ask the question.

"I'd do it myself if you didn't want to do it," he said.

Milton went over to the open doors that gave onto the terrace and gazed at the sprawl of the city beyond.

"When do we start?" Hicks asked.

"Tomorrow," he said. "We make contact tomorrow."

John Milton will return in
'The Man Who Never Was'.
- Winter 2019 -

GET EXCLUSIVE JOHN MILTON MATERIAL

Building a relationship with my readers is the very best thing about writing. Join my VIP Reader Club for information on new books and deals plus all this free Milton content:

1. A free copy of Milton's adventure in North Korea - 1000 Yards.

2. A free copy of Milton's battle with the Mafia and an assassin called Tarantula.

You can get your content **for free**, by signing up at my website.

Just visit www.markjdawson.com.

ABOUT MARK DAWSON

Mark Dawson is the author of the breakout John Milton, Beatrix and Isabella Rose and Soho Noir series.

For more information:
www.markjdawson.com
mark@markjdawson.com